Getting Closure

Aaron L. Ashford

iWrite Publishing

Where Literary Stars are born.

ISBN-10: 0615574076
EAN-13: 9780615574073

Dedication:

This book is dedicated to my daddy; I only wish that he were here to have seen it come to fruition. He wasn't a religious man, but he taught me more about faith in God through his actions. He only had a high school diploma but proved wiser than any scholar that I have yet to encounter. Although words don't do enough to describe his impact on my life I simply say thank you for instilling morals, values, work ethic and the belief in self. In a world where heroes are in short supply I can honestly say that you are still my hero.

The principle of closure is seeking a release from tension. The more that tension builds, the more we desire to find a resolution. The greater the tension, the greater the pleasure in getting closure....

Prologue

James

My heart sang with anticipation of her arrival. I had spent the last several hours making sure that everything was perfect. Perfect like she was. Lilies were her favorite so I arranged a bouquet of freshly cut Oriental Lilies that would greet her when she came in. Najee played softly in the background as I put the finishing touches on our dinner. In the spirit of spontaneity I took my best crack at preparing Spanish Paella complete with shrimp, mussels, and green veggies. It was her favorite meal. I was no culinary chef, but I could hold my own in the kitchen thanks to a few things I picked up over the years. Besides, I would do anything for her.

I poured two glasses of Sangria as I strolled to meet her at the door. Even though it had only been a few hours since we last saw each other it felt like years to me. Being without her was not an option. I opened the door before she could turn the key. Anxiety blanketed her face. "Hey babe." "Hey sweetie." We kissed as I grabbed her jacket and her bag. It had rained earlier which bought the temperature down several degrees. This was definitely snuggle weather. I handed her the glass and began to massage her shoulders. Wanted to take away everything that she was dealing with. I watched her eyes as they looked around our corporate condo. The flowers bought out that smile that I yearned to see. It was the smile that could get me to do anything for her. "James.......you....shouldn't have." I gulped my Sangria and took her hand leading her to the table where we dined by candle light. "Baby, I would do anything for you. Trust."

The fact that it wasn't her birthday or any other holiday worth celebrating went a long way with her. Sharon just made me want to express myself to her with everything in me. It had only been six months since we hooked up, but there was something different. We had chemistry. Chemistry unlike I have ever had with any other woman. She knew it and I knew it. It was mutual. Just the thought of this woman could create movement in my pants. Made my blood flow south. She had cast a spell on me. As much as I hated to admit it, I was open. I could tell that she had a lot on her mind despite her many attempts at denying that anything was wrong. Sometimes it was what a person didn't say that really told the whole story.

We ventured to the sofa and continued to drink Sangria in front of the gas log fireplace. I massaged her feet as she fed me her latest problems. Sharon leaned forward and kissed me deeply. She held on to my lips. Savored them. She did that like they tasted good. The temperature began to rise in a hurry. Her kisses felt like pure electricity. I was wired for love. Sharon began unbuttoning my shirt and pants. Her breathing thickened. Her moans grew with intensity. I removed her blouse and her skirt. Stared at her Nubian beauty. Extra blood rushed to my loins. She was wearing stockings that matched her complexion, no panties.

I took a piece of fruit that had been soaking in Sangria from my glass and traced her nipples. They became stiff. Her breathing picked up some more. I traced her sweet spot with the fruit. Did that until she couldn't take anymore. I fed Sharon her own essence. I ate what was left. She tasted oh so good. I have never had fruit that sweet before. She pulled me on top and put me inside of her. It was as if her vagina molded perfectly around my penis. So warm. So wet. Her hands gripped my back and my ass. She held me close. "You feel so good baby!" Music to my ears. I held my position, helped her reach the top of her journey.

I spread her legs like branches. Stroked her longer. Stroked her harder. Stroked her faster. The more I stroked the wetter she got, and the harder I got. She moaned sweet sounds. Sounded like a musical instrument perfectly tuned. An instrument that I was playing the hell out of. Like Hendrix strumming his guitar once the acid had taken over. I was so aroused. So into her. Sharon and I reached the finish line of our erotic journey at the same time. We began round two on our way to the king sized bed covered in rose petals. I had been with my share of women and then some, but no woman had ever moved me like Sharon did. "I love you" she moaned. "I love you too." At this moment I could have died and gone to heaven, because I didn't think that life had anything else to offer. It was like living a fairytale. As great as fairytales were, they always ended. I guess this one was no exception. Our wedding bands danced as we held hands in a perfect embrace. Sharon looked at her watch to see what time it was. That was when the fantasy ended. We both were slaves to father time. He was not stopping for anyone. With a look of disappointment she told me that she had to go. Her husband was expecting her. I swallowed those words like castor oil. I didn't want her to get into trouble. Sometimes love had to be selfless and not selfish. It was hard to be selfish when you were on borrowed time. That was what I tried to convince my heart of. She went to the bathroom to freshen up before she left to be with her husband and children. "Thank you so much for dinner and dessert baby. I gotta go. Call you when I can." She kissed me and like that she was gone. Seeing her come and go was like dying a thousand slow and painful deaths. I hated the thought of her going home to be with anyone other than me. Didn't want anybody touching her but me, not even her husband. I fixed a glass of cognac and drank it straight with no chaser to alleviate myself of those thoughts. I was surprised that my wife hadn't been calling looking for me. Most importantly, I didn't give a damn. A couple of hours had passed by and she texted me to let me know that she had got-ten home. Her husband was home and she couldn't talk. She said that she had something to discuss, but wanted to do it in person. I didn't exactly like the sound of that, but I responded back to acknowledge receiving the text.

Amanda:

She abruptly woke from her slumber in a cold sweat. Her breathing was heavy, as she had a look of panic on her face. Her husband was not home. She was alone, but relieved that she was just dreaming. She searched for her inhaler that was beside her nightstand to help control her breathing. The woman got up to fix a glass of water so that she could take her Xanax that helped her control her anxiety. She picked up her cell phone and was about to call her husband. She wondered where he was, it was nearly 12:00 am and he hadn't called since leaving work. She changed her mind about taking the Xanax, and calling her husband. The woman lit a cigarette instead. Her anxiety was not getting better, in fact it was getting worst. The woman barely recognized herself when she looked into the mirror. Everyone she met had marveled over her beauty, her model like features, and her rich dark complexion. People often thought that she was African, or Jamaican. Nobody ever asked about London. It was as if they didn't know that black people lived in London. That was the ignorance of many American people. Their ignorance suited her just fine, because she never corrected them. She began chain smoking several cigarettes as she thought about her terrifying nightmares. Her past was haunting her. In that moment she was back in her native land of London. As a child she had seen a lot. She had seen more and done more than a child was supposed to have seen and done. She remembered and adored her father, and her father adored her as well. He always made his daughter promise to make sure that she had a man that would take care of her and give her everything that she deserved. He always told her that she was the most beautiful girl in the world, not just the UK. She smiled inside as she remembered those moments. Every girl loves their daddy, and she was no exception. Not everyone else loved her daddy. In fact most people hated him. They hated him because he had terrified the streets of London for nearly two decades. Her father was a major player in the drug game, and was thus responsible for more death than even she cared to imagine. He was always gentle with her and did his best to keep her closely guarded. "Take my good, and leave my bad." He told his daughter on numerous occasions. She held on to the memories of her father, but couldn't forget that not everyone adored him like she did. The smoke from her cigarettes left a cloudy trail inside of her lavish master bedroom suite and forced her to go outside and sit on her deck that overlooked their boat that was docked on the lake. She enjoyed the peace and the tranquility of the early morning just after midnight. The woman remembered the frightened look on her father's face when he awoke her from sleeping. He grabbed her hand and told her not to be afraid. She had never seen him look afraid before, which made her afraid. He took her to their basement and told her to go inside the safe room that not even his enemies knew about. "No one even knows that this room exists, you'll be safe here." Told her that some bad men were looking for him and that he couldn't allow anything to happen to her. He had given her a handbag which contained a gun, passport and enough cash to last. "Just in case you have to use this to save your life. Don't be afraid. Never count on anyone to do for you, what you can do for yourself. Do what you have to do baby. If I am not back before day break........know that I love you. Everything you need is in this bag." Her father had taught her how to use a gun, so she wasn't afraid. She had seen murder up close and personal. It was common place. It was a lifestyle. She began crying in the present over what had happened in her past. She cried as she relived her agony. Her father never made it back. That was the last time that she ever saw him. Apparently some people less fond of him thought it was time to put a stop to his reign of terror over London's streets. His murder would go unsolved according to the Daily Telegraph and other local papers in the UK. Many believed that his own men had set him up. She struggled to come to grips with those realities. So many mysteries. She didn't really know her mom. Rumor had it that her father had her mother killed because she betrayed him with his best friend. The best friend was killed as well. She dreamed of having a family. Having children of her own, so that she could love them the way her father had loved her. The contents in the bag that her father gave her had currency in the Euro and the American dollar, and airline tickets to the US. Her father knew that he was on borrowed time and made sure even in his death that his daughter would be out of harms way. He knew that his enemies would search her out and kill her on London soil if she remained there. He wanted her to go to America and start her life over. He wanted her to go somewhere that she would never be found, not one of the popular cities like New York, Chicago, Miami or Los Angeles, somewhere that nobody would look to find her. She even changed her name and assumed a whole new identity. Eve Saunders was the name given by her at birth. The young lady affectionately known as the "Black Eve" was no more. She settled on the name Amanda. It would take some getting used to but it grew on her. It sounded American enough, but maintained a UK feel as well. The woman remembered the ring that her father gave her. "Give this ring to the person that you love the most." She never disobeyed her father's words. It was the ring that her mother had given to her father. It was the ring that she had given to her husband when they were married. A look of disgust consumed her being with that thought. She didn't feel any love in return from her husband. In fact she had strong convictions that he was having an affair. She felt that this was not the first affair during their ten year marriage, but that there was something different about this one. She just needed proof. That was what she intended to get. The woman could not stomach disloyalty. It went against everything that she knew. With that thought she flicked her cigarette butt onto the manicured lawn that surrounded her expensive home on Lake Murray in Columbia, S.C. She always wondered if there would be anyone searching for her from her past. This was definitely the last place anyone would look.

The woman grew tired of feeling sorry for herself. She grew tired of waiting on her husband to give her things that she deserved. She needed to get out of the house. She needed to feel alive. She went inside and showered quickly and decided to put on some clothes to feel beautiful again. It didn't take her long to get ready like some women. She pulled her hair back in a pony tail, put on some lipstick, mascara, eye shadow and she was ready to go. The woman put on some skinny jeans, a sexy fitted t-shirt with the BeBe logo and some heels. She absolutely loved heels. With her smaller heels of about 3 inches on she was about 5 "11", which meant her taller heels put her over 6 feet. She avoided wearing her taller heels when she went out with her husband. He was somewhat vertically challenged and it ate at his ego to have her tower over him. She did a lot of concealing herself just to feed his ego. Tonight she would wear her heels and feel like the beautiful woman that she was. She looked in the mirror again, this time she recognized herself. It almost made her smile. She jumped in her white Mercedes Benz and exited her garage in search of something that resembled life. When she let the top of her car down, she felt the cool breeze of a Carolina summer on her face as she put on her favorite tunes. The melodic flow of Joss Stone helped navigate her in search of people doing something in the small city at this hour. Still no word from her husband, but she didn't care. She was hungry for something that he had not provided in sometime. She wanted to feel beautiful. She wanted to feel appreciated, like her father made her feel. Tonight she was chasing ghosts. After making it to I-26 she headed towards downtown away from Lake Murray. The woman decided that she felt like dancing. She always loved dancing to good music. Dancing was not one of her husband's favorite pass times. Even if the music was not that great, she would dance anyway she thought. The woman pulled up to a nice crowd of lively people going inside of the night club called Pure. After she parked her car she walked through the parking lot towards the entrance. The woman ignored the guys gawking at her and soliciting her attention. Deep down inside of her it made her feel good. She felt good that someone else thought that she was attractive; even if they only wanted one thing. She payed the 20 dollar cover charge and made her way to the bar. All eyes were on her as she ordered a Cosmopolitan. Although she wanted something stronger, she wanted to pace herself. The Cosmo made her think of the many episodes of Sex and the City she had watched and nearly memorized the lines to. For a moment she almost wished that she had girlfriends, then she dismissed that thought. Amanda realized that she had trust issues. She believed less of what people said, more of what they did. It was what her father taught her. It was how he lived, and now it was how she lived. She took her drink and sat down at a nearby bar table. She took inventory of the club and found everything in decent taste so far. She loved the décor with the animal printed open lounge chairs and huge wide stretching bar. Behind her a few guys stood apprehensively awaiting the right opportunity to approach her. Everybody gave her that "you are not from around here" look that she had grown accustomed to. After another Cosmo, she began to feel alive. She was glad that she decided against taking her Xanax earlier. She hated taking medicine, it made her feel controlled. It made her feel weak. Her breathing was normal and she was ready to dance. Amanda strolled to the floor and began dancing all by herself in the thick crowd of eager party goers. The DJ had a nice mix going of reggae and calypso music that reminded her of days long gone in her native land in London. Her heritage was that of Afro-Caribbean from what her father told her, although she had never been to the Caribbean herself. She remembered the influence of the islands that dominated his accent, especially when he was angry. She thought about the way her accent had been watered down since coming to America, especially being in the south. The DJ's mix had taken her home with track after track. She rode the rhythm of the music underneath her 3-inch Manolo's. It was as if she was in a trance, she was in a different place; a place that she had not been in sometime, but a place that she needed to be in. The woman danced for minutes that seemed like hours in club time, before she even noticed that she had an admirer that was glued to her back side tight like her skinny jeans. "Damn girl, you dance like you just got outta jail." The woman turned around startled by her admirer. He was attached to her backside long enough to have what Americans referred to as wood. He was erect, and very intrigued by the woman's beauty. He stared at her in a way that she had not been looked at in a while. The woman was grateful, but spooked all at once. She was not afraid of him, but more afraid of herself. In a strange way she was attracted to him as well, which was kinda weird given his makeup. He was tall and skinny wearing baggy jeans, a button down shirt and cuff links. Most of all his hair was braided. A thug wanna be, she thought to herself. Amanda was not feeling him. She began stepping away towards her seat. "Hey what's up? Where you going?" The guy asked. "I am feeling kinda tired, think I need to sit down." She responded. The woman walked to her table hoping that he would take the hint. This man was persistent. He was not very good at taking hints. He met the woman at her table and introduced himself. "I am Reggie, what's your name?" "I am married.. Reggie." "So your name is Married? That's a kinda weird name...don't you think?" The woman laughed. Reggie laughed as well. He was glad that his joke worked. "I was just asking your name sweetie, that's all." "My name is Amanda." "Okay, assuming that's not your club name it's nice to meet you Amanda." "Where is your husband?" He asked while looking around the club. That was a question not even she could answer. "I would not let something as beautiful as you out of my sight, not even for one minute if I was your husband." She found herself clinging to those words. So much in fact that she didn't even mind being referred to as a "thing." She felt bad for misjudging him, he was nicer than she had given him credit for. They conversed for a while before she decided that she was ready to go. Reggie had sparked a noticeable curiosity within her, even though he was looking for her to give him the "Green Light" so that they could get out of there and hopefully get better acquainted. "I have to go" She asserted. The man took her hand in an assertive manner. He was authoritative yet gentle. "When can I see you again beautiful" he asked as he stared into her eyes. "I'm married." "Yeah you said that, but you ain't happy." That caught her off guard. She was amused by his southern accent as well as his boldness. She didn't have a reply. It was obvious that she was not happy. This stranger was more attentive to her than her own husband. The woman was a prisoner to the moment. She left the club with the stranger that called her beautiful. In that moment she didn't see the corn rowed thin man, she saw what she was in need of. She saw someone worthy of her company, even if it was just a one night stand. The man had offered to get a room, but she declined. She didn't feel like being ordinary that night. She wanted to be spontaneous, she wanted to feel free. Amanda and Reggie reverted to their youthful days and they had sex in her cramped Mercedes Benz. The car that her husband paid for. She pulled down her skinny jeans, let them rest at her left ankle to give her legs freedom; kept on her expensive shoes. With her Manolos pointed to the sky, she let Reggie have his way as her legs swayed in the night air. It excited the stranger when he saw that she was not wearing any panties. He wanted her since he laid eyes on her as she walked in the club and now she was his for as long as he could stave off his orgasm. She longed for the days of being screwed with such passion and fervor, even if she didn't love him. It was more than her husband had offered in recent memory. The woman smiled a million smiles as she enjoyed the stranger's girth that filled her perfectly. The thrill of the unknown excited her, helped her enjoy the moment. Fifteen minutes of drunken pleasure felt like a lifetime of enjoyment as she moaned and groaned to his every stroke. Reggie collected all of his excitement inside of the condom he was wearing as they both adjusted their clothes to where they fit best. She asked him to reach inside her glove compartment and hand her some napkins. He saw her now unconcealed weapon resting on its side. Reggie was unphased and handed her several napkins and saved a few for himself. Neither of them were strangers to the steel hardware that rested in her glove compartment. They both respected the power that came with packing heat. An instant respect was born on the backseat of her convertible Benz. The moment would have seemed rather awkward with the talk of guns immediately following sex between two strangers, but it seemed to bond the two of them. She listened after Reggie told her of his street exploits that landed him in prison many moons ago. Amanda was not impressed, neither was she frightened. Little did he know that he had slept with a woman who had forgotten more street exploits than he would ever know and that included what he saw while watching his Scarface and American Gangster DVDs. They sat like two horny teenagers under the stars revealed by her vacant roof top. Reggie handed her a business card that advertised his detail shop. "Bring your car by my shop tomorrow, and I will detail it free of charge. I did kinda help mess it up." He laughed at his joke. She took the card and nodded that she would take him up on his offer. He hopped out and she drove away in total disbelief of what had just happened. She lit up a cigarette with absolutely no regrets as she drove off with fond memories of screwing an *ex-felon* but feeling like this could be the beginning of just what she needed.

James

After the first several drinks I soon lost count. I became a prisoner to the drunken stupor that accompanied too much cognac. No matter how much I tried to cloud my mind from the many thoughts of me and Sharon I couldn't. I felt sick to my stomach with the mere thought of not being with her. I would leave my wife in a heartbeat and not think twice if

she gave me the word. I wouldn't even look back. It was too
much to put up with her secrecy and her night mares and
panic attacks. There was so much mystery to her. So much
I didn't know about her. My wife was definitely a thing of
beauty, she was a sight to behold. Aside from that I didn't
have many other accolades to give her. I wish that she had
come with a warning. Hit it and quit it, or else. Maybe she got
screwed up being raised in multiple foster homes. Too many
to remember is what she told me. She has been pressuring me
to have kids, but I didn't want any kids because I was afraid
they might inherit her crazy genes. I had to make sure that
dream of hers never came true. I would give all the money
that I had to be able to come home to a woman like Sharon
everyday. I remember the first time we met. She came into my
advertising firm for an interview. I made sure that she was
hired just because she was fine. I just had a thing for admiring
beauty. My mother warned me that chasing women would be
my demise. I'd have to take my chances. Initially she seemed
adamant about being into her husband. It made me pursue
her with even more vigor. I simply love a challenge. She had
shot down a number of my subtle advances to have lunch
or to meet for drinks. I had to take a different approach. I
needed more background information on her. It wasn't one of
my prouder moments, but I had my I.T. guy hack her email
account. It had the makings of a soap opera plot. It didn't take
long to find out that Sharon and her husband were having
major problems in their marriage. She had some trust issues
and he didn't exactly help to put her mind at ease. Somewhere
during the course of their relationship he had stopped doing
the little things. He had stopped making her feel special.
Once a woman stopped getting peace of mind from a man, a
man stopped getting a piece of ass from a woman. That was

exactly where they were. There was no heat in their bedroom. They had been reduced to roommates and co-parents. It made me think of my marriage to Amanda. Sure we screwed from time to time. In fact that was the only thing we did get right. I always felt that there was more to a good relationship than just a good screw. It was part of it, but not all of it. My insight about Sharon was more than enough to know how to plant my seed of doubt and get my foot in the door. Misery indeed loves company, so I played that to my advantage. I began to increase her workload little by little to ensure that we worked closely on several advertising campaigns. This made her work schedule fluctuate, which changed her responsibilities at home and further drove a wedge between their relationship. She became more and more comfortable and I baited her to tell me about her marriage, I even talked about mine. People just love hearing that they are not the only ones catching hell. I helped to breath life to her doubts of her husband's infidelity and affirmed her worthiness of total attentiveness. After a few weeks I knew this woman better than I did my own wife, which was sad. I had gained her trust and that was crucial. Sharon was not the first woman that I had had an affair with, but she is the only one that I actually had to put effort into. I knew that she was being tempted when she opted not to go with her family out of town one weekend to stay home and complete a project for work. It was the perfect opportunity to make my move. Sharon met me at Ruth's Chris steakhouse. We sat at the bar and enjoyed appetizers and drinks. I knew that she was not comfortable being out in public. She didn't wanna make it look like we were fooling around. Once she had a couple of drinks she became flirty and loosened up more. She started doing things to her mouth with the fruit inside her drink that made me curious and increased my desire for her even more. Sharon told me that she couldn't remember the last time her husband took her out on a date. It was always them and the kids. He had become so mundane, so damn predictable. She loved the way he was with the kids, but hated the way that he was with her as a husband. Although she loved her kids I sensed a part of her that envied the attention that her husband gave them and didn't give to her. She was almost embarrassed about that revelation. Sharon was under the influence of the Orange Citrus Mojitos that she consumed one after another. I wasn't judgmental towards her. Figured that she had been judged enough. Who was I to judge her or anyone else after what I had done. Part of me almost confessed, but I dismissed that crazy idea quickly. She told me that this had been the first time that she had had adult conversation in a very long time. Sharon finger combed her short hair and began to bite her lip in a very seductive manner. If I would have stood up I would have been embarrassed because the whole restaurant would have known that I was aroused by her. No matter how much I tried to seduce her or spring my trap, it was always women that chose men and not the other way around. That night Sharon chose me, inside of the four walls that enclosed our hotel room inside of the Hilton and I have been hooked on her ever since. She is the reason I am sitting in a condo that I leased downtown simply to give her peace of mind, just so that I could get a piece of ass.

CHAPTER 1

Jason

My mind was thinking about a million thoughts a minute as I listened to the stir of echoes that laced my tri-level home. Hearing the chimes of my antique clock was a reminder that the next hour had come, which made it 4:00 a.m. My mind and body were not on the same page because this brother was suffering from some serious insomnia. Normally by now the TV would be watching me, but not tonight. I wondered why they put all of the infomercials about weight loss on when most fat people were asleep or why people actually called psychics for their Psychic reading. If they knew so much, why didn't they know the lottery numbers or who's gonna win the Super bowl. If this is BET, where did all of the black folks go after Comic View, and Midnight Love? I guess even BET has to pay the man just like everyone else. Scrolling through all of these channels made me regret paying this ridiculous cable bill each month. No matter what time it was, I loved to catch my boy Stewart Scott put his thing down on Sports Center. It cracked me up how he has changed the face of broadcasting. He has got every sports anchor nationwide saying "Boo-Yaw", and wondering who Lucretia's baby daddy is. I could always count on Sports Center to help the time go by. Wonder if Bobby Knight was a black coach, would have been able to get away with half of that crap and still have a respectable name. Not! It was finally confirmed that I wasn't getting any sleep tonight after another hour passed. I decided that I would head into the gym extra early to help work off this stress. As I prepared my things, I remembered to freshen my breath before I left. There is nothing worse than spotting your gym buddy with dragon breath. With my minty fresh breath, I jumped into my Lincoln Navigator in route to Gold's Gym. I just loved the smell of expensive leather, heated seats, and being able to look down on everyone else. A gate that only opened when you scanned your id card surrounded my suburban community. This was really inconvenient when you were rushing like I was. I guess this was one of the perks for living in high society. Between the time it takes to actually drive out of the neighborhood and where the Gym was, I was looking at about a 15 minute commute. On a foggy damp morning like this it would probably be closer to 25 minutes. Everything was alright because I could listen to Rickey Smiley or Russ Parr until I got to the gym. Those clowns were always tripping on somebody, yet keeping listeners informed about what they needed to be informed of. Once I made it to Clemson Road, I knew that I would be at Sandhills shortly. Working out was something that I did religiously, since I could remember. I was relieved to see Kevin's car in the parking lot, since normally I always beat him to the gym. Kevin is my best friend from college, and my workout partner. Sometimes I think that he takes it too serious. I have warned him about taking those supplements that Mark Mcguire and those Muscle Fitness dudes take. They weren't for me, because I was always afraid that I might lose a few inches where it counts the most. When I walked in I saw Kevin warming up on the treadmill.

"What's up bro?"

"Your late bro."

"I don't need you to remind me of that, Mr. I'm always late."

"Hmmm"

"Besides, the show don't start until I get here anyway".

Kevin and I met back in college, and we have been tight ever since then. He was like another brother to me, we had everything in common. It was freaky. After about two hours of chest pounding, triceps extending, and ab doing we both agreed that enough was enough. We concluded each workout by relaxing in the jet spa.

"Ahhh, this almost feels better than sex", I said.

"Hell No" Kevin quickly replied.

"I said almost".

We both shared a laugh at my expense. There was something about the feeling of having worked out before most people even get out of bed; it was like a sense of accomplishment. I just hoped that I wouldn't have an overwhelming case of fatigue later in the day that usually accompanied getting no sleep. It was like clock work watching the city practically come to life as the night evaporated into day. As Kevin and I parted company we discussed plans for later on. After all

it was Friday. Even though he meant well, I knew that all of
his plans would be predicated around his wife and two kids.
Kevin and I were alike in a lot of ways, except the relationship department. He got hooked up with his wife senior year
at S.C. S.U. I just knew that I was not ready for marriage, no
way, no how. Deep down, I respected Kevin for the way that
he devoted himself to Sharon and their two rug rats. Sharon
hated the fact that Kevin and I have remained so close, due to
the fact that he is married and I have no desire to cross that
bridge anytime soon. She thought that I was gonna get him
to run game on the women like we did in college. I've been
accused of a lot of things in my life, most of which is true
but I would never encourage Kevin to jeopardize his marriage. I respected marriage too much, and respect is the ulti-
mate form of fear. Watching Kevin drive off made me laugh.
Laugh to see his muscle bound frame squeeze into Sharon's
Nissan 300. That's just the type of man he is, to sacrifice so
that his wife could push their Expedition. Sacrifices like that
are why I ain't married. I weaved in and out of traffic handling my Navigator like it was a NASCAR. I heard my joint
on the radio. Kanye West and Jay Z were blaring through my
Bose speakers. I wondered how many people knew that Otis
Redding was the originator of this track. Just like every other
phase of life imitation made for great flattery. It sounded good
nonetheless. I knew that getting my groove on would be short
lived as I vastly approached my gated community decreasing
the volume of my music. When you looked like I looked and
you lived in the same neighborhood with over payed under
performing college coaches, physicians, and attorneys you
had to be mindful of certain things. Everyone already thought
that I was either slinging dope or some type of professional
athlete. Professional was right, but athlete wrong. I own my

own private practice as a marriage and family therapist. The daily grind of hearing all of the problems that go on in marriages was another reason why I did not even think about being married. I did not know many brothers who had a successful business, their own crib, a fat ride, and cash that was theirs. Visa doesn't count. Not a bad living for single man in Columbia, South Carolina. By the time I pulled into my driveway and finished waving at my mostly white, extra chipper neighbors I was back inside my crib. Everyone wondered why I needed a 3800 sq. ft. home all by myself. Why not? After all, it's not like a brother was born with a silver spoon in his mouth. I didn't even have my own room until I moved off campus in college. I hustled to get myself together before heading into the office. There was nothing like a hot shower early in the morning. Thumbing through my collection of fine designer suits made me think back when I had to share a closet with my brother and together we could not fill it with clothes. Growing up in a family of three didn't afford many luxuries. Now my closet was bigger than some people's bedroom. When in doubt always go with a nice Brooks Brothers original. All of my suits had to be specially tailored to fit my irregular but nice frame. They just don't have 44 jackets with 35" waist pants. When I wear a suit, I really wear a suit. Morris Chestnut, and Taye Diggs ain't got nothing on this brother. My morning nutrition included a protein shake, and two egg whites. Momma would tell me that I was starving myself, and prepare a buffet of scrambled eggs, grits, pancakes, sausage, and make me eat until it was gone. That type of eating was long gone for me, and it was a huge contributing factor of heart disease and diabetes in the black community. I miss my momma, working all the time I don't get to see her that much. Fridays were always my light day, I rarely

scheduled many appointments because I hated carrying other people's drama into my weekend. A quick glance at the
Weather Channel told me that today would be another typical
mid summer day in Columbia, South Carolina. "Hot as Hell!"
I was dressed and out of the house. One remote armed my
security system while the other one unlocked my luxury SUV.
This gas crisis almost made me second guess my selection of
automobile. It was taking nearly a C-note to fill it up. I love
my truck, but hot weather plus air conditioner equals more
gas consumption. In a place this hot you learn quickly that
AC is a necessity. This was an unusual type of heat laced in
vicious humidity that discriminated against no one and vic-
timized everyone. This heat could make your armpits have
puddles by noonday. I hated to sweat in my good clothes, so
I turned the AC on full blast. By the time I got down town
I witnessed five tire blowouts. Those idiots must not have
gotten the memo about the Firestone Wilderness tires; some
people are just hard headed. Stuck in traffic, I whipped my
Blackberry out and called momma. I knew that she would be
glad to hear from me.

"Hello."

"Hey momma."

"Is this Jason? I think I remember how my son that never
calls sounds, but gimmie a minute to make sure"

"Yes maam, it's me".

"Son, our address hasn't changed. We still love for our
children to come visit?"

"Momma, you know that I've been busy with work and stuff."

"Stop making excuses son. We all get 24 hours each day the Good Lord blesses us to see. It's what you do with them that counts. You know your sister coming to town this weekend".

Momma really knew how to get things off her chest and put them into your head. Guilt was weighing me down. Now she was making the one hour drive from Charlotte seem like a cross country trip. "I spoke with her a few days ago, look; I am almost at work, I just called to tell you that I will be over for dinner on Sunday and to remind you not to try to feed me any pork or red meat."

"Okay boy, I know how to cook I'll let your daddy know you coming. That is if you're really coming."

"See you Sunday Ma."

"See you Sunday, son. I love you."

"I love you too."

I just remembered that I made out of town plans for this weekend with Angela. She would have to get over it; I never break promises to my momma. Angela was probably getting closer than I was comfortable with anyway and I could not take her to momma's for Sunday dinner. Momma would call her by someone's name on purpose just to piss her off, and then I would have to deal with that mess. No matter how many girls I dated, they never seemed to measure up

to her standard with the exception of Samantha. That's just
how overprotective momma was over me and my brother
Darryl. I guess that's why he up and moved away from home
and never visits. Today was definitely another scorcher. It's
a good thing my building is climate controlled. "Jason P.
Adams" is what my personal parking space reads to me every
day when I arrive to work. Finding a park is one less problem
in this black man's life. The time it took me to get out of my
car and into the building was just enough to raise my perspi-
ration level a few notches. Alas, I was at my own desk in my
own office when I realized. I didn't have a damn thing to do,
it was Friday and I had no appointments, only light paper-
work and case reviews which probably meant that I would
do nothing. After fixing a cup of coffee, I figured that I would
peruse the internet and see what was going on in the world.
There were definitely fringe benefits in being your own boss.
Glaring at my parent's picture atop my desk made me think of
how my daddy worked his whole life just so me, Darryl, and
my little sister Tonya could have it better than he and momma
did. Looking at my Masters Degrees and Licenses on the wall
made me thankful for those values that they instilled in me. I
wondered what type of excuse I could think of to tell Angela
about this weekend when I met her for lunch at the Blue
Marlin. Whatever it was, it had to be smooth and sound legit.
Angela was definitely a bonified dime piece. She was an in-
vestment banker at First Citizens Bank. Angela was the type
of woman that most guys only dreamed of having, and most
would lock her down immediately. She had her own money,
car, and stayed in a fancy condo downtown. This was perfect
for me because I didn't want any woman all up in my pockets, and trying to stay at my place for more than one night.
Having my own space was what I desired most. It was about

noon when Maxiene, my receptionist, buzzed my extension. Maxiene was very good at what she did and really made sure that things in my practice worked as they should. She was money well spent and having her around even felt like having a second mother. I needed her more than she could have imagined.

"Mr. Adams?"

"Yes."

"You have someone here to see you."

"Who is it?"

I wasn't expecting anyone and I didn't have anyone on the books.

"You can send them back."

"Okay, Mr. Adams."

I wondered who the hell it was and what was wrong now. Without even asking I invited the knocking mystery person into my office. Before I could even turn around I inhaled a very familiar aroma, an aroma that made my hormones go into overdrive. It was funny how you could equate smells to fond memories and it would elicit the same response whenever you encountered it. There was something about the smell of Chanel Number 5 that drove me crazy and excited me at the same time. When I turned around it was Angela.

"Did you forget about our lunch date?" I got out of a meeting earlier than I had planned so I thought I would stop by to see my favorite guy." Those words flowed from her mouth with all the sophistication that I have come to expect from a woman. She had me at the word go. Much like Adam, I was not built to resist this form of Eve.

Normally I would have expressed my displeasure for her coming by unannounced and violating clear boundaries, but I had to admit it was a very pleasant surprise. As she stood in the doorway the light from the hallway hit her in all of the right places and showcased her hour glass figure. With a devilish grin on her face she closed my office door, and it was clear that she wanted to spontaneously combust. It didn't take long for me to become a willing participant in her jobsite sexcapade. Angela's skirt and blouse were soon a thing of the past, as she unloosened my shirt and tie, she revealed to me a thong that would make Sisqo proud. I unbuckled my belt and let my pants fall to my ankles along with my boxer briefs. She turned around and bent over my desk; showed me a full moon at noonday. She put me inside of her and I rode the rhythm of ecstasy. We both knew that this was not the time to be long, so a quickie was definitely on tap. I had to cover Angela's mouth to muffle her moans and groans of passion.

"Ohh Jason that's the spot."

She was one of those noisy lovers that could really inflate a brother's ego to blimp size. I stroked her longer and deeper. With each thrust I lost control of any rational thought that I may have had. Her ass was perfectly shaped like an apple. She arched her back and begged for more. It didn't take long for me to cum. We had climbed to the heights of pleasure and orgasmed together. This was a different kind of therapy I thought to myself. Moments like this really made me grateful that I was my own boss, thus making sex breaks perfectly legal between consenting adults.

"If you keep on pulling these surprise visits, then I will have to replace my office furniture, I don't want my clients thinking ill of me."

"They might think that your into Sex Therapy."

We both laughed, as we put our clothes back on.

"Are we still on for lunch?"

"I just gave you desert."

"I will take that as a yes."

"Of course we are Jay".

I paged Maxiene to tell her that I couldn't possibly see anymore surprise visitors today, and that I would be leaving for lunch. Suddenly my place of business was overtaken by the scent of Chanel topped with male and female pheromones. Walking Angela out made me suspicious like Maxiene knew that we had just got our freak on in my office, because she didn't even make eye contact as we passed by.

CHAPTER 2

Kevin

There was nothing else possible that could make this day any worse than it already was. I had just spent all week trying to close two mortgage loans that fell through, I got stuck in traffic on I-26, and Sharon was calling me again to pick the kids up from daycare on the other side of town. She said that she was working late again and that she would not have time, something about trying to secure a new account. I was getting sick and tired of always having to pick the kids up and making sure that they ate. They are my kids too, but sometimes I needed a break. Since I was part Caveman, I didn't think that my woman needed to be working this late anyway. I made more than enough to support our family very comfortably. I missed the way that Sharon used to always be home before me, and she used to cook, and she used to meet all of my needs and then some. I reminded myself that "used to bees didn't make honey," right now my wife pretty much only made me frustrated. Oprah had too many women on that "self fulfillment," and "get out and get yours" nonsense. Whatever happened to taking care of your man? Jason was buzzing my phone trying to coordinate plans for later on this evening, and it sounded just like what I really needed. He said that he was on the way home from Angela's and mentioned something about a lunch date that turned wild. I remember the days when I was playing the field and free from any real responsibility, pulling down more panties than Tiger Woods. Even though I loved Sharon and our children there was a part of me that secretly envied Jason's carefree life. Sharon and I dated off and on during college, even though I still did my thing with other women. There was just something about her that set her apart from any other woman that I have ever dated. She was raised up north in Philadelphia, but still had a lot of southern values that most northern girls did not. There was never a time that Sharon put me second to anyone or anything. That alone spoke in volumes. I guess being great in bed did not hurt either. I think that I shocked everyone I knew when I announced that we were getting married. Jason wanted me to have my head examined and told me that I was incapable of being faithful to one woman; it sounded like a sermon that I had given him. Almost five years have gone by and I have been completely faithful to my wife except staring at a few booties here and there but it don't count if you don't touch. It almost felt like everyone was waiting for me to cheat on Sharon just so they would be right about me, especially her girls who only got steady action from other women's men and their battery operated boyfriend. When Sharon got pregnant with India and later with KJ, there was a change in me that would not allow me to ever look at another woman without comparing her to my wife. She had given life to the two most important parts of my life; my children. When I arrived at the daycare I noticed that all of the workers were extra friendly and chatty, which reminded me that they were expecting my monthly check in the amount of 1100 dollars. This was another reason why Sharon should stay home, at least that way the money would be in house and we would not have to worry about strangers taking care of our children. I guess that was too much like making sense. After I finally fought through traffic and rescued my rug rats, I took a shower and changed clothes in preparation for later. I fed India and KJ slices of cheese pizza and milk and put them in front of the electronic baby sitter and decided to take a nap until Sharon got home. I called Jason on his cell phone to see what was going on. He was talking about going to some new club in Charlotte that was supposed to be exclusive. I told him that I would meet him at his house when Sharon got home. Just as I hung up with Jason, I could hear the garage door opening. Sharon came in and KJ and India rushed her at the door with hugs and kisses like she was Santa Claus. She spoke to me and gave me that "hey honey not tonight smile" that I was growing very accustom too lately. Her face wore both worry and exhaustion like it was her make-up. I was growing too accustomed to this new look since she started back working. I didn't mind competing with my children for her attention, but I refused to take a back seat to her newfound career pursuits.

"Are you going out tonight?"

"That's the plan."

"Where are you going?"

"Is this some type of interrogation or something? Last I checked I was a grown man." "Excuse me, Mr. Grown Man have a nice time."

I wanted her to feel my pain and agitation, I wanted to fight but Sharon caved quicker than Enron stock. It was possible to win a fight and lose the war at the same time. I felt bad for snapping at Sharon, but my frustration got the best of me.

"Look, I am sorry…. I guess I had a long day. I am going out with Jason."

Sharon's face frowned when I mentioned his name. I kissed her on the cheek and waved to my children as I exited my place of dwelling. A change of venue was just what I could use, not to mention several stiff drinks. I called Jason to alert him that I was en route to his house. It was becoming increasingly obvious that Sharon and I were having major problems in this marriage. So obvious that Jason was constantly probing and expressing concern that I did not look like myself. I hated lying to him and saying that all was well, but I was not about to let him do that counseling crap on me. Although we were really good friends, sometimes a man had to keep certain things to himself.

"All is well with me and the Mrs."

That could not be further from the truth. As much as I hated to admit it, my marriage was headed nowhere very fast. It seemed hopeless at times, but I was committed to make it work. At this point the children were like Elmer's glue, they kept us together. It seemed as if Sharon was convinced that I was cheating on her and there was nothing that I could do to persuade her differently. In fact I was tired of convincing her that I wasn't. The second a brother tries to turn over a new stone is the second no one notices. There was a point that I was the Man Whore that she accuses me of being, but that was before we got married. I haven't been with another woman in over six years and we have been married for five years. Sometimes I feel like Keisha Cole, "I should have cheated". Maybe that would make her happy. In retrospect the biggest mistake I made was ever admitting that I messed around on

Sharon while we dated. I guess that I had some bright idea that confessing that I cheated on my then girlfriend would signify that I was serious about taking the next step. I thought that starting over on a clean slate would be proof that I was seriously committing. I can still remember the look on her face as she encouraged me to be "honest" with her about my indiscretions. I picked the wrong time to do right and tell the truth. Even though she accepted my proposal and pretended that all was forgiven, I don't think she can ever get the image out of her head about me running game. I think that Usher is getting a lot of guys in trouble with that whole confession idea. That is strictly for entertainment purposes only. Information is on a need to know basis and not everyone needs to know everything. I remember when we made love how her body would quiver at my slightest touch, and the way she would moan the sweet sounds of orgasmic harmony. It was as if she had an itch that only I could scratch. I was so certain that our relationship could only get better and that she was the woman that I would spend the rest of my life with and then some. It was amazing the way things could change in a New York minute. The love of your life could quickly change to a person that you couldn't stand the sight of at times. There would always be a part of me that will love Sharon forever, but there is a bigger part of me that sees we're not in love with one another anymore and that hurts. Her level of trust in me is basically nonexistent. I stopped hanging out as much because I have grown tired of random penis scans. Sharon has insisted that I submit to the "smell your genitals" test to prove that I wasn't parking my car in anybody's garage other than hers. As humiliating as it was I was eager to prove my innocence, knowing deep down that this was no way to live. I was beginning to wonder that if nothing really lasts forever, what made love the exception?

Jason

I was on the phone with Samantha when Kevin called and said that he would be over and urged me to be ready. Sam and I had a very interesting relationship with lots of history. Most of which I'd rather forget. We fooled around off and on but mostly off since Angela and I hooked up. Samantha was still in the rotation, but it was clear that she was no longer the starter for team Jason, although she wanted to be. She was trying to hook up tonight, but I had to brush her off with my plans to kick it with the Kevin.

"Sam let me call you when I get back."

"You always say that and you never do."

"No, I am serious I will call you back."

I hung the phone up and thought to myself that some people just cannot take a hint. Kevin said that he would be over in a few and I was still not ready. I briskly did my man prep which consisted of a shower, shave, and an eyebrow arch concluded by brushing my teeth. I pondered for minutes over what to wear not wanting to be over or under dressed but versatile in case we had to go to multiple venues. I decided to wear a nice black button down shirt with some jeans. I had been dying to wear these new black Louis Vuitton shoes anyway. My phone nearly vibrated off the counter which forced me to answer without looking to see who called, assuming it was Kevin.

"What's up Kev?"

"Excuse me, this is not Kevin."

"My bad what's up Angela?"

It was a good thing I was expecting Kevin to call me saying he was outside of my house and that I needed to hurry up, or I could have said some other girl's name.

"You never said what time we were leaving for the beach on Saturday."

Dang, I forgot to tell Angela that I would have to take a rain check on this one....sex can really cloud a man' s judgment.

"Oh yeah" I hesitated.

"Oh yeah what?"   She replied.

"You have been promising that we would get away for some fun for over a month now, and I know you ain't gonna back out now."

"It's not that, I sorda made a promise to my momma."

"You can do better than that Jason."

"Seriously, my sister is coming in town and my momma is having the whole family over for dinner."

I was hoping that this would be the part that Angela would let the whole thing go and we could get together and make it up another time.

"Why didn't you say so?"

What time is dinner?"

I nearly dropped my phone when she said that.

"I have been waiting to meet your sister and this would be the perfect time."

This was not what I had in mind, but if I said no then I would have to explain why and it really was not worth all that.

"Dinner is around three I think."

"I can't wait until I meet your family, I am excited."

Thank God for interference I thought as I heard my door-bell ring.

"That is Kevin, and I gotta go, I will call you later." She paused.

"Take care Mr."

For a brief second I thought she was going to say that she loved me, and I did not have a response for that. I liked the way our relationship was, no definitive boundaries or titles. We had a mutual respect for one another, and I did not need things getting complicated. Women confuse relationships when they want to apply expectations that are practically impossible to live up to. I opened the door for Kevin.

"What's up black man?"

"I thought I told you to be ready."

"Don't get mad at me because you ain't getting none."

"Man don't worry about my business, let's go."

I could tell that Kevin was uptight when he didn't laugh at my jokes.

"Yo man, you good?" Is everything straight."

"I am good, just tired of your butt not being ready when I gave you plenty of time to get ready. Some of us do respect timeliness."

"My bad massa, it won't happen again boss."

Kevin couldn't help but laugh.

"Man you a fool, let's go. Can't believe you are somebody's therapist."

We hopped in his truck and headed to Charlotte. There was so much trash, car seats, and toys in this large SUV that we had to spend about ten minutes moving stuff just so I could sit on the passenger side.

"Man you need a Maid for your car."

"You know how women are" he replied with an uncomfortable look on his face.

That was another reason that I wasn't married with kids, no way no how. I decided to change the subject sensing that my brother from another mother was in a not so good mood. We had about an hour long drive to get to the spot, and I bought up everything from sports to politics. Kevin and I were in constant debate over almost everything even though we had lots in common. Nobody could debate who was better between Biggie and Tupac like we could even after their untimely demises. It made me think back to our college days when we were freshmen and we competed in everything, even women. "Remember I won that bet our junior year in college?"

"What bet?" Kevin said.

"When we bet who could bang the most girls in one semester."

"That wasn't the bet. The bet was who could bang the finest girl, and I won."

"Whatever Kevin, they say that memory loss is the first sign of old age."

"I got with at least seven new honies that semester all while maintaining a 3.5 GPA." "Well all seven of those girls were no match for Tammy Neismith, who by the way was the queen of our college, and vice president of the SGA."

"Tammy was tight, but she wasn't all that" "Where is she these days anyway?"

"Last I heard she was finishing up medical school and she was engaged."

Kevin's whole demeanor changed as he went into detail about Tammy and their moment in the sun, albeit short-lived.

"She was okay, but I won the bet.....right?"

A man and his pride could blind him from the truth and in this case my best friend was no exception. My GPS tracking guided us to the night spot. It was good to go to a different city for a change of pace and fresh faces. Judging from the outside, either this was the happening place or either they were giving away something free. The line was wrapped around the building and across the street. It was a nice mixture of all races from black to brown and red to yellow. So far this place was living up to its name; this was truly The Melting Pot. It's a good thing we were on the VIP, because this line was not moving. Kevin and I were inside in no time with no wait, which was obviously to the dismay of many of the people who gave us the evil eye that waited in line. The Melting Pot was not your average night spot. There were three levels and each level featured an entirely different theme and catered to everyone's interests. There were at least seven different rooms and dance floors with everything from Hip Hop to Techno music. The second level had a theatre that showcased comedy, live concerts, and spoken word. Tonight Anthony Hamilton was the featured guest performer, so that was where we were going. Even the bathrooms in this place were lavish complete with expensive marble floors and coun-tertops. They even had a guy that works in the bathroom that dispensed the soap for your hands and even gave you a napkin when you were done. This guy had everything from magazines, breath mints, condoms, and even advice. Just like everything else in life, this was not free either. I admired a man that did an honest day's work no matter the circumstanc-es; he could be doing much worse. I tipped the brother just because, and offered him some words of encouragement after I used the bathroom and washed my hands with his good soap. Kevin had found us a table and was motioning for me to come over.

"Good job we are in a nice and discreet spot, like I like."

"Yeah, if you stop being so pretty we could have been had a table."

"I don't know what pissing has to do with being pretty, I had to pee."

My initial glance around the room indicated that there was a serious advantage for men looking to meet women." I had never seen so many men taking off their wedding rings as they saw what I saw. Kevin was the only dude that I could see that was married and not trying to hide it. He was definitely the minority in The Melting Pot tonight. There were some local aspiring poets putting their thing down opening up for the main event for this evening. I thought it was awesome the way good poets can bring their words to life through spoken word, but I was not nearly brave enough to try that.

"Is someone sitting here?" Tapping me on my shoulder was this cutie trying to get a good table for her and her friend.

"Naw, it's just me and my man, there is enough room and we don't mind." Even though I was not looking to meet anybody didn't mean that I didn't keep my options open.

"Hi, I am Jason and this is my friend Kevin."

"Nice to meet you Jason and Kevin, I am Elise and this is my friend Lisa."

Elise was about 5'2' with a slender but pleasantly curvy shape. She had a caramel complection with wavy shoulder length hair and looked like she may have an island influence in her ethnicity. I have always admired a woman that dresses well and takes pride in her appearance. Elise was wearing a hot black halter dress with a circle top near her cleavage and T-strap sandals that were about 4 inches high. Looking at her feet I could tell that she recently got her toes done, and she had reason to show them off, because she was flawless. Lisa and Kevin conversed and we all had drinks and shared each others company until Anthony came on. Elise told me that she recently finished college and that she was contemplating law school. She was only twenty four and a bit too young and unestablished for me. I hated telling people what I did for a living on my personal time, because they always tried to get me to give them advice and assumed that I knew everything. Surprisingly she didn't, in fact she changed the subject which was cool. The whole room focused on Anthony as he performed a medley of his hits before a packed crowd in his hometown. After the show Kevin and I were headed to check out the rest of the club before we hit the road. "Wanna dance?" she asked as she grabbed my hand and lead me to the third floor to dance Reggae. This girl could wind and grind her body in ways that made me have thoughts that I probably shouldn't have. It took some real willpower to control my soldier, because he wanted to salute and stand at attention.

"Are you afraid of me?" She asked.

I thought to myself, this girl doesn't know who I am.

"I don't know, are you psycho?"

She laughed as she pulled me closer to her and began putting her hand in places that people who just met usually don't go.

"Whoa lil momma.....wait a minute."

"What's wrong?"

"Nothing…I gotta go find my boy, we gotta get back to SC."

"You got a curfew of something?"

"Kevin is married and I know his wife don't want him out all night, and I drove."

It was good to have an alibi sometimes.

"I understand, maybe we can hook up sometime."

"Yeah definitely."

She took my Blackberry off my hip and proceeded to dial a number.

"Now you have my number, so use it when you want to hook up."

"Absolutely,… good meeting you."

She was very ambitious and probably a little too straight forward for me, but I had to give her props for persistence. Kevin was not going to believe this one. I went out in search of him, I hoped that he was having a good time while I was being entertained by the bumpin and grinding of cute little Elise. I was getting text messages on my phone from Kevin telling me he was downstairs in the lobby.

Kevin

Th is was exactly what I needed to take my mind off another hectic week, and an escape from the drama that was my marriage. Jason had disappeared with Elise and Lisa and I walked around the club and chitchatted. It was good to talk to someone of the opposite sex with no strings attached and no complications or restraints. This was the most free I have felt in some time. Lisa was coming off a relationship that had been on the verge of marriage, but never materialized past the point of an engagement. I offered her some words of comfort due to the obvious struggle that she was having while discussing her relationship. Lisa was very attractive by most standards. She was into working out and she even taught aerobics at a local gym in Charlotte three times a week. She worked in human resources for some fortune 500 company in the down town area called Dreamers Inc. that invested in start up companies.

"If you can dream it, we can fund it."

She said that corny company catch phrase as if she has said it hundreds of times. Lisa handed me her business card with her company logo and contact information. I almost felt guilty for noticing how fine she was, but like I say being married does not make you blind. Her look was casual; she was wearing denim Capri pants and cork bottomed sandals with one of those button down shirts that tie around the waist with her stomach out. No make up, lip liner with light gloss and a low natural hairdo, French manicure and pedicure with no visible polish, almond complexion, clear skin, and curves reminiscent of Serena Williams in that cat suit. Her ex boyfriend had better be dating Gabrielle Union to let her go, because that was probably the only way he could upgrade. The more she talked I waited for the real drama to unfold, but so far so good. I had to be discrete because I didn't want to let her see me taking a peek at her. Lisa asked me about marriage and what it was like as if she longed for the day to have someone call her wife. Despite my personal experience lately, I responded that it was the best thing that had ever happened to me and hoped that she could not tell that I was lying through my teeth. This was a similar response that I had gotten when I spoke to married people seeking their advice before Sharon and I got married. Not one person ever gave me any negative thoughts or experiences despite their personal hardships. Now I was being one of those people being dishonest and making marriage sound like a piece of cake. Maybe people do that because they want you to experience the misery that they are experiencing first hand. I told her about my two beautiful children and the way that Sharon and I met in college and it was love at first sight and other crap that was the substance of best selling romance novels. I am sure that she was not interested in knowing the daily grind of surviving in my world. With each swig of my Hennessey and Coke the less inhibited I began to feel.

"Let's go see the rest of this place and catch up with Jason and Elise," I remarked.

Lisa was a willing participant as we began to tour this utopia called The Melting Pot. This place must have cost a fortune I thought, no expense was spared. Lisa was from DC and she insisted we dance to go-go music. Not wanting to be rude I reluctantly agreed, all the while praying that I would not see any of Sharon's friends spreading gossip. Even though Lisa and I had nothing going on, some people have a way of making something innocent into a wild affair. Lisa morphed into another person when she heard her brand of music. This was definitely not my scene, but I was doing it in the name of fun. I never really liked this type of music, but people in the DC area swear by it. I guess Lisa could tell that I was not really feeling it and agreed to experience my world.

"Where are you from Kevin?" she asked.

"I am from the ATL shorty."

She laughed at my faint attempt at humor.

"Ohh…Atlanta well show me how they do in the ATL."

I had to take her to the hip hop spot and show how we did it in the "A." It was funny how nostalgic music could be,

I thought to myself as we entered my domain of familiarity. The DJ was spinning tunes that I hadn't heard in years, and for a minute I had gone back in time to my college days. He was doing a hip hop medley of old school that made me miss the days when rap was rap, and not crap. Outkast when they both appeared on the same track, PAC, Goodie Mob, Biggie, Luke, and on and on. Lisa must have been thinking what I was thinking because she had the "that's my jam look" on her face as we both headed for the dance floor. We carved out a space to dance on the crowded dance floor. Lisa could definitely shake her money maker.

"You move well Kevin."

"What's that supposed to mean?"

"I meant to say you're a good dancer."

"Ohh, thanks, you're alright yourself."

We both laughed. It was no laughing matter the way Lisa was winding her body, and before I knew it my nature was rising.   I wonder if she noticed, as I backed off. Some forms of dancing were the closest thing to sex other than sex itself. If this was any indication of her bedroom prowess she had the skills to pay the bills.

"You want something to drink?"

"I'm okay." I needed to create some separation.

"Well, I am kinda thirsty."

That was embarrassing I thought to myself as I ordered bottled water. I definitely needed cooling down. I had probably reached my limit of alcoholic beverages for one night. The last thing I needed was to have my inhibitions to disappear in the presence of this goddess. Besides the sobering reality that I had to go home was more than enough to snap me out of the trance that Lisa's booty had led me to. Obviously Lisa still wanted to get her groove on because she was dancing with some dude that wasted no time corralling her before I could get to the bar. It was cool, she wasn't my girl anyway. I waited on her as a courtesy since Jason was with her girl, I figured we could do an even swap of friends and get back to some type of normalcy like heading home. I enjoyed going out like the next guy, but I could not hang like I used to no matter how much Sharon got on my nerves.

"Did you get your drink?" She asked.

"Yeah, I got some water."

"You ready to find your friend?"

"Sure" I said.

I texted Jason to let him know that Lisa and I were heading downstairs to the main lobby. Lisa and I headed downstairs to swap friends. As weird as it seemed at the time, I couldn't help feeling a sense of familiarity about this person I had met a few hours ago. I could see Jason and Elise waving for us to come where they were. Just before I was about to feel awkward Lisa gave me one of those "thanks for a good time" hugs that was both innocent and yet provocative all at the same time. Meanwhile Jason was looking as surprised as I was with his "you got something you wanna tell me bro?" looks that only he could give. Under normal circumstances as a single man this would have been the part in which we exchanged contact information. I was married albeit not always happily, I didn't exchange phone numbers with women. Sharon was a CSI wannabe always looking for things that didn't even exist. It wasn't even worth the headache. I said my goodbyes to Lisa and Elise and Jason and I headed for the exit. Taking what I thought at the time would be my last look at her lovely assets; I paused for a minute to catch my breath.

"What's up with you and Lisa?"

"What do you mean me and Lisa?"

"It looks like she digging you bro."

"I don't think so.....I was only keeping her company because you left with Elise."

"Sure, as big as that place was you could have found hundreds of things to do." "Whatever Jason, everybody ain't like you man, some of us do have responsibilities like a wife and two kids."

I had to hit him with a dose of reality to get him to stop his relentless probing about me and Lisa. It was nearly 2 a.m., which meant that it would be after three before I dropped Jason off and got home. Whatever fun I thought I had would be short lived once Sharon got her mouth open about me coming home at a decent hour and how Jason was single and didn't have a wife and two kids. Just the thought of her nagging made me think about sleeping in the guestroom, it wasn't like I was gonna be getting any by the time I got home anyway. Jason was telling me about Elise and how she had tried to get better acquainted with him on the dance floor. I didn't know why he was trying to act like he didn't like it.

"Did you get her number?"

"Naw, but she made sure that she got mine."

I didn't quite know what that was all about, but I let him ramble and ramble to help shorten the trip and to make sure he stayed awake. He would probably be calling me next week telling me that he had sexed Elise. That was how he did it, no commitment in sight for that brotha. It reminded me of myself in pre-Sharon days long before marriage and the kids. The commute down I-77 was more crowded than it would normally be, which was thanks to The Melting Pot and eager partygoers like myself and Jason who were all headed back in the same direction. The visibility was not that great, in fact if was foggy and slightly damp at 75 degrees. Summers in the south were no joke. Thunderstorms were in the forecast, and apparently one hit while we partied. I became extra cautious behind the wheel and slowed my Expedition down; even if it meant that I would get home extra late. With both hands on the steering wheel and my seat in proper form I switched from my CD player to the radio for a change of pace. Jason was still talking about how many honies he had seen tonight and how Elise was all into him. I pretended to listen and even throw in appropriate responses like, "naw,"and "boy you crazy," when I really wanted to say, "it's okay if you go to

sleep if that will shut your mouth." Instead I used the opportunity to think about Lisa and how sweet she smelled, how
good she looked, and how nice her body was. I know it was
wrong, but I don't guess I could control what I was thinking. Besides, it's not like I would see her again. Before long I
was dropping Jason off in his gated community. This time of
morning he had to use his gate pass to gain access to his own
home. I thought that this was a little too constricting for my
taste, but it was just like Jason....guarded.

"I had a blast, call me tomorrow." He uttered as he dapped
me exiting my truck.

"It is tomorrow man, but I will hit you later" I said.

"Okay funny man, you better hope Sharon don't kill you
coming home this late."

He laughed. I laughed to, but inside I braced for the
worst. I began what seemed like a voyage home as I prepared
my alibi for Sharon. I would just blame it on Jason and say he
drove and it was his fault as if she hasn't heard that one before. I could just pick up where I had left off with an attitude
and make her think that I was still mad. Screw it I thought,
I didn't have to explain anything to her. When I got home I
opened the door and set the alarm. The house was scented by
plug ins and it appeared that she had done some cleaning. So
far so good I thought as I ventured upstairs to check on my
kids. They were sound asleep in India's room in their sleeping bags. You would swear that they didn't have their own
beds or something. I tucked them in and kissed them both,
turned off the TV and walked away thinking about how much

I loved them both and how I would never risk losing them. I still had one more hurdle to conquer and that was getting in my bedroom, getting undressed and getting into bed without waking Sharon. Here goes nothing, I thought as I entered our bedroom and went into the bathroom to change. I showered quickly and quietly put on fresh boxer briefs and a t-shirt. I brushed my teeth and flossed as whispery as possible. Finally I was ready for bed. Sharon was snoring while lying on her back. She looked peaceful. I gazed at her and thought to myself how beautiful she could be. Sharon had fallen asleep reading some novel by Eric Jerome Dickey. I knew that she tried to stay up and wait for me. It surprised me that she didn't call or text me one single time. Tiptoeing across our carpeted floor I was finally on my side of the bed. I pulled the sheets back and turned off her reading lamp and got into bed. This was too good to be true; she didn't wake up or say anything. I could get used to this I thought as I turned and went to sleep.

CHAPTER 5

Jason

My insomnia was no match for the hangover that I was feeling from yesterday, or whatever day it was. I had fallen asleep on the couch downstairs shortly after Kevin dropped me off early this morning. I wondered if he was still alive or if Sharon had killed him for coming in at the crack of dawn. I mustered up some strength and rolled off the couch to change clothes and shower. My breath tasted like alcohol and Altoids. A hot shower was just what I needed to snap back into things. I had a few errands to run, but no major plans for the rest of the day. I threw on some brown cargo shorts with a white GAP t-shirt and flip flops. I took a few extra seconds to put on lotion because there is nothing worst than an ashy brotha trying to wear flip flops and shorts. I grabbed my dry cleaning and my wallet and headed out the door. It was about half past noon, and this Columbia heat was in full force. Most of my neighbors used Saturday as their yard day or for family time cleaning out the car. I did not have time for either. I had a professional landscaping company to make sure my yard was well maintained. My car was detailed on the regular basis at Reggie's detail shop. Reggie and I go all the way back to elementary school. We played little league baseball and basketball on the same team. He grew up two houses down from me. Reggie ended up doing about four years in prison because he believed in easy money and got caught up. Some people had to learn the hard way. He has owned his detail shop for about five years and he seems to be on the up and up. It was funny how solitary confinement could help people realize that laws were put in place for a reason. Reggie was a major opportunist always looking for the next come up. I turned on my blackberry when I got into my truck and my joint was full of text and voice messages. Angela left me two messages about Sunday at momma's, Samantha text me about hooking up for drinks, and there was a text from a number that I didn't recognize.

"I had a good time, maybe we should hook up sometime......Elise."

It was the girl from the club last night, the cutie that I was dancing with. Now I remembered, it was all coming back to me. This girl was bold; I had to give it to her. I violated the 48 hour no contact after exchanging phone numbers rule, but technically she violated it first. I texted her back.

"I had a good time to; we should get up...JA."

I pulled up to the cleaners to drop off my clothes. They knew me on a first name basis. "You gonna pick up your other laundry while your here?"

"Yes, absolutely."

I forgot that I had anything to pick up. It was some new dress shirts that I bought a few weeks ago and put them in the cleaners.

"Your clothes will be back on Monday after 5pm Mr. Adams."

I spent so much money in this place that they should have my picture on the wall or something. Saturday was my day to get my haircut, but I needed to get my car detailed also. I whipped my phone out to call my barber to see what the wait was like.

"Dre, this Jason, how many you got ahead of me?"

"Yo, what's up Jay?, I got one in the chair and one waiting." "You coming through?" "Yeah, I'll be there in 20 minutes, save my spot."

"Cool."

One in the chair and one waiting was black barbershop slang for it's gonna be a while before I get to you. I had to do what I had to do to maintain my appearance. Sometimes I wish I had a bald head so I wouldn't have to go through this weekly drama. Dre was nice with the clippers, but I swear he could use some business courses and time management skills. Nonetheless, I headed to the barbershop anyway. I had to jump on the interstate headed towards Dre's shop downtown on the other side of town about 20 minutes, but I could do it in about12 minutes if traffic cooperated. Weaving in and out of traffic with the radio blasting, I get another call. This time it's my brother Darryl calling me.

"What's up big bro?"

"What's up Darryl?"

He only calls me when he wants something.

"Dang, you sure don't seem happy to hear from a brotha."

"It ain't like that, I am driving that's all."

"Cool, I was just letting you know that I was in town, that's all. You don't mind me crashing with you? Do you?"

I knew that it was something. The fact that he didn't want to stay at mamma's house means that something is going down.

"No problem Darryl let me hit you back when I get done with my haircut."

"Tell Dre I said what up."

"Will do, keep your phone on."

Just when I thought things couldn't get more interesting, what else was going to happen I thought to myself? When I pulled up to the barbershop, Dre was true to his word. He was about to finish up the guy that was waiting which meant that I was next. Dre has been cutting my hair since I was in high school. He was the neighborhood kid that grew up in the neighborhood cutting everybody's hair under his mom's carport. Finally Mr. Floyd recognized his skills and saw that he wasn't going much further than the GED that he did get and decided to train him as his apprentice. When Mr. Floyd died, he left the shop to Dre because he knew that he was the only one that loved it as much as him. Dre never changed the name, and today Professional Hair Design is still a thriving business in the black community. I guess Dre was doing something right, he was still in business. Although the place needed a facelift, the service was good. The clientele ranged from neighborhood kids with single mothers, to thugged out looking teens with cornrows, and even clean cut business types like me. I remember when my daddy made me get my head cut even all over when I was a kid and how much I hated it. "Cut him low." He would say. "Give him that Even Steven and tape it up." I wanted to get what the other kids were getting. Darryl and I could never get the New Edition haircuts like Ralph and Bobby. "How you want it man?" Dre asked me.

"You know I get the same haircut man, nice and even."

It was funny the more things changed, the more they stayed the same.

"Your boy Kevin was in here earlier with his son."

"Oh yeah."

"He said ya'll had a blast last night."

"Yeah, we had a blast. You gotta check out The Melting Pot."

Dre just nodded and kept on cutting my hair. The barbershop was a unique place to go to. You could hear all the latest gossip before the news could even break the story. All the latest DVDs were there before they hit the theater, and there was always somebody who knew somebody that had a hookup on something. There was a distributor for some hair care products making a delivery to Dre that walked in after I did. I laughed to myself thinking that CSPAN and ESPN should do live broadcasts with the real experts on politics and sports. Everybody had an opinion on every topic that they thought was factual. I have fond memories of Professional Hair Design, this place was like home. I dapped Dre, paid him and proceeded to my car. I always tipped him because sometimes he would slip me in front of other customers who had been waiting before me. My phone was charging in my truck while I was inside. I leave it for one minute and everybody and their momma calls me. Six missed calls from Kevin, Tonya, Angela, and momma. I called Kevin on his cell and got his voicemail, so I called him at home. Sharon answered the phone and before I could say hey, she was saying hold on passing the phone to Kevin. I made small talk with Kevin as I headed to Reggie's to get my car cleaned up. Kevin was lying low spending time with his family watching animated movies. We didn't talk long; I didn't want to seem intrusive. I called my little sister Tonya to see what she wanted. She was dying for me to meet this new guy that she was dating, and yapping about how this may be the one. Like Sunshine Anderson, I had heard it all before when it came to Tonya and wedding plans. I told her that I would meet Mr. Wonderful on Sunday and gave her the "I am busy line" that meant we would talk later. My sister was a piece of work. I had finally gotten to Reggie's detailing shop to have my Navigator cleaned up. Reggie was busy detailing a white Mercedes Benz when I pulled up, so we didn't get a chance to talk much. He just told me that he was about to come up in a major way. I watched him as he tucked the card in his pocket from the owner of that German luxury vehicle. He said he couldn't really discuss it, because there were loose ends to tie up. I really didn't wanna know about his latest plan in the come up department. I tossed him my car keys and decided to give Angela a call to see what she was doing.

"What's up Angela?"

"Hey Jay, did you get any of my messages?"

"Yeah I got em, I have had a busy day of running around."

"Umm huh, I see."

"What are you doing?" I asked.

"Nothing, I was doing some shopping earlier and found some cute shoes."

Angela reminded me of Carrie from Sex and the City; she really had a thing for shoes. I even think she had them color-coded or something. Her closet looked like the shoe department at Bloomingdales. That was one of the things that attracted me to Angela when we met. I like a woman with an eye for fashion. In fact we met each other out shopping. I was in the women's department at Macys shopping for a present for Tonya's birthday. "Ma'am could you show me some of your purses please?"

I asked the lady behind the counter where all the Gucci and Coach bags were. I was trying to make my mind up on which bag to get for Tonya, when I noticed this fine specimen of a woman trying on shoes in the shoe department. She was wearing a nice gray business skirt, with a pink blouse that was low cut. We made eye contact and there was an instant connection. After deciding on the Gucci I purchased for Tonya, I headed into the mall towards the food court. As much as I wanted to I didn't give Angela another look, but I could feel that she was looking at me as I walked off. It was during lunchtime so the food court was crowded. I usually blocked out about two hours for lunch to allow time for shopping and life's other pleasures. Everyone else seemed to be in a real panic as they scarfed down their lunch to get back to work. There were not many vacant tables, but I had one chair available. I was hoping that some weirdo would not come to claim the seat as I thought of something to say in anticipation as this guy approached my table. He appeared to be foreign, about six feet, unshaven, dressed in layers of clothing. I hated to be stereotypical, but since 9/11 you could never be too safe. "Is this seat taken buddy?" he asked with a foreign accent.

With a straight face I looked at him and told him that I was saving it for someone. He looked around as if he had heard that line before. Just then I saw Angela walking with her lunch trying to find a table to sit down and eat. It was totally out of character for me as I motioned her to my table as if we had it all planned. She appeared relieved as she sat down and thanked me for the empty seat. Soon the guy got the point as he walked away disappointed. We exchanged introductions and made small talk over lunch. I explained to Angela that she had kept my lunch from being ruined and how perfect her timing was. She smiled and continued to make small talk.

"How did the bag shopping go?"

I knew where her line of questioning was going as she was implying that I was involved with someone. I replied that I had gotten the purse as a gift for my little sister. All of a sudden her facial expression changed for the better.

"How did the shoe shopping go?"

She smiled and said, "It went well."

Angela explained that she was new in town after taking a job that moved her from New York. She said that she needed a slower pace and a new beginning. Angela told me how much she loved warm weather and walking on beaches. Said she always thought that beaches represented new beginnings. I thought they represented the end, but I let her have her moment. She felt like she had access to both here. She had no kids and hadnever been married. To say that we had instant chemistry was an understatement. We must have talked for about thirty-five minutes before I realized how quickly time had flown by. We exchanged numbers and we have been talking since that day. I watched her walk off as she left and I could only visualize what she must look like naked. Angela was hot. She had Tyra's height, Halle's eyes and complexion, Gabrielle Union's frame, Venus William's torso, Beyonce's smile, Megan Goode's lips, and Kerry Washington's cheeks. I saw all of that when I looked at Angela. She had a stride on her that Ms. Jay on Top Model would envy.

"I am getting my car cleaned up now, and I have to get home to hook up with my brother that's in town."

"Okay, I didn't want anything major, I was just calling." She said.

Angela was obviously making small talk and she was nervous about meeting my family tomorrow. So was I, but it was really no big deal.

"I will call you later Angela, don't sweat tomorrow."

She agreed and we both hung up. Finally, my truck was done and I could leave. Once again Reggie did his thing. My truck was so clean it looked brand new inside and out. He looked occupied like he was in a rush to get somewhere else. He was not the only one. Reggie said something about a meeting he had set up. Talked about some big come up. "It's fool proof, I can't miss." He said with confidence.

I didn't want to hear about another one of Reggie's schemes to get rich. Some people never learned.

"Don't forget about the little people man."

I paid him my normal fee and got on with the rest of my day. It was money well spent I thought as I peeled out of the parking lot in pursuit of my crazy younger siblings.

Jason

6

Sunlight was piercing through my blinds, which was enough to wake me up. I sat up yawned and stretched as I tried to collect my thoughts. I forgot to set my alarm clock and I was running late for church. I guess that I had fallen asleep last night after me and Darryl hung out and shot some pool. Normally I would have taken one of my church cuts and watched T.D. Jakes or somebody on TV, but I didn't want to hear my momma's mouth. I yelled for Darryl so that he could get up and get ready. He was sound asleep in my guest bedroom.

"Wake up man."

He rolled over and looked at me as if I had disturbed a good dream he was having.

"Why are you waking me up so damn early?"

"Maybe because it's time to wake up, we overslept and it's time to go to church."

This reminded me when we were kids and momma would have me wake up Darryl and Tonya on Sundays for church. In those days I was an early riser and I would always get up before them. There were two things that my folks didn't play about and that was school and church. There was no compromising when it came to either one. You had to be damn near dead to be excused.

"Just hurry up so we can leave."

I think he got the point as I adjusted my tone and gave him that older brother glare that meant I was serious. Figuring that he had gotten the point I went to my room to shower and dress. I hated having to abbreviate my routine, but I had no choice. Weather factored into my decision of which suit to wear. A packed church full of black people praising and worshipping had a way of elevating the temperature several degrees. I decided on a nice gray Ralph Lauren three button suit with double slits on the jacket, crisp white French cuffed shirt, and a nice navy and white tie to accent the suit. Black square toed Kenneth Cole lace ups and my black leather belt completed my outfit. At last I was ready to go. I wondered if Darryl was ready. When I turned to leave my closet, he was in my bedroom trying to see what he could borrow.

"Do you think you got enough cologne bro?" I laughed.

"You can never have too much cologne. "Just because you still wear Cool Water don't hate on me for having variety." We both laughed.

"I am consistent big bro, that's all."

I squirted on some Unforgivable to show Diddy some love. Darryl used some of my CK One. He was dressed in an Earth tone linen suit with a collarless shirt, no socks and some shoes that probably could have been Gucci or something like that. Darryl was about six feet, medium build, and darker complexion than mine, bald with a goatee. I didn't think that we resembled each other, but mostly everybody else does when they meet us. I was always told that I looked more like my momma, and that Darryl looked like my daddy. Maybe that was why daddy got along better with Darryl than he did with me. Who knows? We finally left and headed to church. Darryl and I actually had a pleasant conversation as I drove us to church.

"Let me hear that NAS CD" he insisted.

"It is too early in the morning to hear about Hip Hop being dead, besides I like to listen to Gospel music on the way to church."

He gave me that "yeah right" look.

"When you drive we can listen to what you wanna play."

We listened to Tye Tribbet and Kirk Franklin and some other notable artists until we got there. The parking lot was packed when we pulled up, which meant that getting a seat in this tiny sanctuary would be next to impossible. Everybody had on their Sunday best. I wondered if I was the only person that felt like it was too hot to have on a suit and tie in the middle of summer. People were still pulling up and entering the church. Greater Columbia Baptist Church was over 100 years old, and there have been at least three upgrades. It seemed as if there was some building fund every year, even though not much had been built. Me and Darryl got out and headed into church. Once we entered the church I did a quick scan to see if we could get a seat in the back, but they were all filled. We had gotten to church after the call to worship, which meant all the good seats were taken. Everybody had the back seats filled up in case Rev. Smith preached too long and they had to sneak out without being noticed. There was a heavy set sister singing a solo about how much she loved Jesus that had everybody on their feet. I motioned for Darryl to follow me to the balcony, when Tonya was waving us to come sit where she was. This pushy usher guided us near the front of the church to where Tonya was. She acted like she was secret service or something. Tonya was looking pretty, dressed in an off white skirt suit, and stiletto heels that matched her blouse. I hugged Tonya and gave hear a kiss before I sat down. She was so excited to see me and Darryl. Tonya was in her senior year in college at Johnson C. Smith University. Despite multiple major changes, Tonya was on pace to graduate in the fall. Her latest Mr. Wonderful was anxiously waiting for me to acknowledge his presence.

"This is Winston."

Tonya explained as he simultaneously extended his right hand towards me. What kinda corny name was Winston? I thought to myself.

"What's going on man?"

"It's nice to meet you".

He offered the same gesture to Darryl. When it came to guys Tonya was probably as confused as she was about her major. I didn't want my sister spreading herself too thin like some chics that I knew. She was an adult and she was gonna have to learn some things on her own. Momma was glaring at me and Darryl from the choir stand. It was as if she was scolding me for showing up late. I know that look from anywhere. Being the oldest kid I was often blamed for everything that went wrong with Darryl or Tonya. Daddy was in his usual seat where the Deacons sat during service. It was first Sunday and this was when communion was observed. I mentally prepared myself for a long day. After a few selections from the choir, some long testimonies, alter call and the offering it was finally time for the spoken word. I followed along with Rev. Smith and tried to focus my attention on his message. This lady in the back of me was in my ear as if she knew the sermon better than the Pastor. A few people were shouting and it seemed that everyone knew when to get rowdy and when to calm down and take their seats without even being told. This was an interesting congregation comprised of old and young people. People who had three or more generations of family that worshipped here and people who just wanted to come that had never been to church in their life. There were doctors, lawyers and people with some real clout locally. There were also people who didn't have a pot to piss in or a window to throw it out of. The more Rev. Smith preached the more I thought that he was talking to me. It made me do that self-evaluation that everyone does when they are in church. I nudged Darryl to wake up. The older he got the more he stayed the same. Church was a big lullaby for my brother. I looked to my left at Tonya and Winston holding hands and occasionally gazing at each other. They looked

happy. They looked like they were in love. The next thing I
knew Rev. Smith was opening the doors to the church. This
was the part that signified the closing of service. Darryl was
somehow perfectly alert at this point as if he had been a part
of the church service the whole time. After several hugs and
kisses from women that knew my momma and shaking hands
with the Deacons, and Rev. Smith I made my way outside to
cool off and breathe. It was funny how 92 degrees outside felt
more comfortable than the church did.

"Hey Mr. Adams."

I turned to answer the familiar voice. It was Samantha.
Samantha had grown up in this church just like me. It seemed
destined that we would grow up, fall in love, get married,
and live happily ever after. At least that was the sentiment
shared by both of our mothers. I gave her a hug and she
kissed me on my cheek.

"Why haven't you returned my calls Jason?"

Here we go again I thought to myself. Before I could di-
vert her from this line of questioning Tonya, Winston, and
Darryl were coming up. Tonya and Darryl both spoke to
Samantha. Tonya gave her a hug and introduced Samantha
to Winston. For once I was thankful for Winston being here.
I put on my shades to combat some to the UV rays that were
on full blast. Tonya and Samantha chit chatted like they were
long lost friends. Darryl and Winston appeared to be having
small talk. I sat back and observed the scene. There were
a few single sisters gazing my way trying to figure out who
I was here with. It was funny the stuff people had on their

minds right after church. Samantha was looking good in an all white pant suit. Her pants were fitting snug on her thighs and booty. She was making me have some not so churchy thoughts. Samantha and I dated back in high school and some in college. *We had to come to the conclusion that most couples do that distance and college can change relationships.* We agreed that being friends was best. I guess you could say that we were friends with benefits. She knew about Angela, and I knew about every guy that she dated. Samantha had gotten her hair cut like Halle Berry wore hers back in the day. It looked good on her. She had the prettiest smile that I had ever seen, like she could be on a Crest commercial. Her dimples were on full display as if Tonya was tickling her funny bone. Before I knew it Tonya asked Samantha to come by momma's for dinner later on. My heart nearly dropped to the pit of my stomach as I thought about the possibility of having dinner with my past and present girl, both of which I am currently sleeping with.

"I am sure that Samantha has better things to do."

I gave Tonya the shut up and talk to Winston look. She obviously got it because that's what she did. Samantha replied,

"Girl you know I can't turn down your momma's cooking."

I explained to Samantha my concern over the situation and told her that Angela was also coming. She seemed to take delight in my uneasiness.

"In that case I wouldn't miss that for the world."

Samantha gave me a devilish grin and winked her eye at me as she walked away. Somehow I felt as though my momma had something to do with this. Samantha was the only girl that I dated that momma ever really approved of. It was as if momma had struck a deal with Samantha's mother that we would be together. Thanks to Tonya and Samantha, Sunday dinner was going to be very interesting.

CHAPTER 7

Jason

I jumped in my chariot headed home to change clothes before I met up with Angela. My truck chimed to alert me that I was low on gas. I pulled into the 76 station to fill my truck up. The price of gas was not conducive to driving a luxury SUV that required premium gas. Days like this made me wish I had something more fuel efficient. I used my debit card to pay at the pump while leaving my truck running. Damn near pumped a C-note worth of gas just to fill up. I called Angela to give her heads up that I was coming so that she would be ready before I got there. The last thing she needed to do was be late and give momma some ammunition against her. I jumped on 277 to 20 and exited on 82 to get to my crib. On a Sunday afternoon traffic was very light and it only took about twenty minutes to get home. Daryl decided to ride with Tonya and Winston over to momma's house. I was vibing to some Maxwell. He was crooning about having somebody locked up in love until the cops came knocking. It made me think back to some really good times that I had listening to his first album. I wondered why he just stopped making music. I dashed in the house to change clothes. The

Carolina heat had forced me to take a shower. I hated sweating unless I was working out. My brand new dress shirt had some serious ring around the collar on it. I tossed my damp shirt and my suit into my dry clean pile and continued to de-robe myself until I was in my birthday suit. I was cutting it close, so I hurried in and out of the shower. Stayed in long enough to get that fresh feeling back. I threw on some jeans and a tank top from American Eagle. I figured this should give Angela more than adequate time to be ready when I got to her house. I jumped back on I-20 to 277 and exited on Bull St. I was at Angela's condo and I called her from my cell phone to let her know that I was downstairs. I left my truck running to keep the AC going. Angela lived in a nice part of downtown where the city was dumping tons of money into revitalization projects trying to attract corporations and tourism. People around here were used to seeing nice cars and wouldn't be tempted to take my Navigator to a chop shop for some quick dough. I rang her doorbell and waited for her to answer. Her nosey neighbor Marilyn was opening her door with two small bags from Publix in her hand.

"I think that she is home, I just saw her car downstairs" she said.

"Yeah, she is expecting me."

It was funny how some people were so involved in the affairs of others. Angela never said more than hello to Marilyn unless it was absolutely necessary. I wondered how many guys Marilyn had seen on Angela's doorstep waiting to come in. Angela opened the door and gave me a peck on the lips.

"Are you ready to go?"

"I have been waiting on you, let me grab my purse."

Angela's condo was laid. It looked like an interior deco-
rator came in and did their thing. She had a burnt orange
colored accent wall with wall sconces and strategically placed
black art on the walls. Her place smelled like the inside
of a Yankee Candle store. It had a cozy feel to it, but yet it
lacked the warmth that made a house a home. I guess that
was because Angela was like most people who were trying to
have something; she had to work to get it. Sometimes work
yields very little time to enjoy the fruits of your labor. I could
tell she was reading, because she left her book on the couch
turned facedown to mark her page. She was reading some
book about finishing rich and investing. This was the type of
stuff she had to know being a banker. Angela came out with
her Gucci signature purse and Gucci sandals that accented
the sundress that she was wearing. This girl had more shoes
and bags than Joan from Girlfriends and Carrie from Sex in
the City. I was attracted to a fine woman with a mean shoe
game.

"Are you finally ready Carrie?" I said with a smirk.

"Why can't I be Joan today?" She replied with a smile on
her face.

We jumped in my car that was still running. That probably was not the best use of gas, but at least my truck was
not stolen and the AC was very cold. I took the scenic route
through town to get to momma's house. My parents only lived
about ten minute's real time from downtown. Angela was
talking about her church and today's service. She asked me

how my church service was. I nodded and kept the conversation light. My mind was on getting through this encounter with my family with minimal embarrassment. The closer we got to momma's the more my anxiety level increased. I tried to do some positive self talk and all that stuff that I encourage my clients to do, but it wasn't working so far. When we got to my folks house I had to park on the side of the street because my family had taken all of the good parks. I recognized most of the cars so I knew the cast of characters to expect when we got in. I tried to read Angela's face to see if she had some apprehension, but it did not show. If she was nervous she had an excellent poker face. We walked down the driveway towards the front door past my old basketball goal. I remember when my daddy bought that goal home for me and Daryl. I also remember the hours of forced practices that he insisted me and Daryl have.

"You ain't never gonna be like Magic Johnson if you don't practice."

His words were sincere and forceful. Daddy just knew that one of his sons was going to be in the NBA. I opened the storm door to the front of the house. The smell of familiar cuisine overflowed my nostrils. Most of which I probably didn't eat anymore. Angela reached for my hand, and I could sense her anxiety level creeping up a few notches. We walked in the living room and it was the moment of truth. Daddy was sitting in his easy chair, Tonya and Winston were sitting beside Daryl on the sofa. My Aunt Renee and Uncle Frank were on the loveseat. Aunt Renee was momma's twin sister. She was quick to remind anyone interested that she was the younger sister. I introduced Angela to the entire mob that was my family. This was her first time meeting everybody including Darryl. To this point they only existed through conversation to her. Everyone seemed very receptive so far. Darryl, Winston, and even Uncle Frank did subtle double takes of Angela and her stunning good looks. Daddy barked out that he was hungry and ready to eat.

"Yo momma made us wait on you. Can you ever be on time for anything?"

Before I could reply to my daddy's comments, momma had come into the living room to intervene.

"Leave that boy alone."

Momma had always intervened when it came to my daddy. We were like oil and water sometimes. It seemed like I could never do anything good enough for him. Seeing momma made all my anger towards my daddy go away. I introduced momma to Angela and Angela to my momma. Everything seemed to be going well, still no sign of Samantha. Maybe she got the hint and decided not to show up after all. I breathed a collective sigh of relief after thinking that thought. Momma ushered everybody into the dining room to eat dinner. At that moment my relief dissipated. Samantha was already in the dining room setting the table and bringing the food from the kitchen. Our eyes met and she flashed that trademark smile, dimples and all. Samantha approached Angela and introduced herself as an old family friend. I could tell she was sizing Angela up and thinking thoughts that women do when they meet their exboyfriend's new main squeeze. Everybody sat down to a feast prepared for a royal family. Daddy offered the blessing of the food. I lip synched his prayer along with him. It was the same prayer that he blessed every meal with since I was old enough to remember. I wondered if GOD was tired of his redundancy like I was. Momma had prepared fried and baked chicken, macaroni and cheese, collard greens, string beans, rice and gravy, corn bread, and sweet potato pie for dessert. Momma's face beamed with pride that her family was together and eating her cooking. Everyone tossed around various topics of conversation ranging from church, gas prices, war, and sports. Daddy had a way of making every topic a black and white topic. Sometimes I wondered how momma could put up with his narrow mindedness for all these years. "How did you and Andrea meet?" asked Aunt Renee. I corrected my aunt about Angela's name not being Andrea and answered her question. This was beginning to turn into the grand inquisition. Momma fired a series of questions that went from place of birth, line of work, astrological sign, hobbies, and what church she went to. I almost thought that she was going to ask Angela when she lost her virginity. All eyes were on Angela as she answered momma's questions no matter how invasive they were. I did my best to deflect some attention off of Angela. I began my own interrogation and aimed it at Winston. He nearly chocked on his collard greens when I asked him about his intentions for my baby sister. This was the second time today that Winston's presence was a blessing. Order was restored in the universe as the conversation mellowed out and the heat was off of me and Angela. Daddy and Darryl engaged in a side conversation about the NBA finals. They looked like best friends instead of father and son. I wished that I could have one conversation with my daddy without one of us arguing or losing their temper. I helped momma clear the table and offered my assistance with all of those dishes. She gave me one of those kisses on the cheek that said thanks but no thanks and shewed me into the living room. It was as if momma wanted me to get in on the act with daddy and Darryl. Aunt Renee and Tonya pitched in to clean up. Angela asked momma what she could do to help. Momma insisted that she was a guest and that she didn't need to do anything. This was a test from momma. She was somehow testing Angela's character. I was hoping that she would pass it. Angela insisted that she do something to show her appreciation. Although she was fine as hell she was not a stranger to domestic duties. Angela fell in place with the rest of the women and restored the kitchen and dining room to a state of cleanliness in no time. Just when I thought things were going okay, momma pulled out an old photo album. This was one time I did not want to take a trip down memory lane. Momma sat between Angela and I with the photo album. All of the embarrassing photos of me seemed to be in plain view. Naked potty training pictures, missing front teeth, graduation photos, little league sports, and even prom pictures. There were several pictures of me and Samantha from our junior and senior prom. Angela did a double take when she realized that it was Samantha. A look of uneasiness came on her face and for the first time today she was visibly flustered. My eyes met with Samantha's eyes and again she had that signature smile on her face. It was as if momma purposely pulled out all of those old photos of me and Samantha. I waited for the tension to ease and planned our escape.

"I have a busy day tomorrow, and I need to get Angela home."

I even yawned to make it look authentic. We said our good byes and headed back to Angela's condo. There was an awkward silence that said neither one of us wanted to process the events that had just unfolded. Neither of us spoke a word until we got to Angela's. She jumped out of the truck without giving me her lips or letting me walk her to her front door.

"I'll call you later." She said.

"Cool."

I had never seen Angela so....like other women. Until this point we have existed in a place of no drama. I watched her get into her condo, and I pulled off headed towards 277. I thought to myself that the land of no drama was a comfortable place for me. *Not very practical, but comfortable nonetheless.*

CHAPTER 8

Kevin

The weekend for me had come and gone. Other than hanging out on Friday, I pretty much did nothing. Sharon and I took the kids to the movies and dinner on Saturday. I had spent the rest of Saturday mowing my lawn and washing the cars. We had gone to church earlier and out to eat. It was time for my usual Sunday evening routine in preparation for another work week. I had given India and KJ their baths and dressed them for bed. KJ didn't put up much of a fight and was soon fast asleep. India insisted that I read her a series of bedtime stories from her Dora the Explorer library until she fell asleep. I kissed her on her cheek and walked out of her room.

"I love you daddy," she whispered.

"I love you to sweetie."

India was a regular daddy's girl. She even looked like me. Kevin Jr. favored Sharon more than he did me. Nonetheless, I loved my children with all my heart and then some. I couldn't imagine being away from them. I prepared my clothes for work and replaced all of the essential toiletries for my gym bag. Sharon was in the bedroom reading her fiction novel. I set the alarm system and prepared for bed by doing some crunches and push-ups. I had worked up a pretty good sweat and headed for the shower. Sharon was peering at me from around her book as I walked by butt naked heading into the bathroom.

"You see something you like?"

She didn't respond. I jumped in the shower and did my thing. Sharon had turned on some mood music from the satellite TV. Heather Headley was singing in the background about always being some dudes lady. It wasn't long before she joined me in the tub with the look of seduction in her eyes. She began washing my back and caressing my wet soapy frame, she had my full attention.

"I definitely see something I like."

I turned and faced her, palmed her ass and begin kissing her slow and deep, the way a man kisses a woman he loves. R. Kelly was now on talking about the greatest sex. Sharon's breathing picked up, and her nipples became stiff like my manhood. I began kissing her on her neck and then her breasts. I took her nipple into my mouth and sucked it like it was going out of style. Her body was definitely calling me, and I was ready to give her my 12-play. Having two children doesn't afford many opportunities for extended lovemaking and I intended to take full advantage of this one.

"Hurry up and get out of the shower, you know I can't get my hair wet."

We stood face to face outside of the shower, passionately kissing one another. Sharon grabbed my manhood and began to stroke it up and down. She knelt down kissing my nipples and licking my navel with circular strokes. My eyes rolled back inside my head as I uttered moans of inevitable orgasm. Sharon had taken my manhood into her mouth, and bobbed her head up and down at a feverish pace like Mike Tyson on a speed bag. She did that until I released my fluids of ecstasy. Sharon took it all as she headed north on my anatomy repeating the same routine until she tasted my lips and tongue. My wife was the king of fellatio, and she did it with so much pride and intensity. I placed my hands on her waist and hoisted her onto the bathroom counter. My face became buried in between her legs, as I became the giver of pleasure. Sharon was particular about the way she kept her pubic hair. Everything was waxed except for a small landing strip in the middle that ended at her elongated clitoris. It was easy to pleasure my wife, and I knew just how to do it. I began to kiss her lips as I spread her legs from east to west like I-20. I placed Sharon's feet on top of my shoulders and tasted her sweetness. Sharon leaned back as she pulled my head closer into her epicenter. Her muscles tensed as she gyrated her hips, and squeezed her breasts rounding her nipples.

"Ohhhh God, Ohhhhweeeeee, damn…"

I worked her clitoris over, sucking; kissing; my way until she erupted. I stood to my feet and became face to face with Sharon. Her body was trembling as she pulled me close to her.

"I want you inside of me."

She grabbed my pride and placed me inside her warm wet walls as she wrapped her legs around me tighter than a python squeezes its prey. I stroked her slowly in a 360 degree motion as she dug her fingernails into my back.

"I'm cumin baby, I'm cumin," became the only words she uttered.

I grabbed her off of the counter and continued stroking her in mid air as I palmed her ass until my legs began to weaken. I carried Sharon to our bed never breaking our connection.

"Let me get on top."

"Cool."

Sharon mounted me and began riding like a nymphomaniac, as she squatted and bounced up and down like my dick was a pogo stick. I grabbed the sheets and fought back the urge to cum at this very moment as I squeezed my sexual muscles. It was the test of two wills; Sharon's vs. mine and neither of us were giving in. I flipped her over and began thrusting at a ferocious pace. I felt like I was 18 again; can't remember the last time I had multiple orgasms that didn't involve masturbation in the same day. I had the back of Sharon's legs locked by the inside of my elbows as my stride became longer and more intense. We both had worked up a sweat by this time as Sharon's moans and groans grew louder and louder. I almost thought that she was about to wake up the kids as she called out the holy trinity. It was funny how people became religious during sex. "Ohhhhweeeeee baby, I'm cuuuu mmmming."

"I'm cumming too baby."

Despite my urges, I yielded to the stronghold of the orgasm. We both came. I was too weak to move for a few minutes. We lay there embracing one another, sweaty tired and satisfied.

"Damn, I could use a cigarette."

"You don't even smoke silly."

We both laughed. It was moments like this that I missed. This was how Sharon and I used to make love all the time. Felt like I was Superman, and her loving was my Kryptonite. My super powers faded and my once mighty pleasure rod became a mere twig being expelled from Sharon's vagina. I kissed my wife and adjourned to my side of the bed. There was nothing like an orgasm to make you fall sound asleep.

Kevin

I abruptly awoke out of my sleep. It was 1:30 according to the clock. I looked to my right and Sharon was sound asleep with her Eric Jerome Dickey novel beside her pillow like it was the Bible. I had been dreaming. All of the erotic love making with Sharon was nothing more than a figment of my imagination, no more than wishful thinking. My reality was that I was horny and my wife was sound asleep in some "don't touch me" attire. Hardly the stuff that Vickie's Secrets were made of. It had been nearly a month since we made love, and even longer than that if you didn't count quickies. Since she has been working this new job with longer hours, a brother's sex life has suffered tremendously. I needed to get some at least three days a week, so I was in a major slump. Times like these made me understand why some men did have women on the side. Maybe it was what they had to do. Maybe their wives worked long hours and neglected their physical needs. I pondered that thought for several minutes as I tossed and turned and tried to fall back to sleep. When a man had "P" on the brain, it was difficult to think of anything else. I shifted until I ended up on my back with my hand firmly grasped to my penis. Sometimes you have to take matters into your own hand, literally. I didn't need magazines or lotions, just images of previous sexual encounters. I began to think about Sharon and our many encounters over the years. Then my thoughts shifted towards some of my more memorable lovers. I remembered Tammie Veal from my college days. She was definitely top five in my catalog, maybe even number one. I remembered when Tammie would come by my apartment with nothing on underneath her dress but passion and ecstasy. We did it everywhere and anywhere. We made our own historical landmarks on State's campus from the stadium bleachers to the library. We once got busy in a dressing room inside of unisex club bathroom. She definitely brought out the freak inside of me. We were good together. Just thinking about Tammie and the good times that we shared made me get goose bumps. I began to stroke myself up and down with the vivid images of Tammie dancing in my head. I remembered when we got busy inside of her folks swimming pool. It was weird at first, but hydro sex was actually kinda fun. I missed those days; simpler life, no drama or unrealistic expectations. For a minute I had gotten lost in my own thoughts of an adulterous affair all for the sake of a nut. It was what I needed and Tammie once again served her purpose giving me residual pleasure from an act committed years ago. Before I knew it my sleep wake cycle had run its course and it was morning. It was time to go to the gym. I hoped that Jason was not running late as usual. I gathered my gym bag and my clothes for work. I peeped in on K.J. and India before I left. They were sound asleep. I grabbed my MP3 player, deactivated the alarm and headed to get my morning workout in. I passed by several gyms just to get to Golds because despite Jason never being on time, he was committed. That was a necessity when it came to lifting some of the heavy weight that I lifted. As usual I beat Jason to the gym. I took advantage of the lag time and prepared my cocktail of supplements which consisted of creatine, glutamine, protein, and glucosamine. You couldn't get a body like this by neglecting proper nutrition. I began with some stretching and light cardio while I waited on Mr. Reliable to come inside. There were some early risers already working out. Middle aged guys making small talk. Twenty minutes went by while I was tread milling before Jason makes his entrance. He has the look of a man that had a crappy night.

"You okay man?"

"I am good."

"Why did you ask?"

That must have been some of that reverse psychology crap he has learned over the years. "No reason, let's get started I have to drop my kids off to daycare."

I always used Mondays as my leg day. Most people liked to do chest, early in the week. I felt like you built a body from the ground up. Jason and I tossed around conversation about the weekend to pass time between sets. He told me about dinner at his folks crib on Sunday, and about Samantha and Angela being in the same place at the same time. It made sense why he looked like he hadn't slept much. It made me think about my own problems and issues with Sharon. Jason told me how Elise had been blowing him up sending text messages since last Friday. I wanted to ask him if she mentioned Lisa or if Lisa had mentioned me. I ignored that urge and kept the workout moving. Wondered if Lisa would leave her man hanging and use work as an excuse. It tripped me out the way women always claimed they wanted a good man until they got one.

"Oh shit" I shouted as I glanced at the time.

"I gotta go so I can get the kids."

All that talking made me lose track of time. I dapped Jason, grabbed my bag and jogged out to my car. My legs were tight and I knew that I would be sore by tomorrow. I put my 300 in gear and jetted through the parking lot en route to the interstate. I took I-77 to I-20 changing lanes at speeds similar to Nascar. By now the cloud covering had lifted and the sun was getting his blaze on. We were in for a hot one. I was seething all the way home thinking about my current situation, grinding my teeth together making my jaw bone pulsate. She had already put a stranglehold on my sex life, now she is cutting into my work out time. This broad was trippin. When I pulled up, Sharon met me at the door on her way out. It was as if she had timed me or something.

"Bye bye sweetie" she utters as she kisses my cheek.

"I may be home late so feed your kids."

"My kids. Got it boss lady, anything else?"

"Oh, I love you."

".......I....love you too."

I watched her switch her hips to our SUV, skirt fitting nicely with some 3 inch heels. Another reminder of how horny I was. A man hated seeing his wife look that good when she was leaving him. I dropped my gym bag in the kitchen and started making breakfast for the kids. They were still asleep. I jumped when the phone rang in anticipation that it was Sharon. I picked up, but there was no answer. They hung up. Kinda weird I thought as I busied myself with breakfast. Moments later the phone rang again.

"Hello".

There was hesitation. The caller ID revealed that this was a private call.

"Hello, who is this?"

I was about to hang up before the mystery person answered.

"Hi.......is this....Kevin Wade?"

At first I thought it was a bill collector or somebody trying to sell something.

"I am not interested in whatever you are selling, please don't call back."

"I think that you would be very interested in what I have to tell you."

The voice was that of a female. She seemed intent on saying what she had to say.

"Okay lady, not trying to be rude, but I don't have time for this....kinda busy."

"Where is your wife Mr. Wade?"

She had my full attention as tension grew in my forehead.

"Who are you and what concern is my wife of yours?"

I became guarded.

"It is not your wife that I am concerned about, it's my husband."

"Lady, what the hell are you asking me about my wife for?"

There was a pause for a moment.

"Your wife is fucking my husband."

My heart dropped to the pit of my stomach.

"Look bitch don't call my house with that childish bullshit again!"

I slammed the phone to the counter. Anger had consumed me. I was furious. Why did this woman call? How did she get my number? How did she know my name? I needed some answers and I needed them quick.

I headed into the office earlier than normal in anticipation of a busy day. Maxiene had my schedule on my desk along with a hot cup of coffee and the morning paper. The hotter it got the crazier people got, I thought to myself reading about all the rise in crime. The news was filled with murder and scandal. I wondered if anybody did anything good anymore. I guess bad news was what really sold these days. Not many people wanted to read about people doing what they were supposed to do. I put down the paper and logged onto the internet. I checked my email. Besides spam, forwards about ghetto weddings there was not much substance. I got a few message alerts from the world of MySpace. I checked out my MySpace page. Friend requests from people soliciting Viagra and invites to watch them make out with other women. I deleted those requests and marked them as spam. There were two other messages. One was from one of my fraternity brothers named Tony. He was already making plans for homecoming in the middle of summer. Some people never really got college and fraternity out of their system. I replied and told him to keep me posted. The other message was from Elise. The cutie from last Friday. Her email was in all lower case writing. *"well, well, we meet again. lol. had a good time on friday, lets hook up. i may be in your area next week. let me know what you think. peep my pics when you get a chance. take care".* Elise

I checked her pictures out and her profile. Impressive, I thought to myself. They were sassy and cute, just like she was. Elise could really wear a two piece bikini. Damn. I sent her a reply and told her that I would take her up on the offer. Why not, I thought to myself. I had to keep my options open. Maxiene knocked on my door.

"Come in."

"Here is the file for your first appointment."

I scanned the chart long enough to notice that it was a female.

"Is she psycho?"

I joked with Maxiene. She smiled and went to get her. My job had become so routine that I began thinking of the problems that this lady was dealing with without laying eyes on her. Maxiene walked the mystery woman back to my office.

"Mr. Adams this is Amanda Riley."

Maxiene closed the door and headed to the reception area.

"Hi Mrs. Riley it is nice to meet you, have a seat please."

"Nice to meet you as well."

Nervousness and apprehension painted her face and embedded in her body language. When she spoke her accent immediately put me in a mode of curiosity trying to place it. I was sure that it wasn't southern, and even more sure that it wasn't even American. She took a seat on my sofa and began looking around the office the way people do when they are in an unfamiliar place. She stared at my degrees and certifications, at my décor, at my fraternity regalia. I was mesmerized by her beautiful dark skin and model like features. She was an attractive lady, very elegant. She was adorned in a yellow sundress that had a modest split to show off her right thigh. She had legs for days. Her peep toe pumps were multicolored with hues of red, green, and yellow to accent her dress. Lip gloss blanketed her pouty lips and made them stand out. Her hair was shimmery like silk and was pulled back in a ponytail. Mrs. Riley looked like she was made of money. We made small talk to help ease her tension. She told me she was a model; a few magazine covers and runway gigs but nothing major. She still had aspirations of making it big and being the next Tyra Banks. It made me wonder what the hell she was doing in South Carolina. I wondered why she wasn't in New York or L.A. I sipped my coffee, adjusted my posture and got to the point.

"What brings you here to see me today Mrs. Riley?"

She crossed her legs and gave me the fullness of her increasingly exposed right thigh. She placed her keys inside her Prada bag, and then put it on the floor. Sensing my curiosity about her accent she told me that she was born and raised in London. That explained her proper use of English. Her mood became increasingly serious.

"You specialize in fixing marriages don't you?"

She caught me off guard. I increased my concentration to pretend that her exposed flesh was not a thing of beauty.

"I guess you could say that, I am a marriage therapist."

She told me that she had read my column and although she didn't always agree with me she thought it was good. I was flattered that she read my column. I had been writing a column about relationships for the past two years. I had a strong female following, and obviously she was no exception.

"My marriage is in shambles; my husband is cheating on me."

She adjusted her posture and re crossed her legs the other way. Took her right thigh away and gave me her left. It was difficult for her to discuss her marriage. I offered her some tissue in preparation for the tears.

"How do you know that he is cheating?"

Mrs. Riley handed me an envelope from her purse. She had gathered a bunch of receipts from hotels, lunch and din-ner dates. There were no photographs or concrete evidence. "Have you confronted him?"

"Yes, he did what men do, he lied."

"Mrs. Riley, this is a serious allegation.

"Despite the evidence, could there be another explanation?"

She wore a sour look on her face.

"You are a man, and that is a typical response."

"He blames everything on work. It's always work. Said that the hotel receipts were from a conference, and lunch and dinner was taking clients out."

"Couldn't that be accurate?"

"It could, but I don't think so."

This woman had serious trust issues. She had herself worked up in bad way. Beautiful women like her could not take cheating because it was a severe blow to the ego. It was as if they couldn't comprehend the nature of a man and his need to constantly hunt for new talent. She couldn't come to grips with why she couldn't be enough for him. Mrs. Riley talked about meeting with a private investigator later on to-day who had some information for her.   She gave me that *"men are all alike"* glare. I remained supportive and discussed treatment options that could include couples therapy to ad-dress some of their trust issues.

"I am beyond that point."

"What do you mean? What is it that you want for you marriage?"

"Fuck my marriage, my husband and that bitch he is screwing."

"I want to make him feel what I feel. I believe in reciprocity. Nobody makes a fool out of me!"

Mrs. Riley was a woman fed up. She was a woman scorned. She had played the victim one too many times. Momma would always say that "Hell had no fury like a woman scorned." I felt sorry for this woman's husband. She thanked me for my time and my listening ear. We shook hands. Her grip was assertive and forceful. I sensed her sincerity, something was about to go down.

"I will call you back for follow up", she said.

I wished her good luck and walked her to the reception area. I couldn't help but think that this was the calm before the storm with regards to her marriage. I shrugged it off and prepared for the rest of my day.

CHAPTER 11

Kevin

My attention shifted to my children and their needs. I needed to redirect my focus from this woman and her allegations. India and K.J. were awake and they were in full blown morning mania. They were all over the place. I dreaded Mondays like some people dreaded jury duty. As usual India and K.J. were at it about trivial things such as whether or not Dora the Explorer was for boys or for girls. Either way, I could not care less at this point. I got them ready and dressed and fixed them some breakfast. Had to hustle and get myself ready for work despite my own irritable mood.

"Your wife is fucking my husband."

That echoed over and over inside of mind. Just the thought of another man being in my space made me contemplate things that probably would warrant time behind bars. I wrestled with traffic on I-20 headed towards I-26 en route to India and K.J.'s school. I didn't know why we had to take our children all over town for this Montessori school that was supposedly top notch. There was very little disparity in the races and India and K.J. provided most of the color. I felt as though they could get a better education if not equal if they went to an all black private school.

"All black schools are not reality" said Sharon.

I don't know whose reality she was referring to. It seems as though we were the only race in America that conveniently forgot its heritage. Jewish people support their own, as do the Asians, and of course Caucasians. Soon Mexicans would have their own private schools and support them. Blacks would once again feel compelled to forsake their own schools just to feel accepted. This was one of many compromises that I had made with Sharon over the years. I heard that marriage was all about compromise, but no one ever told me that I would always be the one on the short end. I hugged India and K.J. as I took them to their respective classrooms. India always hugged me tight as if she would never see me again.

"I love you daddy."

"I love you more India."

I kissed her cheek as I headed to work. I was probably like the majority of Americans. I hated my job. Times like these made me envious of Jason. I did not have the courage to take the leap of faith he did to open up his own business.

"You have a wife and two kids to think about Kevin. We need consistent income." Those were Sharon's utterances whenever I contemplated opening my own sports management firm. Instead I opted to be a company man. I have done well, but I know that I could do better. I had a pretty decent chunk of change that is doing well in a diversified fund that I managed to keep away from my wife. She has very poor impulse control when it comes to spending money. Long before my reality became a wife and two kids, I had dreams of becoming a pro football player in the NFL. Coming from a small historically black university made my dreams even more of a long shot. I had made the final cut for the Panthers after being signed as a free agent. Things were finally starting to look up for me. I managed to out play some rookies from the bigger universities. The week before the season opens up we were slated to play the Atlanta Falcons in Atlanta. This would be a homecoming for me. I grew up less than 10 miles from the Georgia Dome. On the final play of the final practice I suffered a tear to my ACL and MCL in noncontact drills. Although the injury can be rehabbed physically, there is the mental aspect involved as well. Initially I attempted rehab, but Sharon had other ideas.

"You need to get over it and move on with your life.

"You need to get a real job."

"We have a baby on the way."

I wondered whose life she was talking about. The Panthers gave me an injury settlement which was a portion of my salary. I took some good advice about acquiring some stock and it has done really well even in this uncertain economy. Facing an unexpected child made me put my dreams of being a football star on hold permanently. I married Sharon so our child would come into the world with two parents that had the same last name. I loved her, but I was certainly not in any rush to give her my last name. Looking at my kids made me realize that I loved them more than I love myself and even football. I wished that my daddy would have married my momma. Maybe I would have had it different growing up. Maybe my daddy would not have been the voice on the phone every Christmas and birthday. I was determined to be there for my children. I contemplated as to whether I should confront my wife about these accusations from this mystery lady. I sat at my desk and attempted to focus on getting some work done. After I replied to some emails and visited a few personal websites I was ready to do what they paid me to do. Sometimes it was like working miracles trying to get some people approved for home loans with jacked up credit. The average IQ was higher than some people's credit score. Nonetheless I proceeded to shop these loans to various lenders to see what type of progress I could make. Before long my thoughts shifted to Lisa. I wondered what she was doing; wondered what she had on and how she looked. I became embarrassed that I was thinking of this woman to this depth that I had only met one time. A woman that I wasn't even free to pursue myself. It's a good thing thoughts were not broadcasted out loud.

"I have a certified letter for Kevin Wade."

It was the mail courier looking around to deliver his package and get the signature he needed. I was hoping that it was some documents that I was waiting on to complete some closing packets. This loan processing stuff was for the birds. I waved for the guy to bring me the package. Our office had glass cubicles about 7 feet tall, so privacy was obsolete in here. That included phone calls as well. He bought me the letter and I signed the form he needed. For a minute I thought that he was expecting a tip. My scowl must have alerted him that it was a no go. The letter had no return address and it was sealed with packaging tape. I used my letter opener to open the envelope.

Dear Mr. Wade,

I have attempted to contact you via telephone several times. You have left me no other alternative but to send you a letter. It has come to my attention that our spouses have been having an affair. I know this must come as a shock to you. I am willing to provide you with sufficient evidence to support this assertion. I have obtained overwhelming proof and I would be willing to share it with you. I hate sending this to your place of business, but I couldn't send it to your residence for obvious reasons. Below you will find my contact number if you would like to meet with me. Again I apologize for this news, just thought you should know. (803) 227-5689

Unfortunately,

Same Boat

It was the lady from this morning. This was getting crazier by the minute. How did this lady know my home number and where I worked? She had definitely piqued my curiosity tenfold. I could tell that this was a cell number. I dialed Same Boat's number and set up a time to meet her. I had to see what she claimed to have. I left my office to meet her.

CHAPTER 12

Kevin

Same Boat said that she wanted to meet at Starbucks in Five Points. Of all the places we could meet, I wondered why she chose a Starbucks around a lot of college kids. This was a spot that Jason frequently hung out because it was in close proximity from his office. "How will I know it's you?"

"Don't worry, I will recognize you."

A part of me wanted to turn around and not even follow through with this nonsense, but Same Boat knew too much about me. I had to at least see if she could back up all of this talk. It was nearly lunch time and traffic began to get thick. People were out jogging listening to their iPods in nearly triple digit heat. I circled around the parking lot to see if I saw anyone who fit her voice. It felt like I was the one being watched. I found a park and sat in my car for a while to collect my thoughts. I wondered what I was going to find out. Had to see if there was any fire to go along with this smoke. My cell phone rang, it was Sharon. I sent the call to voicemail, and headed inside to meet with Same Boat. Entering the building I visually surveyed the crowd of people in line ordering over-priced cups of coffee. There were signs of the time when a cup of coffee and a gallon of gas were both about four dollars. I was not the coffee type in the first place. Made me think back to my childhood when my momma couldn't start her day without a cup of coffee. She said she liked her coffee like she liked her men, black and strong. People were ordering everything from Espressos, Lattes, and even Frappuccinos. I had no clue of what any of that was. It definitely made me want to invest in Starbucks. I see why Magic bought a chain of these. I never realized so many people liked coffee, especially in the middle of the summer. I decided to take the seat at a table in the back that allowed me to see who was coming in and out. Now my anxiety began to creep in. I busied myself by reading the newspaper. I saw where two college kids had fallen off of a roof butt naked and died. A policeman gets found not guilty for beating his wife because he had an affair. Mike Vick gets sentenced to 23 months in prison for his role in dog fighting. Maybe he should have just beaten his wife and he would be free. Thirteen years later they were still trying to get some criminal charges on O.J. Simpson. The sad thing was O.J. was making it easy. I overheard two white guys at a nearby table talking about how despicable dog fighting was and how Vick deserved to be neutered. In the next breath they talked about looking forward to deer season. It took everything in me to refrain from adding my perspective. Somehow I could not differentiate the two. There wasn't much that I could find sensitive about luring a deer to a spot and shooting it just to pose for a picture and mounting its head onto a wall.

Struggling to come to grips with that thought was when I was finally joined at my table by Same Boat.

"Hi Mr. Wade."

She said that in a very professional and business like tone. I guess this was somewhat of a business meeting. I nodded in response, mostly because I didn't even know this lady's name. I must say that she exceeded my expectations. She was beautiful, like I was eye to eye with Black Barbie.

"Let's get down to business Ms."

She was sipping some type of icy coffee.

"I should have gotten the Java Chip instead of the Double Chocolate Chip."

"Somehow I don't think we are here to discuss your coffee selection. Can you get on with it?"

I could tell she was a little uneasy like this was difficult for her as well.

"Why did you call my home, and my job? How do you know me? What does this have to do with my wife?"

She sipped her five dollar cold coffee and looked me in my eyes. Reminded me when I was a kid and my daddy told me to always look a man in their eyes when you are talking to them. Guess her daddy told her the same thing.

"Several months ago I grew suspicious that my husband was cheating on me. I began seeing patterns of inconsistency in his behavior and little clues that he was hiding something. I decided to have him followed."

"What does any of this have to do with my wife?"

"You must have a case of Missouriitis."

I gave her a puzzled look that said I didn't know what she meant.

"That's the *Show Me* state Mr. Wade."

She seemed to take delight in insulting my intelligence. Same Boat proceeded to talk and sip and sip and talk.

"I gave that man the best 10 years a woman had given a man. Gave him everything I could give."

Same Boat said that as if she were really hurt. Almost became emotional as she adjusted her posture and broke eye contact. You could tell she was holding in some deep feelings. I thought about giving her Jason's card, she could use it. She reached into her designer bag and pulled out a folder and handed it to me as if she were giving out Christmas presents. My heart rate increased as I thought about what might be contained inside of this folder.

"Before you look inside.......just want you know I am sorry."

I opened up this folder and reviewed its contents. There were pictures of my house, my cars, and the kids playing. I looked at Same Boat with a look of disgust.

"Just keep turning she insisted."

The shit was making me paranoid. Someone was watching me and I had no idea.

"This guy really did his homework."

"Had to be sure before...."

She paused without finishing her statement. I continued to look into this folder and its contents. Initially everything seemed normal. There were pictures of Sharon leaving work and going to work, and there were pictures of a man who I didn't know.

"That's J.R., you may know him as James. He is my husband."

I have heard Sharon mention James; he was her boss the guy that hired her. This guy has even called my home and had conversations with my wife. I even handed her the phone. I began to become infuriated, my pulse quickened, palms got sweaty. There was nothing that could prepare me for this. Pages of emails that started out business, but ended up being pleasure. Sharon had confided things in James about our marriage and her unhappiness. To say that I was pissed off would be the understatement of the century. Same Boat organized the emails and instant messages in chronological order as if she were setting up the sequence where things began to go astray. The one I M exchange that caught my eye was dated two months ago. That was the weekend that I went to Atlanta with the kids to visit my momma. Sharon claimed she had lots of work to do and that she could use the quiet time.

James: *You got plans for the weekend?*

Sharon: *I was going outta town with hubby, but I could use a weekend to myself.*

James: *Oh, so you'll be all alone......hmmmm*

Sharon: *What's that supposed to mean? What you got going on?*

James: *Nothing, I may try to get out later that's all.*

Sharon: *Sounds like fun.*

James: *Could be. Why don't you hang out with me a little bit? You said yourself you will be free.*

Sharon: *I dunno. Don't wanna risk running into someone that I know or that know's me.*

James: *Don't worry I have just the place. I know how uncomfortable you were at the hotel the last time. I have a surprise for you. Call me when Kevin leaves.*

Sharon: *Okay, gotta go. He is getting out of the shower. Call you later.*

I was officially past the point of being pissed off. This dude is setting up rendezvous with my woman and mentioning me in the process. If looks could kill Same Boat would be a memory. She sat and sipped as I continued to discover my fate with Sharon. Welcome to my world was the stare that covered her face.

"Read on Mr. Wade."

"I don't want to see anymore of this shit."

There was a document for a lease on a condo downtown.

"My husband leased this condo in the companies name for the purpose of his personal hotel. This was the surprise he was talking about in the email."

Pictures with dates and times of Sharon and James both arriving to this condo were right there in plain view. Times and dates that she was supposedly working late. She had been at this condo last Friday before she came home. This was beginning to add up. At this very moment I felt like this was some type of role reversal. I was being played and I didn't even have a clue. This woman that always accused me of cheating was the one having an affair.

"How long has this gone on?"

"At least nine months according to my sources."

Sharon had been working for James at his marketing firm for about a year. I guess it didn't take long for them to start mixing business with pleasure. My heart had fallen deep into the pit of my stomach. How could I have been so blind?

"My husband only used work as an excuse to extend his play dates."

My life was turning into an episode of Cheaters. Only this time I wasn't laughing. My expression was visible as I slammed the file shut that undoubtedly would close the door on my marriage as well.

"I have seen enough."

"I know this must be difficult."

"You don't know anything about me lady."

"Obviously I do. There is really something you need to know."

"I don't think that I can take much more at this point."

She sipped coffee and hesitated with her next thought.

"This is not easy Mr. Wade."

Her speech became crisper as if what she was about to say trumped everything that I had already seen.

"Your wife is pregnant by my husband."

She said that without batting her eye. Nodded her head towards the file as if that proof were in there as well. She showed me a recent email from Sharon to James that confirmed what she had said was true. Sharon actually contemplated what to do as if she thought about keeping dudes baby. I would not have wished this hurt on my worst enemy. I was waiting to exhale like Angela Bassett. Felt hurt like a man was not intended to feel. Same Boat had dropped a bomb on me that rendered catastrophic damage. I was having an emotional 9-11 that had me at ground zero. The levies to my emotions had been broken, and the hurt I felt was about to be unleashed in the worst way. I clenched my jaw, grabbed my life altering folder and abruptly stormed out of Starbucks without breaking stride. I was the angry black man that many feared. Gone was any sense of rational mind and logical thinking. It had been replaced by revenge, and vengeance would be mine.

I ignored Same Boat as I walked out headed to my car. My stride resembled Arnold Swartzenneger in Terminator as I made it to my 300. I sped away enroute to Sharon's job. Had to confront her about this bullshit. Couldn't believe what she had done. Needed answers from her. She had to be able to explain what I had seen. I never got married to get divorced, never broke my vows either. How could she give herself to someone else? How could she be so slack and let this dude get that close to her? This dude was running up in my wife with no rubber. All this pussy that I had turned down and refused to hit and this is the thanks I get. I have been jacking off while this dude has been screwing Sharon in hotels and condos. My mind was full of mixed emotions, none of which were good. I was speeding through town on my way to Sharon's office. Didn't even pay attention to the car that was tailing me in my rearview mirror. Just focused on getting to where I was going. My office was calling, but I ignored that as well. I could give less than a damn about a mortgage loan at this point. Every radio station had a song about cheating or being on the down low. I turned it off speeding all the way. Could care less about a speeding ticket. I circled Sharon's office building looking for a park. I decided to park in visitor's parking up front. It was hot and very humid, nearly triple digits. Momma said the hotter it gets the crazier people get. I felt crazy right about now myself. Knew I was not in my right frame of mind, I had raw emotion leading the way. I strolled into the building and bypassed the elevator and opted for the stairs. Took four flights of stairs to Sharon's suite without being winded. Walked by the temp girl who was the receptionist and headed down the hall towards my wife's office.

"Can I help you sir? You can't go beyond this point without authorization. Sir…..Sir!" In my blind rage I didn't even care that she was calling security. I walked into Sharon's office perspiring and frowning. I was pissed off.

"Hey baby…..what are you doing here? Are you okay?... Is everything okay?"

"Don't baby me. You know why I am here."

"You are scaring me. Are the kids okay? Why are you sweating and yelling?"

"This ain't about the kids. You don't get to ask questions! I need some answers."

I had her full attention. In fact I had the full attention of the entire office. I slammed her door shut. It was official I was not rational in the least bit.

"You didn't think I would find out you was fucking your boss? You let this dude all up in your space like that. All this time talking about working late, you was with James. On top of that you got pregnant by this mother fucker."

My words were razor sharp, but they didn't pierce her the way her silence and lack of denial cut through my heart like a scalpel. Tears were her only offering as she dropped her head in shame. There was a knock at the door.

"Is everything okay?"

"Everything is fine, just talking to my husband.... James."

He opened the door and damn near wet his pants when he was in my presence. I stood face to face with the bastard who had entered into my sacred place. He had been where only I was supposed to go. The man who had gotten my wife pregnant. He was small in stature only about 5 "9", maybe 180 with weights in his pocket. James had a bald head, baby face, and dark skin like Wesley Snipes. He was well groomed and impeccably dressed.

"Nice to meet you Kevin."

When he extended his hand to shake mine, I lost whatever sense of reality that I may have been clothed in at that point. I did what any other man would have done who was confronted with the man who tried to take their place by screwing his wife and planting their seed. I kicked his ass. I unleashed a wrath on him that would make Pharaoh harden not his heart and free God's people. My hands got to know his dry-cleaned shirt very well as he was quickly sprung into the air and slammed to the floor.

"You thought you could run around with my wife and I wouldn't find out?

"Pllleease man, you got it all wrong. It's not what you think."

I pounded his pretty boy face with my fist for that statement. I wasn't gonna stop until he looked like Martin did on that episode with Thomas Hearns. Sharon was crying and screaming for me to stop, but I didn't. I only got angrier. Didn't know if she was upset for me or him and that was like pouring gasoline on a fire. I raged on.

"I'm sorry" he exclaimed.

He was begging for mercy and forgiveness and I wasn't about to grant him either. I was in full revenge mode, and revenge tasted sweet. His face became the resting place for my fists of fury. Three security guards and one police officer finally subdued me and pried my death grip from James's throat. I tried to kill that fool. My breathing was thick and heavy as they restrained me. The officer radioed for back up. I didn't even remember being read my Miranda Rights, but I was handcuffed nonetheless.

"If you don't calm down I will taze you sir."

There was something about the thought of thousands of volts of electricity passing through your body at once that could make a person return to their right mind.

"I'm cool."

Sharon wore disappointment and sadness on her face as she wept uncontrollably. James struggled to gain his composure as the temp worker and other employees wiped his face with a towel and tended to his fresh wounds. I had issued him a beat down that would make Tyson proud. Now I was headed to a place where Tyson was all too familiar with. A place where guys that looked like me were too familiar with. A place where I promised my momma I would never end up. I was going to jail. At this point I was numb and void of any emotion that resembled happiness. Later on I would be embarrassed by my actions and subsequent consequences. Now I felt as though they were justified. The cuffs were tightening by the minute on my wrists as this policeman escorted me down the elevator and out the front door to his cruiser. I managed to avoid taking this walk for nearly thirty years. My head was dropped in shame as I walked handcuffed to an awaiting police car that would escort me to the Alvin S. Glen Detention Center. I had passed this place dozens of times going to the highway department. I never thought that I would be issued an all-inclusive stay at this resort. That ride gave me plenty of time to reflect on my actions and my life as a whole. I was too young to be having a mid life crisis, but I was definitely in a state of turmoil. I tried to so hard to avoid the pitfalls that so many brothers fall victim to. My daddy spent most of his life in and out of jail.

"Jail ain't no place for a black man son. It's justified slavery. Keep yo wits about you at all times. Take it from me."

He said the same thing in between stints in correctional facilities in Georgia. I had allowed my emotions to get the best of me and look where it has gotten me. A small seed of animosity had been planted deep in my soul for Sharon and it was growing larger by the second. The undying love I felt for her was withering like a tree with no sunshine or water. I was crossing the thin line that separated love from hate. I was regretting that I ever married her. Aside from my children she has not bought me anything but heartache. She runs around with someone, gets pregnant, and I go to jail. I felt like such a fool. I would probably lose my job with these assault charges. My marriage was over, my family would be broken, and my career very much in jeopardy. I didn't have anyone to call to bail my black ass out. Didn't wanna get Jason involved and I damn sure wasn't gonna call my momma.

"If you get locked up don't call me. I didn't raise you to be no criminal."

Those were momma's words to me when I was growing up in Southwest Atlanta. If I could help it she would never know. I didn't want to let my momma down and break my word. Damn, I hated Sharon for what she was putting me through. She better be glad I don't believe in hitting women. Should have let her feel my wrath like James did. It began to pour down rain as I saw grey skies in the midst of sunshine. Thunder crackled and lightening flashed in the distance. It reminded me of how I felt on the inside. I was hot and steamy and my anger roared like thunder, my actions quick and damaging like lightening. Inside tears began to swell. I fought to keep them back. My life was a clear sky when this day began. Now grey skies and thunderstorms had come all of a sudden. We pulled into the complex to the rear of the building where the precious cargo was admitted. Made me think of books that I had read about the Middle Passage and slave trades. I thought of all the righteous men that had been arrested and spent time in jail. I thought about Jesus and Martin Luther King, Jr. Thought about Mandela, and Ghandi. Even thought about Tupac. Other than Tupac those guys were jailed because they believed in a cause and were willing to sacrifice freedom as a result. I couldn't compare myself to any of them. I was just a fool that trusted his wife; got cheated on and beat the dude down that screwed her. Maybe that is what I will tell the other inmates when they ask why I was there. I was another black man that couldn't control his temper. Momma would always say that if you couldn't control yourself, then someone else would. Times of humility made me reflect back to the lessons that I was taught earlier in life. I went to booking which added further humility. All of my personal items removed, finger prints and mug shots, and Richland County apparel in exchange for my personal threads. I was losing circulation in my wrists from the handcuffs. I was all for jails existing, and I even agreed that some people were better off living in them. But I knew that I was not one of those people. I cherished freedom too much. One minute you are minding your own business getting your kids ready for school and the next minute you are getting ready to go in lockup at the county jail. Life was funny like that sometime. The present is truly a gift. All of my personal items were in a container. I was no longer Kevin Arthur Wade, the name my momma had given me. I was property of Richland County. They told me I had one phone call. One collect phone call. I had been booked. I was an inmate. I didn't wanna call Sharon. I was too embarrassed to call Jason, and I had too much pride to call my momma. Pride could make a man do some crazy things. Pride was part of the reason I was here in the first place. I decided not to part with my pride so quickly. I opted to call Jason.

I gambled that he would pick up. His cell phone wouldn't accept collect calls, so I called his office. Midway through I almost hung up before Maxiene answered. I asked for Jason. She told me he was in sessions and that he was booked until 6:00 pm. That was at least three hours away. It's not like I could get a returned call. I told her it was an emergency and asked her to interrupt the session. Jason came to the phone.

"You better have a life or death emergency interrupting my sessions man."

I hesitated.

"Look….I am in jail. Can't talk long, but I am gonna need you to bail me out. Long story, I will fill you in later."

"Dang, you okay, what happened? You need me to call Sharon?"

"I am cool, no I don't need you to call Sharon. Just need you to bail me out ASAP!" "No problem, I am on the way."

I hated involving Jason, but I did not have many options. I didn't want to be in this place any longer than I had to. I pictured a large communal cell like they always show on TV. Right now I was shackled from head to toe like I was a murderer or a rapist, and I was placed in lock up with the rest of the guilty otherwise innocent citizens of Richland County Detention Center.

I couldn't believe that my anger had gotten the best of me and landed me in a place that I vowed to never go. If it weren't for Sharon I would not be meeting this guy and I would not be in this place. I would be working on those two loans at my office. I had probably prayed about a hundred prayers since being arrested. It was funny how people got extra religious when they were in trouble. I sat on a bench oblivious to others with my head hung low staring at the tile on the floor and watching shoes go by. Time seemed to go slower than frozen molasses up hill in this place. I didn't know how any human being could tolerate this. The agony was killing me by the second and I was minutes from truly snapping. A fucking criminal is how society would view me; no more, no less. I would be branded with that distinction from this point forward. Nobody takes the time to differentiate these days. Either you have a criminal record or you don't. Being a black man with a record is two strikes in America. All I could think of was the humiliation that this would cause my mother and my children. I thought back to the emails, the pictures; and the time frame of her affair. Those words and images echoed inside my head. "Your wife is pregnant by James."

My anger crept back up like a Boeing increasing altitude. It's a good thing I had on handcuffs and shackles. The heavy duty officer broke me from my trance by summoning me to the door of this cage that housed men of various backgrounds who had found themselves on the wrong side of the law and now awaited a Judge's decision. Whatever he was saying, he had my full attention.

"It's yo lucky day son."

Maybe he had me confused with his kid or something. There was nothing lucky about this day for me. It was probably the worst day of my life. His voice was thick and raspy like someone who smoked cigarettes since they were invented.

"You a free man son. Somebody been looking out for ya. It's a good thing too, you ain't cut out for dis place. Hope I don't see you no mo."

I looked up to see if my ears were deceiving me. He wasn't joking; he was for real. He unlocked the door that had me contained. I was free. It took no time whatsoever to put my back to this brief but agonizing chapter of my life; never to return was my state of mind. Freedom felt good. Jason must have really made some things happen I thought to myself. I removed the florescent jumpsuit and quickly changed into my clothing. I don't think that I ever changed clothes faster in my life. My belongings were issued to me. The correction's officer explained that the charges had been dropped and that I was free to go home. I didn't ask anymore questions; just proceeded to the exit to meet Jason. It felt good to be Kevin Wade, and not property of Richland County Detention Center. I walked outside of the building looking for Jason. The grey skies were gone. There was not a cloud in sight. It was still hot as hell, but a beautiful scene nonetheless. I turned my phone back on and got ready to call Jason. I had 15 voice and text messages. Most of them were from work and a few from Sharon. I had a missed call from India and KJ's school. It was after 6:00 and they hadn't been picked up yet. Sharon was supposed to get them today. My car was still at her building and I was waiting on Jason. I called her cell phone. It went straight to voicemail. I wondered if she was with James. I wondered how many times I called her and they were together. I shook those thoughts when I saw Jason pull up.

"Where did you disappear to that quick?"

"What are you talking about? I just got here. Had to postpone several sessions. You ain't the only one with problems Kev."

"How did you got my charges dropped."

"I didn't get any charges dropped. I tried to reach Judge Cunningham, but he is on vacation this week. There wasn't anything that I did"

I grew more confused. If Jason didn't get me out, who did?

"I need you to take me to my car. I gotta pick up the kids, the school called."

"Where is your wife? What were you doing in jail?"

Jason started looking me up and down and noticed my clothes were stained with blood. "What the hell is going on?"

"I will explain the whole thing on the way."

"I will take you to get the kids first and then you can get your car."

That was good thinking on his part. I started telling Jason the whole story from this morning after I left the gym and filled him in on how I got an all expenses paid trip to the detention center. He listened like a good friend does. I kept getting calls from an unfamiliar number. I sent it to voice-mail, didn't need any other surprises today. Talking to Jason and revisiting the events of today got me pissed over again. I got a text message from a familiar number.

"Glad to see that you are a free man Mr. Wade." It was Same Boat. It was becoming apparent that she had gotten my charges dropped, not Jason. I continued telling Jason what happened on the way to pick up India and KJ.

Jason

I sat and listened to Kevin tell me about Sharon's affair with her boss and how he was contacted by some woman he didn't even know. I didn't say it to him but it sounded like the stuff I hear everyday at work. The only difference was that he was my friend and someone I cared about. I could tell that he was hurting. I knew that things were not perfect with him and Sharon, but I did not expect this. I tried my best to comfort him in a way that he could maintain his dignity as a man. I wanted to say that I never liked Sharon anyway and that I told him not to marry her, but somehow I don't think those words would be well received. I know Kevin and it takes a lot to get him to the point where he was at today. He is a very tolerant and calculated person. There is something about a woman that can make a man turn into a savage beast. I glanced at my best friend. He looked disturbed, not at peace. His clothes were soiled and bloody. He wore the blood of a man that has lived in his space for half a year.

"I got some shirts in the back I just got out of the cleaners. You can't go in that school like that."

"Thanks man, good looking out."

This made me think about my relationship with Angela. Normally we would communicate every morning. She said that her morning didn't begin until we spoke. Somehow I didn't think that Angela was still in bed waiting on me to call her. I hadn't spoken with her since yesterday. It was hard for me to give myself to a woman totally. I didn't want to end up hurt like my best friend was right now. I knew that Kevin was a good guy, and I wouldn't have felt bad if he was out getting his groove on like Sharon was. I had seen him turn down sister after sister all in the name of being faithful. That has gotten him no where but hurt and humiliated. I began to assess what Sharon's mental and emotional state must have been in order to allow James an all access granted pass to her goodies. I knew enough about relationships to know that women determine when and how everything plays out. Guys think they have game, but women have all of the game. Guys are merely players in the game, but women actually control the game. Kinda like Kobe and Iverson, both great players but if David Stern says jump they both say how high. It is a woman that allows a man to penetrate her fortress. She must have had an incredible emotional bond to sleep with James without protection. Most women function opposite from men. It is difficult to sleep with multiple partners for women because they equate sex with emotions. Kevin didn't have to tell me, but Sharon had physically and emotionally replaced him with James. That is a bitter pill for a man to swallow. I didn't think that a woman could be reformed once she strayed away and cheated. I would never disclose this to my clients, but it was my personal belief. Women cheated for different reasons than men. A man could stray even if everything was fine at home and not think twice about it. He could conceivably have his body and his emotions in two different places. Women cheated to fill a void, to replace what wasn't there. Once a woman stepped out, it was over. I pondered these thoughts as Kevin went into detail about the pictures, emails, and corporate condo, all of the secret rendezvous and late night meetings after work. I imagined Kevin beating this dude down at his place of business. I wish I could have seen the look on Sharon's face when she got busted. She always hated on me for being single and accusing me of being a negative influence on Kevin. We pulled up to India and KJ's school. I parked far enough away so that Kevin would not draw any attention with his wardrobe malfunction. He looked like he had been hanging out with O.J. Simpson. This had to be my boy for me to let him wear my brand new shirt.

"Thanks for the shirt man."

"Don't worry about it bro, I got your back."

He got out and secured his kids. I wondered what would keep Sharon from picking up her kids. The last thing Kevin needed was for child services to get involved. This dude has had enough brushes with the law today. I began to think of how this day would forever affect the lives of India and KJ. Every kid wanted their folks to be together regardless. Kevin had grown up without his daddy in the home. Always talked about making sure his kids had their dad. All of that was in serious jeopardy. I watched Kevin as he and his kids came back to my truck.

"Uncle Jason," India exclaimed.

"Hey India and KJ."

They called me uncle because I told Kevin that I wasn't down with the "Sir" title yet, made me feel too old. They had no idea their lives were about to change one way or another. Kevin attempted to mask his hurt and humiliation in front of the children. He kept looking down at his phone, it had buzzed a few times since we have been in the car. He was quiet for the rest of the ride, plotting his next move I suppose. When we got to Kevin's car I helped him get the kids inside. He didn't say much, but I know he was appreciative of our friendship. I wondered how he would react when he got face to face with Sharon at home in front of the kids.

"You sure you don't need the kids to crash at my crib for the night while ya'll work this out?" He hesitated for a minute and struggled to make eye contact.

"Naw, that's okay...I appreciate the offer. I will figure something out."

I gave him that half hand shake half hug that guys do to avoid looking gay.

"Call me if you need anything, and keep your head up."

He just looked at me as if he knew that I meant don't end up in jail again. I watched my friend for the second time today drive off. Only this time I really didn't envy him, didn't wanna have to face a woman that cheated on me and got me arrested for it. Kevin was out of sight and I was headed in the other direction. I had to go by the office to shut some things

down that I had left unattended to when Maxiene interrupted my session. It was nearly 7:00 p.m. and the temperature
outside was still in the nineties. Maxiene was already gone
for the day, but she had left me some messages from clients.
There was no call from Angela. She must really be pissed at
me. All of my clients that had to be rescheduled were taken
care of. There were three messages from Mrs. Riley to return
her calls. It was the lady from this morning, my new client. I
telephoned her back at the urging of her messages.

"Hi Mrs. Riley, this is Jason Adams....you asked me to call
you back."

There was silence for a few seconds.

"Mrs. Riley."

"Yes, I am here. Thanks for returning my call. I have had
a long day and I really need to come and see you sooner than
next week."

Her voice sounded desperate and sincere. I glanced at my
schedule and told her that I had an opening first thing in the
morning.

"Thanks."

She hung up abruptly. Pretty weird I thought, but so far
this day was a bit out of the norm. I collected my files in
preparation for Tuesday's clients. I decided to bring home
the digital recording from this morning's session with Mrs.
Riley. On the way out of my office I pulled my phone out

to call Angela and break our silence. Before I picked up my phone to dial her number I was getting an incoming call from Kevin. He was almost frantic when he told me to meet him at Richland Memorial Hospital and hung up. I knew that it was serious so I headed there immediately.

Kevin 15

It had only been moments since I had gotten into my car with my children. Moments ago I was handcuffed riding to jail. This was definitely a surreal feeling. There were reminders on my wrist that this was definitely real.

"Where the Hell was Sharon? Why didn't she pick up the kids?"

These were the thoughts I pondered as I headed home. My day had already been full of surprises and just when I thought things couldn't get worse, they did. I answered the phone out of frustration without even checking the caller, thinking it would be Sharon. I was ready to give her a glimpse of my verbal assault that was to come. It wasn't Sharon. It was an operator from the hospital. She informed me that Sharon had been in a car accident and that she was at Richland Memorial Hospital in the Trauma Unit. They had been trying to get in contact with me for some time. That explained the numerous missed calls from the unidentified

number. She didn't provide many details, but urged me to
get there quickly. A feeling of numbness blanketed my entire being. I didn't know what to feel or what to think. I
knew that I could not allow my children to see their mother in this type of condition. I called up Jason and told him
what was going down. I would probably have to take him
up on his offer to allow the kids to crash with him tonight.
This was one of the many disadvantages of living in a city
where you were not from. I had very little support in terms
of people to reach out to in times like this. I fought back
thoughts of Sharon being seriously injured as well as guilty
feelings because I had wished her harm for what she had
done to me. There was so much I didn't know at this point.
I felt helpless and scared all at the same time. That explained
why she didn't pick the kids up. Maybe she was too upset to
drive. Maybe she would not have gotten into this accident
if I would have handled things differently. Jason was in the
parking lot when I pulled up. His office was not far from the
hospital. I gave him the report that I had gotten from the
operator. When I said trauma his entire expression changed.
He looked serious, but at the same time he didn't want to
alarm me.

"I got the kids man, don't worry about a thing. Call me
when you know something."

I wanted to give him the whole checklist of things to remember considering he didn't have kids. Wanted to remind
him of dinner and baths and wrapping India's hair up at
night. My paternal instincts were in full gear. I hugged India
and K.J. tight as if I were not sure I would see them again.
Nothing about my life was predictable right now.

"I love you guys. Listen to Uncle Jason. I will see you in the morning."

My kids were comfortable with Jason. Probably because he didn't enforce many rules. People without kids were always fun to be around. They just didn't know any better. I watched my kids drive off and headed into the hospital to see what was going on. Hospitals have this way of making me very uncomfortable. Made me think back to the last time I had gotten a phone call that a family member was in the hospital. It was when me and momma got word that daddy had been taken to the hospital. That was the day my whole world turned upside down. Even though my parents were not married and didn't live together, every kid loves their father. My daddy had a habit of loving other people's women. It was a habit that eventually cost him his life. Daddy had been seeing this woman in Decatur that proved to be his kiss of death. Sometimes the lessons we learned from people was what not to do. I watched my momma cry many nights over my daddy. She always held hope that he would reform from his ways and make her his wife. Momma always thought that what my daddy did was her fault that she had to be more of a woman to him. My daddy was stabbed 10 times when his girlfriend's boyfriend showed up unexpectedly. When he got to the hospital he was in intensive care and had lost massive amounts of blood. Despite all the women he had run around with, it was my momma who was there as he lay on his death bed holding his hand. It's funny how the people we take for granted the most have a way of showing up when we need them the most. It does something to a 16 year-old boy to watch his daddy die right in front of his eyes. He wasn't much to most people, but he was everything to me. I guess in hindsight that was the day that I became a man, the day I made a promise to never take a woman's heart for granted. I didn't want to end up like my daddy. I saw firsthand the devastation that his actions had on my momma. Damn near drove her crazy. Had her on Prozac and Xanax. I wanted to prove to my momma that there was good in men, and that not all men cheated. Wanted to show her that everything would be okay. I had a lump in my throat when I walked through the emergency room entrance. Didn't know what I was walking into. I prepared myself for the worst. Figured that way there could be no surprises. Richland Memorial was a county hospital which meant that they accepted any and everybody. The emergency room was packed with single mothers, homeless people that probably wanted a meal, and a few people that looked like they thought crack was cool. This hospital did have the best trauma unit the state had to offer. I checked in at the information desk to find out where Sharon was. I was promptly asked for insurance information as her spouse and next of kin. Hospitals were all about business.

"Can't this wait Ma'am?" "I need to see my wife."

"Unfortunately Mr. Wade, it cannot."

I had to fill out forms to authorize our insurance to cover the hospital visit, along with ambulatory services. There were even forms that wanted to know if it would be okay to resuscitate and provide blood if needed. All of this was alarming to me. I wore my displeasure on my face as I looked at the receptionist. She looked back at me as if to say you can do better than that. She was not impressed. I completed the forms as quickly as I could and handed her the plastic clip board. I was used to filling out tons of forms in my line of work, but this seemed a bit out of order . Little Ms. Sunshine explained how to get to the trauma unit. It was funny how they treated a Blue Cross Blue Shield Card as if it were a platinum credit card. I was now a preferred customer. I was greeted in the trauma center by a middle aged female. Her name tag read Libby. Libby explained to me that she was a case manager in the trauma unit and that she coordinated the care of her assigned patients.

"I just wanna see my wife."

"I understand honey, but I gotta explain procedures around here."

Libby told me that she had been the one calling me from the hospital since Sharon had been admitted. She told me about the accident and asked me all types of questions about her medical history. She said it was important to know if she was on any prescription drugs or recreational drugs. There was nothing that I could think of or knew of, but as this day grew longer I wasn't really sure about much.

"None that I am aware of."

"Your wife has been assigned a trauma number once she entered the Emergency Department. This is to protect her identity and no one can have information about her without this number."

She gave me the number and urged me to pass it on to anyone in the immediate family. I asked her to call Sharon's parents in Philly to explain what happened. Thought that they should know what was going on. According to Libby, Sharon's SUV struck another car and flipped a couple times before landing in the median. She had to be cut out of the truck and air lifted to the hospital. When she arrived she was in and out of consciousness due to the impact of the accident.

"I need to prepare you before you go back to see her. She may not be awake yet due to the medication for pain. Your wife also has scars from the broken glass as well as a broken femur and some tender ribs. She is in a lot of pain."

"Is she going to be okay?"

My anxiety crept in and I was feeling vulnerable. This would be the second time today that I have fought back tears. My emotions were getting the best of me. I couldn't help but think the worst. Somehow I could not help but blame myself for her condition.

"The doctors remain cautiously optimistic about her condition. She has some slight swelling of her brain that makes it too early to determine her long term prognosis."

My eyes began to water when she made that statement. Libby grabbed my hand to provide comfort sensing that I needed it. She did that like it was natural and sincere but yet her job at the same time.

"She is hooked up to several machines that will help us to monitor her accordingly. Don't be alarmed honey."

She guided me down the hallway to Sharon's room. All I saw was families at the bedside of their loved ones with looks of despair and gloom written over their faces. The reality would be that not all of us were getting good news. I had emotionally been taken back to that sixteen year-old kid that held onto to hope that his father was going to survive intensive care only to watch him lose his battle with the Grim Reaper.

"I will leave you alone with your wife honey Is there anything I can do for you right now?"

I pondered that thought for a minute, wanted to ask her if she could wake me up from this nightmare. I simply nodded instead. Sharon was lying there so helpless yet peaceful, like she was in another place. She had tubes and IVs hooked to her with bandages on her face where she had been pierced by glass from the windshield. I did not know what all the beeping meant from the machines, but I know she was breathing into a respirator. I held her hand. There was no response from her. Tears streamed down my face like a waterfall. Thought back to the first time we held hands when we were dating, back when things were much simpler. I leaned over to kiss her on the forehead to let her know that I was here and that everything would be okay. A few hours ago I was contemplating doing harm to my wife and now I was wishing that I could take her place so that she wouldn't have to endure this pain. There were so many questions going through my mind. I thought about my kids, my marriage, my career, and Sharon's health. I didn't have a single answer for either one. Times like this momma would tell me to keep my faith in God. I began to pray for Sharon to make a full recovery.

I prayed harder than a Baptist Preacher on Easter Sunday; prayed like a starving man prays for food. I prayed like a sinner on judgment day; harder than a slave prayed for freedom. I prayed so long and hard that when I opened my eyes and saw the light in the doorway I thought I saw an angel, but it was Libby. She was back checking on me.

"Just made some coffee, want any? It looks like you ain't going anywhere."

I wasn't a huge coffee person but I figured it wouldn't hurt anything.

"Yeah, that'd be great."

I needed to call Jason and check on the kids, and Sharon's family, and my momma. She would want to know as well. I followed Libby back out of the room. She took me to their break area where the coffee and vending machines were.

"You will be able to use your cell phone in here honey."

"Thanks Ms. Libby."

"Oh honey, please everybody else calls me Libby."

She winked her eye at me as she left to go back to her office. Libby had a certain maternal instinct about herself. I pulled out my phone to make my calls as I sat and sipped hot strong coffee from Starbucks and contemplated who to call first.

Jason 16

contemplated to myself about what Kevin must be going through as I prepared his children for bed. It was no problem because I had babysat for him and Sharon on several occasions when they wanted to go out. We even had our own routine for baths and bedtime. I just let them do what they wanted to do and they eventually wore themselves out. India and KJ was the closest thing I had to my own kids. I called Angela and told her what was going on and asked her if she would mind coming over. Sometime in life a tragedy provided the perfect segue to mending things that needed to be mended. There was no way that I could do India's hair no matter how hard I tried. I really needed her help. I was hopeful that Kevin would call to provide at least an update. I guess no news was good news. Angela showed up shortly after I had given the kids dinner and a bath. I wanted to gauge her emotions after the way we ended things yesterday. I wondered if she was still upset about that whole Samantha situation. Angela was very casual. She had her hair pulled back in a scrunchie, fitted sweat pants, a halter top, and some sneakers. I could tell that she had already settled down for the night. Even without her makeup she was beautiful. She was definitely wearing her best poker face, because I could not decipher her emotions whatsoever.

"Hey Angela, thank you so much for coming."

She nodded to dignify my response. There was no embrace like she normally does.

"I am here for India and KJ, not for you."

Her words were razor like and her tone filled with resentment. She immediately came in and engaged in motherly duties with the children. In minutes KJ and India were dressed for bed. Angela did India's hair and wrapped up her head in a scarf that she had bought with her. She took them to the guest bedroom to rest for the night. I watched Angela as she interacted with my best friend's children. She did it so effortless as if it was second nature. I thought to myself that she would make a wonderful mother some day. I left Angela with the kids as I began to prepare for my day. I had a million things to do prior to getting to my office. When I missed half a day, I really missed a lot. People think that being in business for yourself was a walk in the park. They had no idea of the amount of responsibility it took to make sure everything went accordingly. Not to mention the responsibility it took dealing with clients who never want to be the case that you happen to have the bad day with. They never understand me being sick or not at my best. With that thought in mind I remembered my session with Ms. Riley from this morning. I had to review the audio from that session to make sure I was on my game for her next appointment. I wondered what prompted her to schedule a follow up within a 24 hour period. I listened to our session to see if there was anything that I may have over looked from this morning while I completed my clinical notes. I remembered her bitterness and resentment towards her husband and her strong convictions that he was having an affair. "I want to make him feel what I feel."

Her words echoed over and over through my headphones. I was actually looking forward to our next session to see what she had done. I didn't hear Angela calling me as she was coming down stairs.

"The kids are asleep, so I am headed home."

"Do you have a minute Angela?"

"It's getting kinda late Jason, and I gotta get home."

I could tell that she was not being affectionate because she called me Jay and not Jason. She was being formal with me to let me know she was irritated still. Women were some of the best psychologists ever, it must have been innate.

"I wanna talk about last night at my folk's place."

"What is there to talk about?"

"I know that you are pissed off, but…" She cut me off in mid sentence.

"Save it Jason. You allowed your mother to attack me and insult me the whole night and you said nothing. Then you parade around your little high school sweetheart around like she is your family."

Angela was even pretty when she was mad.

"Look I didn't even know Sam was gonna be there. That's why I ain't wanna take you to dinner with my family."

Angst grew on her face as she responded.

"What…are you ashamed of me or something?"

"You know that it is nothing like that."

"What is it then?"

"My family is just crazy okay, they are crazy. I don't go there much myself much either when they all gather. Don't take any of that personal. Momma has been mispronouncing the names of every girl that I have dated."

She sucked her teeth and rolled her eyes.

"She seems to know just how to say Samantha."

I guess it was official that we were in a real relationship because this was the first major spat that we have had. I absolutely hated arguing with women. They would never admit they were wrong. Angela sat beside me and took my hand. She looked me in my eyes. "I wanna ask you a question Jason."

No man ever liked when a woman prefaced a question with a tone setting remark. I didn't think that anything good could come from this question. I sat and listened anyway. "What do we have?"

My puzzled look let her know that I needed her to re-phrase the question.

"I want you to define our relationship. Tell me what we have, because I need to know." "I like what we have, the way we can just kick it with no stress or drama attached, and the sex ain't bad either."

My feeble attempt at humor was not well received.

"I see. Well let me ask you this. Do you love me Jason?"

A lump formed inside of my throat and took me back down memory lane. I had a similar feeling the first time I had ever really kissed a girl. I was in the 8th grade at a school dance. Keisha Miller told me that I needed to give her a real kiss if I wanted to be her boyfriend. I guessed just carrying her books to class were not enough? A boy had to do what a boy had to do. With that lump in my throat I leaned forward and tilted her head opposite from mine and gave it my best soap opera impersonation. After about thirty seconds of teeth gnashing it was over, and so was our 8th grade romance. Angela's bold question had taken me to that place in time once again as my moment of hesitation was more than enough response for her. She stood up and took my hand. Angela paused me before I could say a word. I wasn't even sure what that word would have been. She leaned forward and kissed my lips. This was not the type of kiss that ignited a sexual encounter. This was the type of kiss that would seal the fate of our relationship.

"I love you Jason, but I can't invest anymore time in something that we don't both want. I hope you understand."

She turned and walked away like it was the toughest thing she had ever had to do. It was hard for a man to see a fine woman like Angela walk out of his life. Numbness consumed my entire body. I was paralyzed by uncertainty. What did I feel for her? Why didn't I have words to say anything? Why did things have to be so complicated? I was left alone with all these thoughts to ponder.

Kevin 17

That strong coffee had me wired like a zombie on crack. My head was throbbing nonstop like I was amped. I could literally hear my own heartbeat. I wondered why this crap was legal. I had finally gotten through to Sharon's parents to bring them up to speed on what had gone down. It wasn't easy to deliver that kind of news to someone about their child. I could hear the emotion in her momma's voice when I told her what happened. I wondered how many times I would have to rehash this story about her accident before everyone got up to speed. Her folks were catching a red eye from Philadelphia to Charlotte and then drive down to Columbia. I guess that was the thing about being in a small market. There were not a whole lot of direct flights that came into Columbia. They would be here by early morning which was good considering the distance. I would need to run a few errands and prepare the guest room at the house for their stay. The one good thing about having in-laws over 600 miles away was very infrequent visits. I was already thinking about how not to discuss the big fight that Sharon and I had gotten into prior to the accident. I didn't need my in-laws poking their noses somewhere it didn't belong and trying to draw conclusions to something. I called my momma to tell her the news. I didn't like calling her at this hour. The last time she got a call at this hour it was about my daddy getting stabbed. Momma always said that only bad news came this late over the phone. I called her up to let her know what was going on. I decided to keep the part about me going to jail to myself and even Sharon's affair with her boss. Times like this made me wish I was a kid again. I felt like I needed to hear my momma say that everything would be okay. I just needed something positive to believe in at this moment. I had to get myself together. I had to be composed when she answered. I didn't wanna seem weak or broken by this situation. I made myself a promise to be strong for my momma when my daddy died.

"Hello."

"Hey momma."

"Baby why you calling me this late? Is everything okay? You not in jail are you? Are the kids okay? I told you I ain't coming to get you if you go to jail."

"I am okay. I am not in jail and the kids are fine."

A few hours earlier and I would have been lying about that whole jail thing. That would be one secret that I would carry to the grave.

"Momma I called to tell you that Sharon was in a car accident and she is in the hospital." "Ohhh my God......Is she okay? What happened?"

I waited for her to summon God in every name that she knew along with a few disciples before I answered her questions. Momma had a way of getting herself worked up like Ms. Payne on Martin.

"The doctor is waiting for her to regain consciousness, but they are optimistic she will be fine. I just wanted to call you and let you know. Her nurse is calling me now…..I gotta go ma. I'll call you later on. I love you."

"I'll be praying baby. It's gonna be okay."

I hated lying to my momma, but this conversation had the potential for being a long one. I just wanted to make sure that she was in the loop. I was about to check in with Jason when Libby came to check on me.

"Did you get enough coffee honey? There is plenty more." She smiled.

Libby had that coffee drinker's smile.

"Trust me. I have had enough. Thanks anyway."

"Your wife's doctor will be making his rounds shortly and he will want to talk to you." "Okay, thanks again Ms. Libby."

"I've told you just call me Libby."

It was right at daybreak and I needed to make two more calls before I went in the restricted call area. I checked in with Jason to see how my kids were doing and to get him caught up on Sharon's status. Even though he and Sharon never blended well, I knew that he would never wish her any harm. He told me that everything went well and that Angela stopped by to help out with them.

"She is a keeper bro; you better not screw that one up."

He didn't offer much of a response, he only chuckled.

"I'll let you go so you can get back to Sharon. Don't worry bout nothing."

I could tell Jason was sleep deprived because he was using a totally different vernacular. "Thanks again." We hung up.

I decided to leave a message at my job that I definitely wasn't coming into the office. I hated letting people into my personal business, especially people that I worked with. I headed back to Sharon's room to be by her side and await her doctor. She was still not conscious. The machines continued to do their thing beeping and dripping. I held her hand but there was still no response from her. I was determined to stay by her side until she awoke.

"Good morning, you must be Mr. Wade. I am Dr. Glading."

It was Sharon's Dr. He was way too perky for this time of the morning. I observed his large cup of coffee in his left hand as he extended the right hand to shake mine. I was full of anxiety waiting to finally get an update on her condition. This nervous feeling in my stomach reminded me of being a kid and waiting on my momma to punish me after I had done something wrong. I stood up to shake his hand.

"Hey Dr. Glading, I'm Kevin. Is my wife going to be okay?"

He gave me that firm look that meant you couldn't tell if it was good news or bad news. Dr. Glading was the head of the trauma unit and he was nationally renowned. Libby told me that when I first got here. She said that aside from God, that Dr. Glading was Sharon's best possible option. He proceeded to outline Sharon's condition pretty much the same way that Libby had. She was lucky to be alive, but they were really optimistic. They put her in a medically induced coma to help minimize the pain that she was feeling. Dr. Glading said that he was confident she should be conscious shortly once the medication wore off. He advised that there was still no guarantee that she won't have damage to her brain. I had to compose myself as I thought of all types of scenarios, none of which were good. He had just dropped the bomb on me and he said it as if it were nothing. I watched as he sipped his coffee and reviewed her chart. I contemplated jacking him up just to get him to take back those words. My better judgment prevailed knowing that he was just doing his job. The nurses were coming in to start their rotation for the day.

"Mr. Wade why don't you go to the cafeteria and have some breakfast, the nurses will be in here for a while. It might do you some good."

As much as I didn't wanna leave her side I figured that Dr. Glading was right. Besides I didn't need to see them having to do everything for my wife that she normally does for herself. I headed to the elevators to go down to the hospital cafeteria. This was one of those days that I wished I was just having a bad dream and when I awoke my life would be normal again. As much as I didn't feel like eating, I knew that I should try to get something down. Otherwise I would not be able to maintain whatever energy I may have had. I decided to get a plate of grits, scrambled eggs, and hash browns. They didn't have turkey bacon so I passed on the pork. It was a pleasant surprise that food from a hospital cafeteria actually wasn't bad. I was a typical southern brother so I loved grits. In fact I liked my grits the same way that I liked my women; nice and thick. Breakfast just wasn't the same without grits. Sharon was from up north so she didn't really grow up on grits. Her mom fed her oatmeal and cereal. I had to teach her how to make grits like my momma. To her credit she was a fast learner. In my opinion no matter how fine a woman was, if she couldn't make grits she lost a couple of points. Halfway through my breakfast I received a few text messages. Same Boat sent me a message. *I need to see you!* Anger crept back into my conscious as I thought back to the way my life had changed since I met that woman. Sharon's parents sent me a text to let me know that they had landed in Charlotte and that they were getting on the road. That was a half hour ago, so they should be here really soon. I would have a chance to leave and handle some things. I needed to tie up some loose ends with Same Boat. Jason also text messaged me to let me know that the kids had been dropped off at school. The thought of Same Boat served as a reminder of all the dirty little secrets that my wife had kept from me while she was screwing James behind my back. That thought ended when I was tapped on the shoulder.

"Come quick, Dr. Glading says your wife is awake."

It was Libby. I would recognize her southern accent any-where. Finally some good news I thought to myself. I left my plate and followed her lead. She acted as if she was the one getting good news. I headed back upstairs with Libby to check on Sharon. Suddenly I felt a rush of anxiety not know-ing what to expect. When I entered into her room I hurried over to her bedside. Dr. Glading was asking Sharon all types of questions.

"Hey Sharon. How are you?"

I wasn't even sure how I should approach her. I am hu-man so there was a part of me that wanted to pick up where we had left off at on yesterday when I was at her office con-fronting her about James. The other part of me wanted to embrace her with a blanket of warmth to comfort her and let her know that I was glad that she had survived the accident.

"I am fine baby, just a little sore."

She spoke those words like it pained her to talk. I noticed that they had changed her dressing and removed the breath-ing tube from her mouth. For a minute she almost looked normal. Sharon would never be caught dead without her hair and makeup done to the Tee. That's what I liked about her when we first met. She was always presentable. She practi-cally lived at the beauty salon and the MAC counter at the department stores. Sharon reached for my hand. Without thinking I accepted her hand and embraced her touch. Life had a way of putting things in perspective for you. Momma always said to be careful what you said, that it just might happen. While I never wished that Sharon got into a car accident, I said some pretty hurtful things to her and probably wanted to hurt her myself. I finger combed her hair to give it some resemblance of the style that she normally wore.

"What happened? How did I get here baby? Where are my children?"

She began sobbing uncontrollably. I assured her that the children were fine and that they were at school. Sharon didn't remember the accident. Dr. Glading asked me to follow him outside of Sharon's room. We stood outside of the room in front of the window looking in on her. She was taking inventory of her injuries as if she had just discovered her full damage. Dr. Glading began outlining her condition to me. He talked about the head injuries that Sharon suffered from the accident.

"Your wife entered into the trauma unit due to her head injuries. She was unconscious when she arrived which made it difficult to fully assess her brain functioning. She has total motor sensory functioning and there does not seem to be any risk of impairment, however we do not know about her short term memory."

I tried to follow him as best I could, having taken a few psychology courses in my day. "What does that mean? She remembers me and our children."

"You are right Mr. Wade. She does not remember the trauma itself. She probably does not remember the last 72 hours of her life."

I found myself envious of her condition because I couldn't forget the last 24 hours of my life. For a minute I wish that I could forget them like Sharon has.

"Is this going to be permanent?"

"It is too early to say, we are still running tests. The most important thing right now is that she remains calm. Stress at this point could set her into a deeper state of amnesia. The brain has a way of protecting itself from trauma by embedding memories deep within the sub conscious mind until the person is better able to cope with the emotional or physical pain. In your wife's case it seems a bit of both. She is stable now and like I said only time will tell."

I was not sure of what all that medical mumbo jumbo was, but I guess that now was not the time to deal with Sharon's affair. I accepted Dr. Glading's advice and sealed the deal with a handshake. Her parents were getting off of the elevator with a panicked look on their face. I eased their worst fears by letting them know that she was okay. I asked Dr. Glading to get them abreast of what was going on and to emphasize the importance of remaining calm. Sometimes my in-laws needed to hear things from other people. Their perception of southerners was less than flattering. I told them that I would be back later on and watched them go into the room to assess their only child's condition. I knew that Sharon would be okay with her watchdog parents there, besides I had loose ends to tie up.

CHAPTER 18

Jason

No w I knew what the other half felt like as I had to do my best at multitasking in order to get India and K.J. off to school and beat traffic to be at my office on time. One kid wanted cereal and the other kid wanted grits. I figured that a compromise was in order, so we went to McDonalds instead. I needed a cup of coffee myself. The actions of last night were weighing heavily on my mind. I didn't exactly plan on getting dumped by Angela, or having to turn into Super Nanny for Kevin. I contemplated many thoughts as I wheeled and dealed my way towards India and K.J's school. After I fought through traffic in Northeast Columbia, I met more when I got to I-26 headed to Harbison before I dropped the children off. Kevin had put me on the pick up list so they were not alarmed to see me. I explained to the director what I felt she needed to know regarding the situation. I asked her to give me a call if anything came up. It still wasn't clear if Kevin would be able to leave the hospital. Didn't know how that whole situation with Sharon was gonna play out. Figured he'd call when he got a sec. I pulled out of the drop off lane once the kids were safe and sound searching for my own destination. It was kinda weird having to be responsible for anyone other than myself. Wrestled with the thought of what it would be like when I did settle down as I sipped my liquid pick me up. It didn't take me long to snap back into reality, my reality. That was I am a single man with major trust issues and that wasn't likely to change. Angela was further proof of that. Every time things are going well, something always happens. I had learned over the years mostly anything that could happen, more than likely will when it comes to relationships. I haven't been wrong yet. There was no such thing as the perfect woman. No matter how good they looked, or how much they seemed to have it together, or how good the sex was, they were pretty much all the same. They didn't know what the hell they wanted.

"I want you to define what we have. Do you love me Jason."

Her words replayed over and over in my mind as I got high on coffee from McDonalds. It was funny how weeks ago we had the exact same thing and she seemed as if she couldn't get enough of it. All of a sudden the same thing needs to be redefined. I saw that crap everyday with my clients. Things start out one way and they head south in a hurry. I have often wondered if it was all worth it. Truth be told I had strong feelings for Angela. Since we met and connected there has not been a day that I haven't thought about her. Our connection was indescribable. I have never bared my sole to a woman the way that I have with her. Besides her super model looks I was most attracted to her inner beauty and intellect. I learned many years back that a bangin body and dynamic bedroom etiquette only go so far. Been there done that many times and then some. She could have been Mrs. Adams. That thought even startled me, but it was the truth. Maybe this was for the best I thought. Maybe a breakup with more time invested would have been more difficult. There would be more women like Angela I thought. I had convinced myself of that, so much that my next move would be even more stupid. I dialed Samantha's number. There were several ways to get over your girlfriend. I preferred getting on. Old reliable. Every guy needs one.

"Hello."

"What's up Sam?" She paused.

"I didn't expect to hear from you Jay."

"What you saying, I can't call you?."

"No, it's not that. I thought you'd be talking to Ms. Angelique."

I had to refrain myself, I had almost snapped. She said that on purpose to strike a nerve. Women loved a pissing match; so typical.

"Naw, it ain't like that. I was calling to see what you had going on later on. Maybe we could hook up."

Damn I hated putting myself out there like that. Didn't wanna seem desperate.

"I ain't got nothing going on, hit me up when you are wrapping up your day."

"Cool, I will call you later."

Samantha and I had so much history it was crazy. My momma even had me sold on her prophecy that we would "fall in love and get married." She even had me believing that fallacy. Momma has still not given up on that one yet, but I had. We represented a series of firsts. First kiss, first relationship, first time having sex, and first love. We were even voted cutest couple by our senior class. Back in those days a two year relationship seemed destined to end in wedding vows; young and dumb. We even thought that we could survive the whole distance thing when we left for college. I had her pictures, letters, and panties posted on my dorm wall my freshman year. I was so naïve that I wouldn't even talk to another girl without feeling guilty. I was too worried that my girlfriend would find out. My daddy told me that God looks out for fools and babies. I guess I was the biggest fool around. At first the long distance calls and letters began to slowly decline, then we started visiting less and less. Deep down inside I kinda figured things were not as they seemed. I rode down to Atlanta with Kevin for the weekend to surprise her at Spelman. I did surprise her, surprised the hell out of her. I walked right up on her in front of her dorm sitting in between some dude's legs like she was born to be there.

"Jay......what .....what are you doing here. I didn't know you were coming here."

My heart went south quicker than the Titanic. That was a bitter pill to swallow. Here I was being "Mr. Committed" and Samantha was spreading herself around like Chicken Pox. I tried to remain cool and not let my outer actions reflect my inner emotions.

"My bad Sam. Did I catch you at a bad time? Didn't know you were busy."

I really wanted ole boy to say something to me so I could kick his frat boy ass. I couldn't believe she was seeing this pretty boy Christopher Williams looking dude with the red and white frat shirt on. To this day I still despise him and his entire fraternity; not something I'm proud of. Guess I can hold a grudge. I walked away and headed to the car where Kevin was waiting. This was one of those moments you wish had gone differently. I was about ten feet from the car when Samantha came from around the dorm.

"Wait Jason......it's not what you think. Wait!"

Her breathing picked up while she attempted to further humiliate me.

"I think that you are fuckin ole boy. Did I get that part right."

She dropped her head as if that statement had resonated with her. Tears raced down her cheek, she struggled to maintain eye contact.

"You weren't supposed to find out like this. Things have been really stressful.....and.....I....things happened. Don't be mad at me. I love you Jason.....really I do. I guess I always will."

"Guess you have a really fucked up way of expressing your love. We don't have to make this out to be what it's not. Now I know. It's been real Sam. Get back to loving ole boy. Have a nice life."

I left her right there with her current lover. This was a feeling that I have vowed to never feel again. Never again would I allow myself to be that damn vulnerable. Kevin was my roommate freshman year so he knew how I had played myself for Samantha and didn't talk to any girls on campus. He told me the best way to get over one girl was with another one. That was exactly what we did. We went club hopping in Atlanta with some of his old classmates from high school. Kevin hooked me up with some prospects to choose from that night. That was the beginning of our bond. He had seen me exposed and he extended the olive branch to save me. You couldn't trust people you thought you knew and you could trust people you really didn't know at all. Either way the room that I had gotten for me and Samantha ended up being used for me and some chick named Carla. While she had been only the second person I had sex with, she would be the first of many one night stands. From that point on I really didn't even want to get close to a woman to feel that type of hurt. This was the new and improved Jason.

Jason 19

I couldn't believe that I had called Samantha to hook up with her later on. There was a small part of me that took pleasure in taunting her with a reality that would never be. She thought that we might possibly get back together, but that was not gonna happen. We have managed to be friends with occasional benefits over the years. You only get one chance to crap on me. I have found value in the evolution of our friendship despite our past. It was proof that titles were unrealistic and served as major barriers to any relationship between men and women. I had seen dozens of my couples get divorced or break up and then go on to have the most cordial relationships towards one another. It usually only takes two sessions before I was able to assess a couple's long term compatibility. There have been numerous divorces that I have helped people come to grips with. They thank me to this day and maintain that they have never been happier. Happily ever after is what you make it, and it is not always found in the confines of marriage. I have ruffled more than my share of feathers among my colleagues when making these points in various lectures. You couldn't argue with results. I was finally at my office. Pulling into my park I noticed an unfamiliar car in the parking lot reserved for my clients. It was Mrs. Riley. She was early. I gathered my things and headed into my entrance. She was making a call and didn't appear to notice me. I despised people waiting on me when I got to work, which is why I showed up early. Needed a moment to vent and check my email and read the bad news daily. I met briefly with Maxiene to get a feel for my schedule and to monitor the comings and goings since yesterday. I sat down at my desk and turned on my computer to kill time before Mrs. Riley came inside. After I had visited Myspace, Yahoo, and CNN, I logged onto Bulldog Roundup. This site was specifically designed to connect alumni of South Carolina State. My friends list was growing by the day. Everything from former honies, old friends, and frat brothers. All trying to recapture a glimpse of their youth. That moment in life when you were grown, without really being grown enough to take on real life responsibilities. That bridge between being in high school under your parent's rules and paying bills and having grown folk problems. Man those times were sweet. Maxiene's knock at my door served as a wake up call that those times were a thing of the past. I was definitely in the real world now. She escorted Mrs. Riley into my office and closed the door. I greeted her in typical therapist fashion with a hand shake and a smile. I tried to read her expression and gauge her mood searching for her reason for returning this soon. Minutes passed by with small talk back and forth. She could deflect questions as good as Hillary Clinton in a debate. She was sharp. It felt like two boxers in the ring feeling each other out before they swung a punch. I decided that I had had enough. Decided to take the best approach. The direct approach.

"What can I help you with Mrs. Riley?"

She maintained her poker face. Her silence covered the room like a blanket. She raised her head and spoke.

"I didn't have anywhere else to go. I have done a terrible thing."

She had piqued my interest.

"What terrible thing have you done?"

Her face wore concealment and worry. She ran her fingers through her hair, and licked her lips as if she had cotton mouth. Today she didn't have on lipstick, looked like she was sleep deprived. I hadn't noticed yesterday how dark her lips were. It looked like she wanted a cigarette now to help calm her nerves. I offered water instead. She accepted. "Tell me what you have done."

"I have given him chance after chance and he didn't take me seriously. Now he knows I am serious."

"Who are you referring to?"

She gave me an agitated look which assumed I was smart enough to know that she was talking about her husband. I learned to never assume anything in therapy, had to be sure. "My husband. Are you even listening to me?"

"You have my undivided attention Mrs. Riley".

"Good Mr. Adams. I believe I have his as well."

Now she had made eye contact with me. Mrs. Riley talked about when she and her husband first met. She was born and raised in London, which explained the British accent. Her parents sent her to America so that she could escape the racism in her country. I guess they didn't get the memo about racism over here. She had dreams of being a model and an actress that have not quite worked out. She put all of her dreams on hold for the sake of her marriage. Her father encouraged traditional roles when it came to marriage. "I ignored the obvious signs that he was cheating....thought that we'd be different. I have tried for years to get pregnant. We have been to fertility clinics and all. The shit has caused me to suffer from panic attacks."

Things were starting to make sense to me.

"What brings us to this point?"

"What brings us to this point Mr. Adams is when I found out the bastard has been giving me birth control without me knowing it for all these years. He had no intention of having children, all the while maintaining that he did. I feel like such a damn fool."

She saw the look of confusion on my face and knew that I wasn't following her. Mrs. Riley said that she had been taking Prozac for anxiety and depression over not being able to conceive children. She said her psychiatrist ordered blood work and it revealed elevated hormone levels.

"He had been insisting that I take what he called multivitamins. The shit was birth control."

She left me speechless with those words. So much venom in her words.

"Are you divorcing him? It sounds like you would do pretty well in alimony."

"He had me sign a prenuptial agreement, I can't get a dime. He is worth $2.5 million in total assets alive, it doubles if he dies. My attorney verified this to me."

"You aren't planning to kill him, are you?"

I said that in jest, but sometimes in life the truth could be found hidden in jest.

"Of course not, but sometimes accidents happen. People die everyday."

She went further discussing how she had hired a private investigator to follow her husband around to get proof of his infidelity that somehow could get the prenup voided on those grounds. So much pain laced her words.

"That's how you found out that he was cheating."

"No one can accuse you of being slow Mr. Adams." One more insult and she was about to be cussed out. Her husband had been seeing a number of women according to her sources. She even showed me pictures as proof. The man had good taste. I stopped looking after I thumbed through at least five pictures.

"You should take a look at his latest prize Mr. Adams."

"I think that I have seen enough, besides one of them could be a client of mine and I don't want to have that burden of maintaining confidentiality."

Mrs. Riley was definitely a woman scorned. She had played the fool for too long, and she was auditioning for another role. If she left her marriage even after 10 years she had no claim to any of her husband's assets and there wasn't a thing she could do about it. It was nearly time for our session to end before I thought about her opening statements. "What was it that you did that got his attention?"

She smiled for the first time during the session.

"Let's just say that I got his attention."

In therapy sometimes less was more in terms of words being said. Somehow I figured that she was saying something more despite the simplicity of her statement.

"You'll call to reschedule won't you?"

"I just might, I have the number."

We exchanged pleasantries as she left my office. I could honestly say that I was not sad to see her leave.

"42 CFR Mr. Adams. Don't forget."

She was referring to the federal laws that mandated patient therapist privileged consent. She wanted me to know that she knew that what happened in here stayed in here. Kinda like Las Vegas. I couldn't help but feel sorry for her husband. She didn't actually threaten harm on his life, but she implied it all the same. Unfortunately, implications were not enough to void confidentiality and warn him of impending danger. I still had to consider that I was bound to confidentiality and I couldn't tell if I wanted to. This was not the Tarasoff case I was dealing with. It wasn't worth it. I tried divorcing myself from those heavy thoughts. My phone was blowing up, it was Kevin calling but he hung up before I answered. He sent me a text instead to let me know that Sharon's parents were in town and that he was running errands. He wanted to hook up for a late lunch after some meeting that he had. I replied "cool" and left it at that.

"He's worth $2.5 million."

Her words echoed in my head over and over. I knew guys that would make that problem go away for a fraction of the cost. Hell it even made a rational guy like myself contemplate it for a few seconds. Just couldn't come to grips with prison blues and getting tested by dudes. Wasn't worth it to me. I shook recurring thoughts of Mrs. Riley from my head and prepared for my next client. 'Please, be less drama" I said to myself. Didn't know if I could handle another Mrs. Riley today.

Kevin 20

The sun felt warm on my face as I left the not so cozy confines of Richland Memorial Hospital. Seemed like I had been there for an eternity. I squinted my eyes in search of my car. Had a million things to do in a short amount of time. I never could have forecasted this storm cloud moving into my life over the past 24 hours. Between me finding out about Sharon and James, going to jail and her near death experience, I didn't think I could handle anymore. The only thing consistent was this record high temperature that made my leather seats hot to the touch. This weather was no joke. Felt like Satan was sun bathing it was so damn hot. I had to meet with the insurance adjuster about filing the claim on our SUV. From the sounds of things it was totaled anyway. Sharon was not cited in the accident because she was in the right. Mike my agent said that they would pay the truck off. I was supposed to meet the lady who hit Sharon after I left the collision place that now housed my gas guzzling Expedition. My thoughts shifted to Same Boat. Wondered where she was; if she was following me. That woman had me paranoid. She always seemed to be everywhere all at the same time. How did she know that I had gotten arrested and why did she get me out? Nobody does anything without expecting something in return. Something was not adding up. I put a call into my office to let them know that I would be taking indefinite leave pending Sharon's condition. "Take all the time you need Kevin. Keep us posted."

Somehow Steve's words just didn't sound very authentic. I really was not the company man type anyway. The more I lived, the more the American Dream seemed like a nightmare. Here I was helping to build this guy's business exponentially and I was profiting in small fractions. Jason definitely had the right idea about working for himself. This was for the birds I thought to myself. When I pulled up to Haye's Collision Center to meet the insurance adjustor, my assumptions had been confirmed. The truck was totaled. It was a miracle that she didn't suffer worse damage than she did. That once huge SUV folded like a piece of aluminum foil. They didn't make em like they used to I guess. I helped myself to my valuables such as my CD's and child restraint seats. Those were the only things not damaged. Couldn't shake the thought of "what if" my kids would have been in this truck during the accident. I became angry and grateful all at the same time. All was well that ended well. My Tupac and Outkast catalogs had been spared along with my other classics. The Hip Hop Gods were looking out for me on this one. Looks like I didn't have many options regarding what to do with my Expedition, it was a foregone conclusion. The insurance guy explained that I would get a check from them after the remaining loan balance was paid in full, they would get the title and I would have to go back in debt for another car. Didn't quite see the silver lining in this one, but lately I didn't see it at all. I nodded in acceptance to what was said, shook hands and jumped into my only piece of transportation that was operable and left. Had to keep moving, time was growing short. I needed to get some things done before the kids got out of school and before I went back to the hospital. As much as I appreciated Jason looking out for me, I had pride and didn't like depending on anyone but me. Guess I learned that growing up. I didn't have any siblings or close family members. My daddy was not very reliable himself. It was funny the way some people could teach the best lessons of what not to do without saying one word. The time on my Movado watch let me know that I had to do some serious multitasking. It also reminded me of my wife. She bought this for our anniversary. I wasn't really into jewelry but she insisted. Made me think if she had bought nice things for James. That made me feel pissed off all over.

"Your wife is fucking my husband."

Tried to shake those words from my head as I realized Same Boat was texting me.

"Can we meet?" I replied yes.

"Where?"

She sent me an address to a downtown coffeehouse. This lady had a thing for coffee that was sure. It was too damn hot for me to swallow something that warm. I headed that direction to meet with my new acquaintance. After circling the block a few times I decided I would have better luck on foot. I knew that I was close. Her directions had taken me to the heart of Five Points. I guess that she had grown tired of Starbucks because this place was only across the street. She wanted me to come to a place called The Gourmet Shop. It was a sidewalk café that didn't offer much privacy at all. This was not like the woman I had met yesterday who seemed so guarded and covert. This time I had her waiting on me. Guess I surprised her because I was on foot. She was looking around expecting to see my car. Thought I would wait and watch her for a change. Study her mannerisms. See how she operated from afar. Same Boat was wearing a multicolored sundress with some sandals on. They were white. She was constantly looking around for me and then to her watch. Same Boat pulled out a cigarette, lit it and took a drag. She blew smoke from the side of her mouth in a very lady like fashion. There was elegance about her. I wasn't a fan of smokers, especially women but she made it look sexy. I decided to stalk her like a lion in stealth mode searching for its prey. I had crept up on her like I was Jet Li on some ninja type stuff. Before she knew it I was right up on her. She reacted in both surprise and disappointment; disappointment because she was a bonified control freak that liked having her way.

"You shouldn't smoke, those things can kill ya."

She didn't like my comment, I could tell.

"There are millions of things that could kill someone Mr. Wade."

The sidewalk was crowded with people carrying on their own lives. There were people shopping at nearby boutiques and consignment shops. Others were drinking coffee and having lunch around us. Our server came to take our order.

"You guys look so great together. Can I take your order?"

She must have seen our respective wedding rings and assumed that we were married. Neither of us bothered to correct her. I opted for water with lemon and Same Boat ordered a cup of coffee with a veggie croissant. She was a pretty woman, despite the fact that she was a smoker. I hadn't even noticed the darker hue of her lips that normally accompanied many smokers. Today trouble owned her face moreso than yesterday. "Been trying to quit. Stress makes me smoke..... damn gum doesn't work."

Obvious tension rested between us. We were both trying to get comfortable with the elephant in the room that was James and Sharon's affair. Their dirty little secret had inadvertently drawn us together. I was short on time so I decided to cut out the small talk and get down to business.

"How did.....Why did you bail me out of jail? She looked at me.

"Felt like I was the reason you were there in the first place.

"You followed me to the office. Why?" There was silence between us.

"You left so angry, I thought you might do something stupid." "How is your wife?"

"So you already know about Sharon's accident." Same Boat was like Einstein she knew everything.

"James's nose is broken and his ego is shattered."

She said that like I cared. There was part of me that wishes that he was hurt worst. I could have killed him with my bare hands.

"We had a scare, but she is going to be okay."

"James was persuaded not to press charges on you Mr. Wade, I saw to that. I followed you to the police station once I had spoken with my husband. "Karma has a way of rearing her head in situations like these."

I wasn't a believer in Karma. If that were the case why would I be having all this shit happening to me when I have not done anything wrong? The waitress bought back our orders. Same Boat sipped her warm coffee on this hot afternoon while sitting at a table with an umbrella atop at an outside café while chatting with the husband of the woman who has been sleeping with her husband. Life had its own unique sense of humor sometimes. We just didn't always appreciate it. She reached for another cigarette.

"Do you mind Mr. Wade?" I nodded.

Didn't think that it would have mattered anyway. Her teeth were incredibly white to say that she habitually drank coffee and smoked. Same Boat took a drag and followed that up with another one. Still blowing her smoke out of the side of her mouth as if she were whistling. She exuded elegance and even made a nasty habit kinda sexy.

"Mr. Wade, how do you feel knowing that your wife has betrayed you with my husband? I am sure that you don't like it. Men handle affairs differently than women do. You looked pretty pissed off to me yesterday when you got that confirmation; looked mad enough to kill someone."

Outlining and re-emphasizing my pain and affliction, she looked directly into my eyes as she smoked her cancer stick. . The truth was that she was dead on the money.

"I was...am extremely pissed about what has gone on. I can't even put into words the way I feel. I could have killed James yesterday without even batting an eye."

"Why didn't you?"

Her words caught me off guard. I waited for her to re-frame her question, but she did not. "Why didn't you do it? Nobody would have blamed you. It would have been hard to make a conviction based on the proof of the affair. A crime of passion is not premeditated. A good attorney could have gotten you off."

I was still in disbelief over her line of questioning.

"Are you serious? You wanted me to kill James?"

I had to look around in suspicion that others might be eavesdropping. She remained calm and calculated.

"He did fuck your wife. More than a few times from what I gathered. You could have done it. You should have done it."

Same Boat took the final drag of her cigarette and held it longer as if she was savoring its flavor. She exhaled through her nose and her mouth this time, like she was hitting her smoker's stride or something. She flicked the butt onto the street in total disregard of Columbia's attempt at reducing litter. What she would say next trumped any and everything that she had said to this point.

"I have a proposition for you Mr. Wade so I will get right to the point. We both have a common denominator here. We have both been fucked literally and figuratively by the same person. This problem needs to be exterminated. What would you say to a very handsome reward in exchange for killing my husband?"

Not once did this woman even bat her eye. There was no hesitation or anything. She was dead serious, no pun. It was as if no soul rested within her. There was obvious hesitation painted my face.

"I am offering you 1 million dollars. No small change here Mr. Wade. That much money could make all of your problems go away. You could start your whole life over if you wanted to. I don't give a damn what you do with the money personally."

That thought traveled through my mind as I struggled to give a response. I was no murderer, but a million dollars was not something to take lightly. India and K.J. entered my mind and helped me to come back to reality. I couldn't imagine my life without being able to see my kids. I loved them too much. I even loved them more than money.

"I am not a killer lady. Think you got the wrong guy."

I had grown up with guys in Atlanta that would do this job for far less than a million dollars with no questions asked. She didn't like being told no. Control issues.

"I will give you half up front and the other half upon confirmation of his demise."

She made it sound like this was easy. Even though I had almost killed him with my bare hands I was no murderer. I had no love lost for James, but didn't know if I really wanted the dude dead.

"Why me?"

"Because... we are in the same boat. Equally vested in this. I don't trust anyone else with this."

"Same Boat, huh."

I chuckled, sat back and sipped my water. Needed something way stronger than water to make this go down. I have never taken the bar exam, but I knew that I would be a primary suspect having just beat the dude down in front of several witnesses. Had seen enough Lifetime with Sharon to know how that worked. The thought of my wife made me remember that I was meeting Jason for lunch before I went to pick up my kids. Sensing my hesitation she responded.

"Just think about it. I'll be in touch."

Same Boat got up and dropped a crisp 100 dollar bill onto the table where the tab was and walked away. Reaching into her purse she pulled out another slim cigarette and lit it up. The waitress returned when she got up.

"Keep the change."

Maybe she had dropped that money like that to show me that she was serious. Maybe she was like Jay Z and money wasn't a thing. Either way she had made this waitress's day with the tip she had collected for an 8 dollar tab. I would be lying if I said that her proposition didn't have me curious. People got away with murder everyday I thought to myself as I got up to leave.

Six patients after Mrs. Riley, it was time for me to leave for lunch. I was supposed to meet with Kevin somewhere downtown not far from my office. It felt kinda funny not to have had any messages from Angela. We normally kept in contact throughout the day texting each other. Both of us had too much ego to break the ice by reaching out to one another. I did have an email alert on my Blackberry from Elise. She was contacting me to let me know that she would be in Columbia for two days interviewing with the University of South Carolina's Law School. They were recruiting her and would be hosting her for the next few days. Elise wanted to get up if I had some free time. Suddenly all I had was free time. I emailed her back to let her know that she could call when she was done. Her earning potential was about to take a serious climb when she finished her law degree. I was at the point in my life where compatibility was measured in many areas, and finances were one of them. Leaving my office AC to go to lunch was a reminder of the heat wave we were going through. Not even a sports car could go from 75 to 100 faster than the mercury just did when I stepped outside.

I jumped in my black truck and cranked my AC to full blast. Listened to Raheem Devaugn talk about his affinity for women as I drove to meet Kevin at Liberty for a late lunch. Thought about the women in my life. Thought about my momma and my baby sister Tonya. Thought about Angela and Samantha. Their differences. The things that set them both apart. I thought about a lot of women that had crossed my path throughout my life. Sometimes I wondered if I would ever trust again enough to let a woman get close to me. I could thank Samantha for that lesson learned in life. My concentration was broken when I saw a familiar face sitting in her car waiting like I was for the light to turn green. It was Mrs. Riley. She was smoking her cigarette minding her business. I had seen enough of her today to last a while. It looked like she was coming from Five Points near some familiar places that I frequented from time to time. Kevin's call made my phone vibrate and took my mind off of what consumed it the most. He was letting me know that he had gotten to the Liberty Tap Room and that he was waiting on me.

"I am pulling up now, looking for a park."

"As usual you are late."

"Save the speech on punctuality Kevin....see you in a minute."

I found one of the metered parks, put in some quarters to feed it and rushed inside. It was funny how people always regarded someone wearing a bowtie. It seems as they always confused them with being Muslim or something. Small minds I guess. I was sporting a nice orange and white bow-tie, white French cuff dress shirt with matching cuff links to accent my three button Joseph A. Banks original tan colored suit. As usual I was GQ cover worthy. People were breaking their necks to sit outside in this humidity laced heat, which made the dining area inside almost vacant. The hostess took me to Kevin's table where he was waiting.

"Bout time Farrakhan."

"You got jokes I see. It is not illegal to wear bowties you know."

"That's okay I'll pass, but I'll take a Bean Pie though."

He laughed at his own joke. I laughed too. We were both laughing. Kevin needed a laugh after all he had going on lately.

"Seriously, you look nice man. You can pull off that look. Probably wouldn't work for me."

"Thanks."

It was hard for guys to compliment one another. He must have really been feeling vulnerable. We just didn't give out compliments the way women complimented one another. I tried to keep the conversation light. Didn't wanna press the issue about Sharon's affair. Decided to talk about subjects that guys could relate to best like sports, women, and more sports. Somehow I could tell that Kevin didn't care much about the NFL or the NBA lock out. Here goes nothing I thought to myself.

"Hey man, you look distracted. Wanna talk about it?"

Normally he would brush things off and tell me that he wasn't one of my patients and to stop analyzing him. All the things that I had grown accustomed to hearing from people who weren't my patient, but needed to be someone's.

"I got a lot on my mind. A lot going on right now."

He hesitated while playing with his silver ware.

"I should be glad my wife got into that accident after what she did to me with James, but I can't help but sympathize with her right now. Part of me wants her to feel the pain that she has caused me. The other part feels that I would trade places with her in a heartbeat. What kind of husband wants to see his wife in pain? What the hell is wrong with me?" "Stop beating yourself up over this thing. I know you love your wife, but you are also hurting because of what she did. We don't always make the best decisions in the face of emotional hardship. It's okay for you to be angry at her for what she did bro. What you are feeling is normal. Remember, you didn't cause Sharon's accident."

"That's just it........maybe I did."

"What are you talking about Kevin? You were in jail remember?"

"Maybe if I hadn't confronted her at work........maybe she would not have been that upset and maybe she would have been more alert."

"Listen, I know this is gonna sound kinda harsh but here goes. Maybe if she would not have slept with James you would not have had anything to confront her about."

There was silence. That dose of reality hit him like a Ray Lewis tackle on a wide receiver going over the middle. He was emotionally knocked out and unable to respond for a minute. I wasn't trying to hurt him but sometimes reality was that bitter pill we all hated swallowing. Here he was blaming himself for something he had no part of. The thing about affairs was that the innocent partner always somehow blamed themselves instead of their partner for the affair. I was his Best Man in his wedding and I still had to have his back through these turbulent times of his marriage. Even to the end if that's what it took. I had his back. Our waitress came back. I ordered a Caeser Salad with Salmon and water with lemon. Kevin got the Crab Cake sandwich with whipped sweet potatoes. He had water as well, no ice. We made small talk while we waited for our lunch.

"You know, studies show that it's better to drink water at room temperature than with ice. Cold water travels through the body's core pass several organs even the heart which could cause problems."

"Oh yeah. Well right now the temperature outside is in triple digits. My body core is hot and if it is okay with you I will take my water with ice, okay."

Kevin was really reaching with that one I thought to myself. At least it made him laugh at himself so that was good. Normally I had envied my best friend. He had what looked

like the perfect marriage, two beautiful children, a nice home
and a promising career. The only thing missing it seemed
was a dog. Today he has a cheating wife, he's trying to sell
houses in this up and down market and he's thinking about
room temperature water. The only constant was his two children; my pseudo niece and nephew. I thought about my life.
Sure I had a nice career and a few material things. I looked
good on paper. Had good credit, and my own money. Had a
house that many would envy. Still there was something missing from my life. Seeing what Kevin was going through right
now no longer made me envious of him. Sharon had confirmed my suspicions and made me right. Marriage the way
that most people vision it is just a myth. It doesn't exist. It
was nothing more than a glorified partnership to combine in-
comes and have babies. Where was the commitment? Where
was the fidelity? Where was the friendship? I know for a fact
that Kevin has never cheated on Sharon. Women were always screaming, "where are all the good men?", and here you
have one sitting in anguish talking about the benefits of room
temperature drinking water trying to get his swagger back.
He was better than me. I would have my attorney drawing
up divorce papers and have that hooker served right in that
hospital bed; amnesia and all. Maybe that would help jog her
memory. I was not a fan of Sharon's to begin with. Even back
in college I saw her manipulative ways a mile away. She was
an opportunist from day one, and Kevin was an easy target.
Never trust a big butt and a smile. Those were the words of
Bell Biv Devoe's hit song. Guess Kevin wasn't a fan of them.
Saw that she was poison from the start. I feel partly responsible having introduced them to one another. One of the best
decisions I ever made was taking a pass on Sharon. I had
banged a few of her suitemates, and I never got a good vibe

about her. Don't get me wrong she was fine. Tight body and could dress her ass off. I just wasn't feeling her "I'm from up north and I am smarter than you" type of attitude.

Black folks tripped me out thinking that there was some type of distinction between north and south. In America one thing was certain. Black was black no matter the area code. She got interested in Kevin once he became the full time starter on the football team and his potential NFL stock began to rise. I am surprised she even stuck around once he got injured and had to retire even before he career took off. It seems like getting pregnant with India happened to coincide with his free agent contract with the Panthers. Thought she would seek half of that injury settlement and run back up 95 until she got to Philly. I wondered how much loot James had to lace her with before she became wet and willing to get her freak on. In the end we were who we were. People rarely, if ever, changed and the best indicator of future behavior was past behavior. In fact, we mostly wore masks anyway. Masks that showed the world who we wanted to be seen as. It is underneath the mask where the true person lies. We were all actors that auditioned for various roles in life on a daily basis. Just like in Hollywood, some of us were better at our craft than others were. I guess Sharon was right up there with Halle Berry and Nicole Kidman. She was Oscar worthy. She acted like she was in love with Kevin. She had fooled him, but I was not impressed at all with her performance. I finished my salad as I thought those thoughts. Kevin only ate half of his sandwich. His appetite had left him, much in the same way as his wife had left him emotionally to be with James. You almost had to be a fool to be in love knowing that this was a possible consequence. He was making me depressed and I wasn't the one going through what he was. Funny. I checked my watch. Saw that I was running short on time before my afternoon rotation. Kevin looked at his watch too. We were both slaves to father time. We both had our own agendas.

"We all get the same 24 hours in a day; it's what you do with it that counts."

Those were my father's words. They were likely his father's words and his father before him. They now were my words and I knew that I had lots to get done with what remained of this day. For a brief moment my thoughts shifted to Angela. I realized that it was less than 24 hours since we talked, but I knew that it would be longer than that before we talked again. The waitress brought our check and I gave her my debit card without looking at the tab. Did that before Kevin could reach for it. Figured he had bigger issues to deal with.

"I can pay my own tab man. Don't need no handouts."

"Easy big guy, it's just lunch. No biggie."

There was nothing like a man with wounded pride. It makes him extremely defensive. It was hard for a man to deal with his woman stepping out on him. Sharon had drop kicked his pride in the groin area with 3 inch heels. We stood up. He dapped me up like we always did when departing.

"I'll hit you up later Orville Redenbacher. Thanks for everything."

That one even made me laugh. I was glad to see his sense of humor hadn't left him. Normally I would have had an equally smart comeback. Today I took a pass.

"No problem homey. Call me if you need me."

Kevin left before me as I waited on the waitress to return with my card and my receipt. I left her a decent tip and headed for my truck. I dreaded the suffocating humidity and triple digit temperature. Hell can't be hotter than this weather.

Jason

I crank all eight cylinders of my gas guzzling luxury SUV and turned the AC on full blast. Used the rear AC as well to help cool down the interior before I left. I had about 20 minutes before my next session started. That was plenty of time to get back to the office. Decided to listen to the radio on my way back. Economists were bracing for $5 dollars a gallon for gas. My tank held about 30 gallons to fill it up. I multiplied those figures in my head. The oil companies had us by the balls. Consumers couldn't even stage enough gas boycotts to do any damage to their bottom line. Gas was like air. We had to have it. I shook my head and flipped on my digital tunes to lighten my mood. I shifted the playlists to some ole school Prince; the Purple Rain CD was classic. Some joints sounded better on the vinyl and this was one. They just didn't seem to make true artists anymore. I sang along with Prince. Matched him word for word and even tried to match him note for note as high as my baritone voice allowed. I wondered if he was talking to Vanity or Apollonia when he wrote The Beautiful Ones. Either one he wasn't lying. Both were banging by any standard. He seemed so desperate to convince her that he wanted her and no one else would do. In my opinion that's what made the song so believable. It's what made it great. I had never opened myself up to a woman and been so vulnerable. I had never lost control; never gave in. Guess I never dated Vanity or Apollonia either. I couldn't even tell Angela how I felt about her when she confronted me. Maybe things were better this way. Maybe I should just leave things the way they were. She needed someone to be straight up with her and open themselves up. Didn't know if I was capable of that one. Shook those thoughts and made Prince disappear into his purple world when I turned my truck off. I was at the office for the final stretch of my work day. All day long I talked with people about what was wrong in their relationships and I couldn't even fix my own. Some days I feel like such a hypocrite. I spoke to Maxiene as I headed past her on the way to my office. Looked at my phone messages and decided who I wouldn't call back before my first afternoon appointment. After several hours of "he cheated, she cheated" and "irreconcilable differences" I was wrapping up my work day. Samantha texted me to find out what time I would be over. Before I could respond Elise texted me again. She was finished with her meeting and wanted to hook up for dinner. I liked having options. Normally I would side with the logic that "a bird in the hand beats two in the bush." These were not normal times. I decided to give her a call to see what she had in mind. Elise was downtown about five minutes from my office. I wasn't sure if I wanted her to know she was that close. I was a bit pressed for time but wanted to change; wanted to relax a bit. She told me that she was staying at the Hilton and she was headed back to her room.

"What do you feel like eating?"

"I don't know. Haven't had sushi in a while. Do you eat sushi Jason?"

"Actually I do."

"Cool. Sushi it is."

"I know a nice spot not far from where you are staying."

"I can be your way around 7:00 is that good for you?"

"That's fine. See ya at 7:00."

That would give me plenty of time to wrap things up at the office and go home to get out of this suit. I needed a shower. Samantha would understand that something came up. We were cool like that. I would leave the door open just in case things turned out disastrous with Elise. Every man had to have an ace in the hole. Something to fall back on when times got tough. I shut down my office and headed out. Maxiene was wrapping up her day as well, taking care of all the administrative duties that made my office run smoothly.

"See ya in the morning Maxiene."

"Have a good evening Mr. Adams."

I intended to have a good evening, one way or another.

Jason 23

I headed towards 277 away from the downtown traffic. Headed to the nearest freeway like many other commuters that worked in the city and lived in the suburbs. Columbia was not a big city, but it had its share of big city problems. Crime was getting out of control and there didn't seem to be an end in sight. Made me wanna start packing heat. Considered that thought as I accelerated past slow motorists driving like they were taking a Sunday stroll. I merged onto I-20 looking for exit 82. Didn't have long to go. That gave me time to call momma and Kevin. Almost called Angela, but I decided against it. Had to make sure everything was okay with Kevin and my pseudo niece and nephew. Momma wasn't doing much aside from reading her bible. She and daddy had already eaten dinner. She nearly caught me off guard when she asked about Angela.

"How is Agatha doing?"

"Angela....is doing just fine. Not sure about Agatha."

Momma kept on talking as if I hadn't corrected her, and made small talk. I decided to cut this conversation short. I was pressed for time.

"Tell daddy I said hey. I will catch up later. Love ya."

Wasn't even sure if she said bye before I hung up. I was at my house. Had to pull a rush job to get showered, dressed and back down town by 7:00. Here goes nothing. I was in an out of the shower in no time. Adorned in dark Sean John denim, a black Ralph Lauren polo shirt with the supersized horse and number on the right sleeve, complete with a pair of black Aldo loafers that slipped on. I had on more designer labels than Macy's; guess I was a brand whore after all. I was chillin. Sprayed on some R.S.V.P by Kenneth Cole and headed back to my truck. Not bad I thought. I would be to Elise by 7:00 or shortly thereafter. I retraced my steps until I-20 took me to 277 and delivered me downtown on Bull. I called Elise to put her on alert that I would be there soon. She sounded ready and said she would be downstairs waiting in the lobby. The closer I got the more this felt like a blind date. I vaguely even remembered how she looked. Alcohol can do that to you. Needed a backup plan in case she was hideous? What if she was jacked up? The things we get ourselves into. I cautiously pulled into the parking lot looking around for any sign of someone who resembled a Gremlin. My head was on a swivel as I waited for her to come out. There was a tap on my driver side window that startled me. It was the valet parking attendants. I let the window down to tell him that I wasn't staying. When I turned my head back, there she was. To my delight she was far from a Gremlin. She was hot. Now I remembered that caramel complexion. I remembered the good looks, those curves on her petite frame. I even remembered the texture of her hair but didn't remember it being that way. It was cut in an asymmetrical style with highlights that reminded me of Rhianna. It was different. Different was good in this case. She hopped inside. We spoke and exchanged pleasantries. Elise was rocking low rise jeans, a fitted t-shirt and some "keep on" pumps that would really accent her birthday suit. No doubt four inches. They were red and matched her belt and writing on her t-shirt. The writing outlined her breasts and had an arrow pointed towards her face reading "My eyes are up here." It was the kinda shirt that draws attention. She seemed like the type. Her exposed belly button sported a piercing. It was cute. It definitely got me. I hadn't remembered her rack being that nice.

"You like my hair? Had to cut it.....too hot this summer."

"If you like it, I love it. I smiled.

"It looks good on you."

I literally drove us a few blocks to this place called Tsunami. We could have walked, but not in this God awful heat. I found us a five dollar park and we got out. Elise was like a mile a minute with her talk game. I knew every detail of her day as if I had asked. I nodded and did all those head gestures to suggest that I was paying her attention. I was really checking her out. Liking the way she walked. Liking the way she looked. The place had a nice dinner crowd but we were able to get a table rather quickly. Elise and I sat down and ordered some drinks while we looked over the sushi menu. I ordered a Red Stripe and she surprised me when she ordered one as well.

"I like beer."

That was different. Angela would never drink beer. She was strictly a wine drinker. White wine at that. I could appreciate different. We looked over some sushi selections and circled a few. Elise wanted Yellow Tail, and Mahi Mahi. I ordered a Rainbow roll. I liked variety. Time passed and we went from distant strangers to closer friends while we drank Jamaican beer and ate Japanese sushi. It made for quite the cultural blend. She was easy to talk to after four beers a piece. This girl could hang a little bit.

"You wanna do something?"

That slipped out before I had time to clean it up.

"That depends on what you have in mind." She smiled.

"There is this place not far from here that does live poetry tonight. I haven't been in a minute, but it's cool......if you like that."

"Hey, that sounds cool. I'm down."

It was just after 10:00 when we headed to Hush. I parked my truck at her hotel parking lot and decided to walk since the temperature finally dropped. It was a clear sky and you could see every star in the sky. Wondered what was in the stars for me and Elise. Wondered what was in the stars for me and Angela. I had the feeling that I would get one of those answers sooner rather later. Her heart shaped booty had me in a trance as she switched her hips in those skinny jeans. She was doing Baby Phat major justice. We walked in. No cover, decent crowd, but not packed wall to wall. There was a table by the bar that was surprisingly available. I grabbed the seats before they got taken. I did that faster than the former Governor of New York could get a hooker. I liked hearing the poets put their thing down on the mic. It would take a lot of Red Stripe for me to conquer the inhibitions that I had when it came to public performances. I have presented at dozens of conferences in front of hundreds of people with relative ease, but somehow the thought of doing spoken word made me nervous. Normally I would have turned down another beer, but I followed the flow of the evening allowing myself to have one more of Jamaica's finest. I was feeling nice. Felt relaxed. I listened to poetry and watched Elise. She was enjoying herself.

"You know my girl is really good at this."

That came out of nowhere. I gave her a puzzled look.

"You know my girl Lisa. The one that was with me at the club last week when we met. Lisa is one of the best poets in the south. She opened up the set that night at The Melting Pot. Been trying to get her some national exposure. Maybe even Def Poetry or something. She's tight."

That jogged my memory.

"Ohh yeah, I remember now."

"She has been talking about your boy nonstop since last week. How is he doing anyway?"

He has seen better days I thought to myself.

"He is doing fine, I will tell him she asked about him."

Now I wondered if Kevin wished he would have explored other options like Sharon did. I downed some water to keep myself from feeling dehydrated in the morning. Had to pee. I got up to use the bathroom. Left Elise enjoying poetic words being spoken over the soft notes played by a live band. I noticed a couple of guys checking her out as I walked away. They were waiting for their opportunity to mark their territory. Her t-shirt was a hit in more ways than one. It made me laugh. I had handled my business and headed back to the table. What I saw next would set the tone for the rest of this evening. There were hotties in here, but one stood out from the rest. She was even hotter than Elise. There was beauty, elegance and grace perfectly woven into one being. I was especially familiar with this woman. My eyes had to adjust to ensure me that they were not being deceived. She was raising her wineglass to her lips when our eyes met. It was Angela looking at me with equal surprise in her expression. She wasn't alone either. Guess she was moving past me in pretty much the same way that I was moving past her. I had to keep my cool. I couldn't let her think that I was bothered. I decided to speak and keep it moving. She could do much better if that guy was my replacement. He definitely looked off brand to me. It was like she had gone from Air Jordans to Starburys. I kept it moving and headed back to Elise. All of a sudden I didn't feel like listening to poetry.

"You ready to get out of here? Got a long day tomorrow."

"They were about to bring the headliner out........but we can leave. You okay? Look like you saw a ghost or something."

"I am good, kinda tired though."

I spat that lie so smooth that I believed it myself. Threw 20.00 dollars on the table which was more than enough to square away the few beers we had. Didn't even wait for the change. Didn't even look back at Angela and her new beau. I decided that I needed to head into a new direction in much the same way that Angela had.

Jason 24

It was in that moment that I had been taken back to my freshman year in college. I was surprised like this in Atlanta by Samantha. Angela had proved me right again. Women were equally as scandalous as men. Maybe they were worst than us. Every time I try to allow someone into my life they disappoint me. I only knew one way to deal with these matters of the heart. I was determined to stay ahead of the game. So far tonight I was off to a good start. Elise and I walked back towards her room at the Hilton. She sashayed her lovely lady humps and we made small talk recapping what was a lovely evening prior to seeing Angela and her wish he was me, corny as hell date. Nonetheless my radar was always working. I was picking up very high frequency signals that Elise was not ready for this night to end. That was just the resolution that I needed. We stood out in front of her hotel. This was the awkward moment of the evening. Didn't wanna be presumptuous and blow my chances of scoring a home run. I was definitely swinging for the fences tonight. It was all or none with this one. That was when her flirty nature took control and began to take the lead.

"You wanna come up and make sure I get in okay?"

That was the million dollar question I had been waiting for. I wasn't good at extending myself. I couldn't stomach rejection very well.

"I'd like that."

She grabbed me by the hand and walked me through the hotel lobby towards the elevator. "Can you believe they put me in this fancy suite? You think they want a sistah or what?" As soon as we got on the elevator and the doors closed Elise turned into a straight up super freak. She pulled me close and planted one helluva kiss on me tongue and all. She totally ignored the fact that we had eaten sushi and drank beer. Soon those various tastes of sushi and Red Stripe blended into one. It became delicious. Our tongues danced as if they were two kids at the senior prom on the song you wanted to last forever as we ascended to the 8th floor where her room was. It was like we were walking on air or either in some type of trance because I don't even remember making it to her room. We remained locked at the lip. She opened up her door without looking and it was on. Our clothes hitting the floor were a blur. Elise kicked off her 4-inch heels and didn't care where they went. Standing face to face I could see her true height without the shoes on. I don't ever remember getting undressed this fast. I unzipped her skinny jeans and pulled them off. She was sporting a pair of lace boy shorts, red to be exact. I was developing a quick affection for this color. She undid her matching bra and allowed the twins to join the party. Her body was banging. Clothes did not nearly do her the justice as her birthday suit did. Damn! Elise pulled down my Calvin Klein boxer briefs. She marveled at my package.

"I see someone is happy to see me. I didn't know you had a six pack Jason. Your body is so sexy."

"Thanks, I could say the same about you."

She was blushing. I kissed her lips and then her neck as I massaged her breasts. Made Elise sit on the bed and I knelt down in front of her. Became eye to eye with her breasts. Her nipples were standing erect much in the same way as my manhood. She began to moan. I put my mouth on her plum colored nipple and teased them to her delight. Made sure I took in her entire areola. Did that over and over and made her moan louder. She palmed her left breast and with her right hand she reached down to her buried treasure. Touching her clitoris and then she began to finger herself. I pulled her panties down. Let them rest on her right ankle. She kissed me. This time even more intense than before. Elise was getting more and more aroused. It was like she was a volcano that was about to erupt at any moment. I had enjoyed being a voyeur just as much as she enjoyed being an exhibitionist. It was time to rejoin the cast of this erotic feature film. Elise fed me her fingers. I sucked all of her off them. She wanted me to taste her. She tasted good. I positioned her feet atop my shoulders. Made her lie back. Buried my head between her legs. I became the giver of pleasure and I delighted in accomplishing that task. Took her swollen clit into my mouth. Sucked it like I was trying to bring about world peace. That sent her into another world. Felt her body pulsate. She grabbed the back of my head and spewed obscenities. Did the same to her lips. Made circles in both directions and concentrated where she liked it best. Spread open her lips and tasted what was good. That sent her to the point of no return. Elise was like a levee that could no longer hold back the raging waters that became her orgasm. She was cumming long and hard.

"Ohh shit......damn.....ohh shit, I'm cumming Jason. Damn......you ain't have to do a sistah like that."

I was just glad she finally relaxed her well toned thighs from around my head. Thought she was gonna suffocate me. I reached into my jean pocket and pulled out my stash of condoms. Had to be safe.

"You just knew you was getting some pussy, huh?"

"Better to be safe than sorry, that's all. Besides what if I didn't have any?"

"Great minds truly think alike."

She pointed to the condoms that she had on the nightstand. She grabbed the condom from my hand and opened it up.

"Magnum, huh?"

I stood over her at the foot of the bed. Elise slid closer to the edge and tasted my erection. She explored my texture with her tongue. Didn't miss one inch. Made more blood rush to that area. I needed to be inside her. She rolled on the condom with her mouth, no hands. Did that like she had done it before. Made sure it was down as far as it could go. She pulled me on top of her. My erection was like a heat seeking missile hot on the trail of my target. I was locked in. She tensed when I entered into her sacred place. It was at that moment we communed with one another. Her with me and me with her. Elise was so damn wet, I thought I was on a slip and slide. Wet and warm. I got on my knees. Pulled her legs open. Pinned them down. Wanted to give her all I had to offer. Stroked her hard and long. Slow and fast. She made the sweetest sounds. There was no way the people in the other rooms were getting any sleep. Bet they knew my whole name by now thanks to her. I pounded Elise with all that was in me as she begged for more.

"Don't stop……..ohhhhhhh….don't stop…..i'm almost there. Damn you about to make me cum again."

That gave me even more incentive to keep up the intensity. Each thrust I began to feel relief. Relief from Angela and Samantha. Needed to get the past off my mind. Needed to be about my future. Needed to focus on giving Elise a proper welcome to Columbia. Once again I had taken her to that wonderful place. I needed to go there myself. I needed to cum. Needed to feel good right now, but I was tired. I stopped. Elise's legs trembled with the aftershock of sexual healing. She got on top. Still wet. Still warm. She mounted me. At that moment we were dancing at the Melting Pot. It was the same soulful rhythm that she had displayed then. It was even better this time around with no clothes. Elise was in full control giving me all I could handle. I grabbed her ass like handle bars on a bike trying to get a grip. Trying to win a fight that I didn't have a chance to. I had thrown in the towel and declared my orgasm the undisputed champion. I came hard.

"Damn....shit."

That was all I could muster up. Cumming for a man was different than a woman. We needed time for the blood flow to leave our penis and return to our brain to make any sense whatsoever. We lay there, sweaty, naked and most of all satisfied. Two strangers who had crossed the boundaries into sexual intimacy. I had seen enough to know that good sex meant nothing more than good sex. It wasn't a guarantee for anything. I got up to pee. Had to make sure all my little Jason's got deposited in the nearest ocean. I cleaned off my penis and wiped myself down. When I returned Elise was sitting up in the bed. She had put on a robe to cover her assets. This was the awkward part. I knew I wasn't gonna spend the night, but didn't wanna make her feel cheap. I put my boxer briefs back on and reached for my jeans.

"Was that your girlfriend back at Hush?"

That caught me off guard. She must have seen my exchange with Angela. Elise responded before I could say anything.

"It's cool. Just saw the way that you looked at her that's all. Only a man that loves a woman looks at her like that. When did ya'll break up?"

"Who said that was my girlfriend?"

"You just did....... Look its okay. I know what this is Jason. Trust me. I am not looking for anything."

I was more impressed with Elise by the minute.

"She is somebody from my past. Life goes on. You know?"

"Yeah I know....... Just saying man, you only live once dude. You only get one true love, don't miss out"

I was being schooled by a young 24 year old woman on her way to law school about the laws of love. I accepted her words as I proceeded to put my clothes back on. Elise gave me a hug and kissed me on the lip and then my cheek. This time there was no tongue. It felt like one of those thanks for the sex we probably won't hook up again hugs. I had seen those too much in my past.

"I will be in town a couple of days. You know how to reach me."

I let myself out and she headed to the shower.

CHAPTER 25

Kevin

It seemed like this storm cloud known as my life couldn't get any worse. I picked up my kids and took them to see Sharon in the hospital. She was dying to see them and I knew they missed her. Dr. Glading said that there was no change with her condition as it related to her ability to recall the events leading up to her accident. I was forced to put on a happy face and pretend that all was well for Sharon and for my in-laws. India and K.J. acted as if they hadn't seen her in years. They were extra clingy to her. I let the kids visit with Sharon and decided that I needed to get home to check on some things. It seemed like I hadn't been home in ages. Everything was exactly as I remembered it when I left for work on Monday morning. Twenty four hours and counting and not much has changed. My bed was calling me and I wanted to answer in the worst way. I logged on to the internet to check my email while I played back all of the voice messages on the phone. Aside from family calling about Sharon there was nothing out of the ordinary. I pulled up an email from Steve at the office. It seemed kinda weird for him to email instead of calling me on my cell. I had just spoken with him this morning.

"Don't worry, take all the time you need."

Those were his words when we spoke. Reading his email,
I got a totally different version. Steve emailed me to let me
know that my services were no longer needed. He blamed
the decline in the economy and said that it wasn't personal,
just bad timing. He said that if things picked up that I could
have my job back. My anger returned. Steve did offer me a
severance package which mostly consisted of bonus money
he owed me anyway. That was about fifteen grand, which
was far from enough to maintain my household very long. I
thought this was some kind of sick joke. I've got this cheating ass wife that's can't even remember she cheated in the
first place. With Sharon being hospitalized and out of work
herself, things were about to be tight as hell. I had to figure
something out. I truly felt vulnerable. My economic prosper-
ity lied in the hands of republicans that despised democrats
to the point that they refused to even participate in the gov-
erning process. I was doomed for sure, and needed to figure
something out quick, fast and in a hurry. This Bush shit was
putting a squeeze on mortgage brokers everywhere. I needed
to come up with a plan, and quickly. Urgency became my implied motto. I logged onto my savings account to see where I
could move money to stay afloat until things got better. There
was only about five grand in my savings account. I could
use that until I figured something out. No way was I touching India and K.J.'s college money. Hell, I didn't even wanna
touch the money I had growing in my mutual fund that I got
from my brief N.F.L. career. Twenty grand would be able to
sustain me for a minute, but I knew that living off savings
was not something that could last very long. My overhead
monthly was about forty five hundred dollars. Quick math

told me I had about four months of breathing room. I needed to make something happen sooner than that. I thought about the million dollar bounty that Same Boat offered me in exchange for her husband's death certificate. Thought about the way that all of my problems would disappear as soon as I made his pulse stop.

"I will give you half up front and the other half when the job is done."

Thought about that offer long and hard. Thought about several ways of making James a memory in this life. I was about to dial her number. Had my cell in hand when I looked at my children's picture atop the computer desk I was sitting at. We were all at Disney World last summer. We looked happy. We looked like a family. Once again my children served to be my wake up call. They kept me sane. I dismissed that thought with the quickness. I got up and paced around and did some crunches and pushups until I had worked up a sweat. Took my clothes off and jumped in the shower. The shower was where I did some of my best thinking. I washed away thoughts of committing murder while I brainstormed a way to come up on some serious cash that didn't have a possible jail sentence attached to it. That's when it hit me. I needed to be doing my own thing. This market was so screwed up that foreclosures were taking place quicker than people could get mortgages. All I knew was how to do mortgages and play football and neither one of them seemed like a viable option right now. That's when it hit me. This was the perfect time to do what I have always wanted to do. Do what I knew Sharon would have never supported me on. I have always wanted to open my own sports management firm. There were too many guys getting ripped off in sports by white collar types looking to cash in on another dumb athlete. The way that I wanted to do it would be first class, no cutting corners. I would need a team of professionals to make sure that my athletes had the very best of the best. I'd need agents, trainers, doctors, even therapists. My team would have to be comprehensive and give the players a true sense of family. There was no feeling worst than a guy walking away with nothing once he could no longer play the game. I took all of my thoughts and began putting them down on paper in the form of a business plan. This type of thing would require some major financing. It's a good thing I payed attention in college and still remember how to do a top notch business plan. I was even proud of myself. I vigorously worked for the next two hours until it was finished. I just needed someone with deep pockets to believe in my concept the way that I did. Needed them to put their money where their mouth was.

"If you can dream it, we can fund it."

Those were Lisa's words. I remembered her smile and her stunning good looks. Most of all I remembered the company that she worked for. I remembered that she had given me her business card. I went to my wallet and pulled out her card. Dreamers, Inc. "If you can dream it, we can fund it." It was right there in plain sight. It was time for me to follow my dream. Time for me to step out on faith and go against the grain. I had to follow my dream like Dr. King. It was time to divorce the fear that enslaved me and kept me from my dream. I decided to dial that number with the (704) area code on Lisa's card. There was a lump in my throat as I heard the phone ring. What would I say? What if I got nervous?

Maybe she would think that my idea was stupid. Maybe she would laugh. I dismissed those thoughts, shook them off. Five rings later I got her voicemail. It was after five so most people had already done their quota of hours worked for the day. Fought the urge to hang up, decided to leave her a message. I made her remember me, told her to call me about a business opportunity. I decided that if today was the first day of the rest of my life that I was going to have a better life. I was going to follow my dream.

Kevin 26

I made sure that things were suitable for my in-laws before I went back to the hospital. In the midst of my storm I felt a small measure of victory. Even though technically nothing had happened, I still felt a measure of success. If nothing came of it, at least I tried to put my best foot forward. In this moment of time I was outside of the box. I called to check on my momma while I drove back to the hospital. I fought with my feelings of guilt being an only child moving away from home. Even though it was only three hours away, it felt like at least a time zone difference. I told momma about my attempt to follow my dream. She provided me with the encouragement that only a momma could give her child; especially her only child. That further validated me which gave me more determination to succeed. When I got to the hospital I pulled into the crowded parking lot where I had left earlier. Shook off ghosts of years past. Ghosts that reminded me of my daddy's demise. I had associated only bad things with visiting people in the hospital. Now my hospital memories would be accompanied by a cheating wife with amnesia. Anger and frustration wrestled in my mind to see who was going to prevail as my dominant emotion. They were taking turns and at this point it was a draw. Had to hide those emotions and put on a happy face as I got into the hospital before my in-laws, my children and my memory deprived wife.

"Daddy's back." India and K.J. exclaimed when I came into the room. They had the power to make all that was wrong take a backseat at a moment's notice. I picked them up and held them tight. As usual I was cordial with my in-laws. After all they had done nothing wrong. They were not the source of my discontentment. We discussed Sharon as they apprised me of her condition. Although she was in and out of consciousness due to medication for pain there was no significant change in her condition. She still had not regained her short term memory. Sometimes no news was good news. I gave my in-laws the house key and we said our good byes. They took the kids home for the night. I was going to spend the night at the hospital. Even though I was grateful for Jason looking out, I felt better that they would be sleeping in their own beds. The more normal the better I thought as I watched them leave. I stood over Sharon and watched her sleep. Thought of better days that we had seen. Wondered what were the thoughts that she was keeping. Wondered what made her turn to the arms of another man. Wondered if I could ever get past her infidelity and love her the same. Those thoughts left me when she opened her eyes. She looked dazed for a minute as if she didn't know where she was. I was afraid that she was losing even more of her memory. Then she spoke with a raspy voice.

"Where you been handsome?" She made me smile.

"I had to run some errands and get some things together."

"You look troubled....is everything okay?"

I thought about all that had gone on since I had gotten Same Boat's letter. Finding out about her affair, me confronting her at work, beating James down, getting arrested, her accident and injuries, and me losing my job I wasn't sure about which bit of trouble had influenced my expression. I made good use of the art of lying and told her that I was just tired and that everything was okay. We talked for about two hours before she was back in dream land under the command of her pain medication. Made me think of days long gone when we could pass hours just talking about nothing at all. I kissed her forehead and sat back down. I busied myself by looking over my business plan and researching some sports management companies on my laptop. Moments later Libby came into the room. She had a troubled look on her face. "How are you honey? I am so sorry to hear about your loss."

It was as if she was speaking a foreign language because I didn't comprehend.

"I am sorry that your baby didn't survive the accident."

Libby put her hand on my shoulder to comfort me the way a mother comforts a child in pain. Her words became the latest dagger that pierced my side. I didn't want to let Libby know that I didn't know what she was talking about. That this was a huge surprise to me as well. I had taken my share of disappointment in the last 24 hrs. She left me with those words and a pat on the back.

"The baby didn't survive the accident."

There had to be a mistake. Couldn't remember the last time we had sex in the last several months or so. James had gotten Sharon pregnant. She had lost his baby. My wife was pregnant with another man's baby and lost it in the accident. That shit didn't even sound right formulating in my mind. My anger returned ten fold. It had become my dominant emotion. I wanted to kill James and I didn't give a damn about the money. I wanted to send him to meet his maker. I called Same Boat to let her know that I would accept her offer.

"I am glad to see that you reconsidered Mr. Wade."

She told me where he would be and even texted the address. At this point it wasn't even about the million dollars. Sometimes revenge could cloud rational judgment and make you do things that you wouldn't regret until later. I told Libby that I would be downstairs making some phone calls. Everyone was capable of murder given the proper circumstances and I was no exception. My thoughts even became the thoughts of a calculated killer. I told Libby that I had to run to my car and to call me if Sharon's status changed. Libby would make a great alibi in case things got traced back to me. It was time to end the life of the man who helped himself to what was mine.

Kevin 27

I would have to make his death look like an accident. It needed to seem random. I needed him in the perfect place so that I could ambush his punk ass. It had to be quick and deadly. I needed a weapon. Nothing that could get traced back to me. Every man had his breaking point and James had pushed me past mine. Men have been killed for a lot less than what he did. Same Boat's directions had led me directly to her husband. I recognized this location when she had given me the address. It was the condo that he had leased as his private hotel. This was no doubt the place where he had sexed my wife. The site where he conceived a child with another man's wife. My wife. I hit the lights on my car. Made sure that I was parked out of site. Decided to observe my prey like a skilled hunter in the wild. My heart rate increased. My nerves were getting the best of me. I had to pee really bad. I got out of the car and took a piss behind my license plate, remained out of sight. There was a chorus of Mother Nature's nocturnal symphony playing. In the distance dogs howled as crickets chirped. Momma would say that dogs howling meant another soul was leaving this world going to the next one. I was determined to make her a prophet tonight. Same Boat said that she was gonna call me back once she lured James out of his safe haven. He would be in the open with nowhere to run. I could follow him without him even suspecting me whatsoever. I'd sit and wait on James. Sit and wait on Same Boat to set this plan in motion. My phone rang, heart damn near jumped out of my chest. I looked down to see the number, almost positive it would be Same Boat. I looked crazy at that number. It wasn't from the (803) area code that I had expected. It was from a (704) area code. Who could this be I thought to myself? Apprehension and curiosity both competed to see who would win the battle to be my dominant emotion. Curiosity had won by a narrow margin and I answered the phone.

"Hi....this is Lisa Ellis returning a call. Did someone call me from this number?"

I paused for a few seconds. I despised when someone asked if a call was made from the number that showed up on their caller ID. That was when it hit me. This was the fabulous looking Lisa that I had met at The Melting Pot last Friday. "As long as you can dream it, we can fund it." I remembered her body; the way she moved and became the music. Most important I remembered my reason for calling her. I wanted to see how her company could assist with funding my dream.

"Hey, this is Kevin Wade. We met the other night in Charlotte..........I was giving you a call....you gave me your card.....I wanna discuss something with you."

That seemed like the hardest thing I ever had to say. It didn't take her long to place my voice and remember who I was. She sounded like she was glad that I called her. Lisa and I played catch up and she explained to me how her company worked. I told her all about my big dream and how I even had my own business plan. For a minute I had forgotten that I was parked outside of some guy's condo waiting for his wife to give me the word so that I could kill him. I didn't even have a concrete plan for how I was gonna do that. Just knew that once again James really knew how to bring my anger to a boil. At this moment talking to Lisa Ellis made all that was wrong seem right. This small measure of time seemed like a piece of heaven to hear her angelic voice. She told me that she really wanted to sit down with me, see my proposal and present it to her board for consideration. Lisa sounded almost as excited as I was. She wanted to know if I could be in Charlotte by 10:00 a.m. tomorrow. Said she would rework her entire morning if I could be there.

God looks out for fools and babies and here I was on the verge of being the biggest fool ever.

Those words spoke to me. Here I was about to be a fool in a major way and miss out on the possibility of a golden opportunity. Truth be told, it would be worth the trip just to see her again and be in her presence.

"I am no murderer."

My logical mind had returned to me. Those were my words when Same Boat initially propositioned me for her little murder for hire venture. India and K.J. resurfaced and suddenly my true purpose became crystal clear. I couldn't have them growing up without a father the same way that I did. Couldn't have them coming to visit me in prison. Not even my strong hate towards James could allow me to put them through that type of torture. I started my car and escaped from that place where 187 almost happened. I talked to Lisa all the way from outside the condo until I was back in the hospital parking lot. Lisa had given me directions to her office as we confirmed our 10:00 a.m. meeting. After making small talk it was obvious that we both had to go. I felt like I was back in high school talking to someone I had a crush on and not wanting to be the first one to hang up the phone. Same Boat beeped in as I hung up with Lisa. She was calling to give the okay to send James on an all inclusive trip to the coroner's office by breakfast time. "Changed my mind, I thought I could …..even wanted to do it…….can't do it."

Those were the words that I had given to her. Silence fell among us. For the first time since I had known this woman she could not find words to express herself. With a solemn tone she replied.

"I understand Mr. Wade. Looks like I will have to go another route to find my closure. I wish you well."

She hung up the phone before I could even reply. For a moment I felt sorry for Same Boat, but she would have to solve her own problems. I had my own to solve. For the first time in days I had something to look forward to. Back upstairs Sharon was awake busying herself watching TV.

"Where have you been baby?"

"I had to make a few calls and set some things up for work."

She was looking at her right thigh. Studying her wound.

"I feel so.....ugly. My hair is a mess. I want to take a shower baby. I want to go home. Take me home Kevin."

She had become emotional as she rubbed her hand over the stitches that had closed her skin after doctors inserted a metal plate and screws to repair her broken femur. Most broken bones healed in six weeks, this could take longer given the fact that the femur is the largest bone in the human body. Sharon would require physical therapy once she was released. No matter what, I would not abandon her in this condition. I rubbed fresh ice chips over her dry lips, brushed her hair back with my fingers. Helped to make her feel beautiful. She was beautiful. Even without her hues of make up, lip stick , and eye liners that she customarily wore.

"You are beautiful Sharon. You have always been beautiful. Everything is going to be okay."

Tears began streaming down her face.

"I love you Kevin.....I am so fortunate to have a husband like you."

Her words stung. Stung like a pissed off yellow jacket. I wanted to confront her about her affair with James. I needed to know why she had betrayed me.

"Sharon......I have something to ask you."

Before I knew what I was saying the words had popped out of my mouth. Dr. Glading's words entered back into my mind. His warning about stress being a factor in Sharon regaining her memory. She tilted her head in my direction, focused her eyes on mine and struggled to talk. Her meds were starting to get the best of her again.

"What did you wanna ask me baby?"

"Just wanted to know if I could do anything for you?" She smiled and said.

"You already have."

Sharon turned her head back towards the TV and let her pain medication become her lullaby. I decided to go back to work on my laptop. Swallowed that urge to know my truth as I watched her sleep. I took out my laptop, had to make sure that I was fully prepared for my meeting with Lisa. I couldn't help but get distracted when I thought about her. Tomorrow would be a good day. I would begin my own pursuit of happiness.

I had gotten off of my normal routine since Sharon's accident. Had done my part to chip in and help Kevin with the kids as best I could. This insomnia continued to abide in me. I hadn't had a full night's rest that didn't include a drunken slumber since I could remember. I decided to take all of this stress that I had into the gym and let it burn like a California wild fire. My workout would have to be adjusted because Kevin was not coming. He had sent me a text about some major meeting that he had. Something about a new venture. I had no idea what he was talking about. I decided to run on the treadmill to get warmed up. Felt the burn in my hamstrings. Made me remember why they were sore. Made me think of Elise and that good workout that she had given me the night before. Then I thought about Angela. Thought about the nerve she had to be in public with her new beau. I guess she felt the same about me and Elise. Turned my iPod up high to drown out any thoughts I was having about the women in my life. I needed to focus on getting a good workout. Needed to feel normal again. Everyone was crowding around the flat screen monitors in the gym. They

seemed intrigued. More bad news, it appeared that someone else
had been gunned down in this little city with big city crime. The
volume was muted and all I could make out was that police had no
suspects and thought that it was a random shooting. Maybe it was
gang related. Trying to read those closed captions that fast made
me frustrated. I turned away from that news report. Thought
about my own issues. I turned up the intensity of the treadmill
to make it incline. Made it burn more. Thirty minutes later I
decided that enough was enough for this workout. I did some ab
work, stretched and called it quits. I went home and completed
my normal routine in preparation of another work day. Ate two
egg whites, fresh fruit, showered, dressed, and was back in pursuit
of another day where I had to be on top of my game. I had the
type of job that nobody wanted to be that patient when you had an
off day. Always felt added pressure to be perfect, even when I was
going through my own problems. I wish sometimes that I could
sit on someone's couch and pay them to make all my problems go
away or give me some perspective. No such luck. Every station
on the radio was talking about the recent homicide that took place
last night during the hours where most of us slept. I didn't catch
the information about the victim and easily dismissed it due to
the frequency of violence in today's society. All they said was that
he was survived by a grieving widow. Same old story I thought to
myself as I decided to listen to one of my playlists instead of the bad
news network that had become local news. My life was beginning
to mirror Bill Murray's life when he played in Groundhog's Day.
Everyday was pretty much a carbon copy of the one previous to
it. Every Monday looked like the last one and so on and so on
until the weekend. My patients showed up the same time on the
same day and pretty much said most of the same stuff. The only
thing that changed was my clothes, the date, and the weather
each season. Even their co-pay amount remained the same. I was

thirsty for change. Thirsty like a man who would trade breath for water. I listened to Alicia Keyes, Corrine Bailey Rae, and Chrisette Michele as my iPod fed me random tunes. Their unique sounds blended together like a musical ménage trios. Their styles so different and yet their messages similar. These women weren't afraid to express themselves to the person in life that meant the most to them. The person that they wanted to be with. The person they wanted to go to sleep and wake to everyday. I had long lost faith in that type of feeling. I had become that guarded person that I discouraged my patients from becoming. It had been over a decade since I played and lost at love. It was such a huge gamble that didn't pay off for me. I had lost that game on the campus of Spelman College. It was that same place that I made myself a promise that I would never be hurt like that again. I'd never be made a fool of again. I thought of all the women I had been with. All of the women that I never allowed myself to give anything that wasn't physical. I had met some great women and Angela was the latest representation. So many I couldn't count. I had shared a bed with so many women I couldn't remember them. Most of them had offered love. I only returned sex in exchange. That was like trading the U.S. Dollar for a Peso. Somehow it just wasn't a fair exchange. I had grown weary of my same old routine, but I felt trapped in a sense. I kept on doing the same 360 degrees, never truly changing. I needed to do a 180 so that I could see things different. I was tired of the women who haunted me in my dreams. I needed to do right by them. Needed to do right by me before it was too late. At that moment I knew what I had to do. I had to go to the root of this problem. I had to evict the skeletons that resided in my closet. Those thoughts remained on my mind throughout my day as I saw my clients. I had dinner plans this evening so I left the office particularly early today. This would be a special dinner where I would put my chef hat on and sharpen up my culinary skills. I stopped at the Fresh Market on my way home to compile my grocery list. I grabbed fresh garlic, asparagus, salmon, spinach, and a bottle of pinot noir. Tonight was going to be special. I prepared grilled salmon atop a bed of spinach, with rice pilaf, and steamed asparagus spears. The dinner was set on low while I prepared myself for this special evening. I set the table after I got dressed, poured two glasses of wine at room temperature. The TV was turned to soft jazz on my XM radio channels. The tone was totally set for this evening. All I was waiting on was the guest of honor. The doorbell rang. I looked at my watch.

"Right on time." I said to myself.

I opened the door and there she was. It was Samantha. She accepted my invitation for dinner.

"It's about time you stop blowing me off Jay. Can a sister get a hug?"

I hugged her and invited her inside. She sat down on a bar stool while I finished setting the table. I handed her a glass of wine. When you had as much history as we did it was easy to relax and feel at ease. So many memories. That became the theme while we talked over dinner. We had gone back down memory lane. It made me appreciate that chapter of my life. Made me realize that the good truly outweighed the bad. I had come to grips that I needed to let go of that bad feeling that I had for her. Needed to forgive her so that I could move on. So that we could both move on. I needed to bring that chapter of my life to a close.

"That salmon was banging boy. You must have been paying attention to your momma when she cooked."

She drank her wine, savored its flavor. I cleared the table and put the dishes in the dishwasher. Normally this would be the part of the evening where some clothes would be coming off. That was not going to happen tonight. I had to slay this dragon inside of me. We moved into the den. I bought the bottle of wine with us. Samantha had gone through my DVDs and put one on. She played Love Jones. It was my favorite romantic movie.

"Remember we went to the movies to see this?"

"Yeah I remember going, don't remember seeing the ending."

We both laughed. The movie played in the background as we drank wine laughing about yester year. I realized that while the past never changes, it didn't have to dictate the future. In a moment of clarity it came to me that the good certainly outweighed the bad where we were concerned. That's when I grabbed her hand and looked her in her eyes. I told her that I loved her. She blushed. I did love her, but not quite the way she was thinking.

"I will always love you. You will always have a special place in my heart. Even when I tried to hate you I really couldn't. I need for you to forgive me for something."

"What do I need to forgive you for, you haven't done anything."

"Just hear me out. I have not done right by you. I have toyed with you all of these years and led you to think that we would one day be together. I wanted you to feel that same hurt that you made me feel all those years ago in college. I am truly sorry." Silence rose and filled the room. She wasn't laughing anymore. Darius (Lorenze Tate) was giving Nina (Nia Long) his spoken word on screen while I was giving Samantha my words in my living room. The dimples were gone, and now the tears were cascading down her face. I really felt like shit knowing that she was hurting like this. This was not the feeling that I thought I'd be feeling all those years ago. Revenge was the tool of the weak and carried a burden that I wasn't strong enough to hold; didn't wanna hold. My words had served as confirmation for her.

"Jason.....I have had to live with that for over ten years now. I don't blame you......I am the one who jeopardized our relationship. I didn't return your trust. You have no idea what it is like to have to wake up to that reality everyday of my life since then. You can't fathom what it's like meeting great guys and knowing that they don't compare to you. I screwed up. I am sorry."

I wiped her tears with my hand. Hated seeing her crying. I knew deep down inside I had to let Samantha go because she would have never let me go. She would have never let go of the hope that we'd live happily ever after. Get married at the church that we both grew up as kids and got baptized at. She had her perfect wedding day all planned out from color scheme to the first song to dance to at the reception. Everything was in place except for me as the groom. I wanted her to be happy. I wanted her to have a man that would give her kids a ring and a house with a white picket fence. Most of all give her a commitment. We sat on my sofa and drank wine while we watched Love Jones. This would be our happy ending, a new chapter, this would be our closure. I had been carrying around this burden for over a decade that grew exponentially by the day. I felt it immediately subside. I felt free.

Kevin

I was running on pure euphoria on my way up I-77 north towards Charlotte to meet with Lisa. Sleeping on a couch at the hospital wasn't exactly what I would call a desirable thing. My crooked neck and stiff back were indications of that truth. The last time I had to do that my two children were born. This time Sharon was in the hospital because of injuries she had suffered during a car accident. India and K.J. had been dropped off at school and my in-laws were sitting at the hospital with Sharon. I looked over my business plan and my proposal a hundred times to make sure it was on point that I felt like I had OCD. I just hoped that Lisa was as confident in my work as I was. Hoped her board members were more excited than both of us were. Felt like my 300 was floating on air the way I was accelerating. Before I knew it I was doing 90 miles an hour and climbing. My better judgment prevailed and I set my cruise control on 75 mph. Didn't wanna push my luck. That kind of speed could earn you an automatic trip to lock down facilities. That was not a return trip that this brotha was trying to make ever again. I was in Charlotte in no time. Blended in with rush hour traffic. People hustling to get to their nine to five. No doubt miserable like the average American who hated their job to. I was making this commute to put an end to that reality in my life. I wanted the freedom that Jason had. I wanted to be my own boss, and call my own shots. Most of all I wanted to do something that I loved doing. My GPS tracking device took me right to Lisa's office turn for turn. I pulled in front of the building in a visitor's park. "If you can dream it, we can fund it." It was written on their door as I walked into the building. I felt that crook in my neck as I looked from the bottom up at this huge skyscraper that housed Dreamers, Inc. The security person made me sign in and told me to take the elevator to the 28th floor to get to Lisa's suite. Normally I would have opted for the stairs, but 28 flights probably wasn't gonna happen today. September 11th has made me paranoid about being in tall buildings. After the elevator rocked and zoomed me to her floor I got out and headed towards Lisa's receptionist to let her know that I was here. Our meeting was at 10:00 a.m. but I knew that I needed to be a little early. It was 9:45 as I glanced at my watch and waited on Ms. Lisa Ellis.

"Ms. Ellis will be with you in a moment."

My anxiety made me stand and pace. I adjusted my suit, buttoned and unbuttoned a few buttons and made sure my tie was straight. As soon as I turned around I saw Lisa walking towards me. That was too much, too fast. I took her in from head to toe. The almond skin, the beautiful face, aerobically fit body, and curvaceous hips. I had seen Lisa in casual dress; today she was dressed for success. She flashed her million dollar smile as she extended her right hand towards mine.

"Hi Kevin, how are you?"

I wanted to take her into an empty conference room and give her something she could feel, but I settled for a handshake.

"I am good, how are you?"

Lisa walked me to her office. She said that she was look-ing forward to looking over my business proposal. I was look-ing forward to looking her over. Lisa was a reminder of how horny I was. It had been a minute since I had sex. Sharon had let James play with my toys. I remained cautiously op-timistic as Lisa sat and reviewed my proposal and business plan. I tried to read her eyes to see if I could gauge her ex-pression, but she remained composed and business like. This must be what it feels like when an author submits their work to a potential publishing company. Everyone had a project that they felt strongly about, but not everyone else felt the same. I glanced around her corporate office. Saw her degree in business from Howard University. She had won employee of the month a few times. I looked for pictures of her ex boy-friend, or any other significant people in her life. There was one picture that caught my eye on her desk. It was Lisa and her father at her college graduation. She must have seen me looking at the picture. "That's me and my dad. She paused, sensing that I was gonna ask about her mother. "My mom died when I was 12."

"I'm sorry to hear that. Your dad seems very proud of you."

She nodded as she kept on reading. For a moment I felt awkward about her having to explain that to me. Then I felt as if we kinda had a connection. Maybe she didn't explain that to everyone. Maybe she thought that I was special. A few moments later Lisa cleared her throat. She did that to get my attention.

"Kevin......I absolutely love your entire concept. I can see your vision the way that you articulated it on paper. They must have taught you something at SouthCarolina State."

She laughed at her joke. My smile was ear to ear in response to her feedback. "Wow....you really like it. I am glad."

"I am just wondering why you haven't acted on it sooner?"

My facial expression told her that unless she had all day that we had better change the subject. Lisa said that she would definitely present my project to her board for serious consideration. We made small talk discussing everything from work to friends. She told me that her friend Elise was contemplating moving to Columbia to go to law school. "You wanna go to lunch Kevin? My treat."

She surprised me with that question. I would go anywhere she wanted me to go with her. "Yeah, I'd love to."

Lisa and I left for lunch.

"I'll drive my car since you drove up here."

I didn't object to her driving. Lisa hit the button on her keyless remote; made it chirp. Her silver CLK Mercedes Benz lit up as we walked towards it. Lisa had her own parking space as if she owned the place. Someone here really likes her I thought to myself. With a body like hers I didn't blame 'em. As we rode in automobile luxury with German engineering, we continued to have pleasant conversation. Lisa drove us to South Park mall. We ate at the Cheesecake Factory. That was one of my favorite restaurants. Reminded me of being home in Atlanta. There was no such luck finding one of these in Columbia. It seemed that Lisa and I had known each other for years given how easy our conversation flowed. She told me all about her mother and how she had lost her battle with breast cancer. It made her and her father become closer. I shared a similar story with her. Told her about my daddy being killed and how I was close to my momma. We both thought that it was kinda ironic that we had no siblings and that we had lost our opposite gender parent. Lisa and I both had salads topped with grilled chicken. I liked that she worked out and ate well. For the first time in days I actually had an appetite. She was able to make the connection to my dream of having my own sports management firm when I explained to her that I was on the cusp of N.F.L. stardom before my knee injury. Lisa identified with the hurt in my eyes, much as I had identified with the hurt in hers. We were proof that bad things happened to good people. When the check came, out of habit I reached for my wallet to square things away. She stopped me.

"I said that it was my treat. You have gotten used to these southern belles that won't pay for their own tab, huh?"

She said that with a smile. A friendly reminder that she had not conformed to the south just because she lived in the south.

"It's just a habit, that's all."

I had to admit that I was a bit more traditional and I felt like the man should take care of a woman. It was what came natural to me. It was like trying to condition an eagle not to fly with healthy wings; not gonna happen. We left and got back into her German chariot. Lisa dropped me off at her building. It was hot as hell standing outside. I would have melted just to be in her presence a little longer.

"I will meet with my board and present your proposal Kevin."

"Thank you so much Lisa."

This time we hugged. Nothing inappropriate, it was one of those not quite business not quite friends hug. It was enough to create slight movement in my pants. Not enough for her to notice. We parted company and I got back inside of my car. I wondered if she had looked back at me but I didn't turn around to see. I left my meeting with Lisa sure of two things. Sure that she liked my proposal and sure that we had some definite chemistry. Before I knew it I was back on I-77 headed south towards Columbia, S.C. again with thoughts of Lisa Ellis dancing in my mind.

Kevin 30

I had done good matriculating my way from Charlotte to Columbia. It was just after two p.m. and I had plenty of time before I would have to get my kids. Sharon didn't know about me being laid off work so technically I was working. Somehow I didn't care anyway, but for her own good I would play along with this marriage hoax until she got better. Still wasn't sure how this thing would play out but I knew that I would have to figure something out. I wouldn't do anything to jeopardize her memory loss being permanent. Decided that I would go to the gym to get a really good workout going. I headed to do this afternoon what I normally did in the morning. I kept gym clothes in my bag because I never knew when they would come in handy. In no time I was changed from my corporate America look to my let's get pumped up look. I had on a grey tank top with burgundy shorts and my Nike Air Max sneakers. I turned on my MP3 player and scrolled over 1000 tunes to inspire my work out. It wasn't an iPod, but it did the job all the same. I needed to do some heavy weight so that I could feel the burn that I needed to feel. I needed to work my body to muscle failure. This was a

great source of stress relief. A day like this I could really use Jason
to spot me, but I had to do what I had to do. After some light
stretching and fifteen minutes on the stair stepper I was ready to
go. It was comforting that I didn't know this cast of characters
in the gym during this time of day. I didn't feel like talking
to anyone I knew anyway. I focused on chest, back, arms and
abs. Took on a workload that would make Lee Haney question
my sanity. Did set after set of bench press until I got up to 350
lbs for five reps. That was all I felt confident doing without a
spot. Made blood gorge my body parts. I was pumped. Felt
that high that weight lifters get while working out. When I
had finished super setting my exercises I completed my ab work.
Pounding that steel took discipline and violence that not many
people had. It took me going into a zone mentally to do that
work physically. When I came out of my zone I noticed that I had
several spectators looking on and marveling at my exploits. They
were in here to talk while I was in here to work out. This is why
the gym was not effective for everybody. I carried those thoughts
with me as I wiped my sweat, grabbed my gym bag and headed
for the heat that waited outside. My arms were almost too heavy
to hold the steering wheel. I managed to drive anyway. Thank
God for power steering. Lisa remained heavy on my mind. Not
even the gym could make her fade to black in my mind. When I
pulled up to my house I observed something unusual. It was the
rental car that my in-laws had. Why weren't they at the hospital
with Sharon? What was going on? I pulled in my driveway in
search of answers. When I opened the door I didn't see anyone.
I put my keys and my gym bag down and searched my home.
My father in-law was napping in the recliner in front of my big
screen TV. I decided to let him get what looked like some good
rest. I proceeded to my bedroom. That was where I discovered
my mother in-law. She was not alone. Sharon was home. This

was feeling like the twilight zone. Did I miss something? When did she get released? I carried a puzzled look with me inside of my bedroom. I know that HMOs were trying to shorten hospital stays but this was crazy. Evidently I startled both of them by their expressions.

"What are you doing home so early Kevin?"

"I could ask you the same thing Sharon?"

My mother in-law spoke and headed towards the den with her sleeping husband.

"The doctors agreed that I was ready to be released. They said it might help my memory to be in a less stressful setting. Felt like I could heal just fine at home. I wanted to surprise you."

"I am surprised. I am glad that you are out of that hospital. I know the kids will be thrilled."

I didn't want to tell her about my meeting with Lisa. Didn't want her to know about my plans to pursue my own sports management firm. I didn't want her negative vibes all over me. Utilizing the art of lying I told Sharon that I had taken half the day off because of a few deals that I closed last week. Told her that it was Steve's way of rewarding my hard work.

"Has it helped so far being home?

"What do you mean?"

"Have you been able to remember anything?"

"So far I don't remember much past last Friday. I just remember getting home late after work when you were sleeping....just before you went out. Couldn't tell you what happened between that and waking up in that dreaded hospital room."

The worry and panic began growing in her face.

"It's okay. Don't stress yourself Sharon, it'll come back."

I grabbed her hand while looking down on her. She smiled. I looked into the eyes of a woman who'd deceived me and didn't even know that I knew. Those thoughts would be stored in my mental database for an unspecified amount of time. I let her hand go and headed for the shower that I desperately needed. She asked me to hand her the State newspaper that rested upon her dresser. It was the most current edition. I executed her request. My life with her could never be normal again; some things that were done could never be undone. I carried that sentiment with me and took a long hot shower. The pressure from the shower head pulsated on my body and didn't miss the tip of my penis. I began to feel stimulated and instant growth had taken place. It was as if mentally Lisa had entered into my shower with me. I could still smell her perfume as we embraced. Remembered her softness; wanted to squeeze her breasts; wanted to taste her; all of her. I stroked myself at a violent pace, up and down until my seed flowed into the shower drain. This was further proof that I needed some pussy in the worst way.

For the first time in a long time I slept; slept like a baby. I felt a peace that I haven't felt in years. I didn't even stay up to watch the 11p.m. edition of Sports Center. My insomnia had been linked to years of unresolved issues that stemmed from the hurt that I now know was unintentional. I hated it took this long for me to confront my demons of yesteryear, but now I was glad that day had come and gone. Samantha and I both would be better for getting things out in the open. It was time for her to move on to bigger and better things. It was time for me to let go of the past that held me captive to it and move on myself. Angela was the last thing on my mind when I closed my eyes and she remained in my thought process even while I slept. She invaded my dreams in the best way and it was her that I thought of when I opened my eyes. It was as if the veil was lifted and now I could see. Things were now more crystallized. I was not about to let her go without a fight. I had to show Angela that I could return the love that she had given to me. My fear kept me from answering her question when she asked me how I felt for her. I was afraid to tell her that I loved her. Afraid that she would disappoint me in the manner that Samantha had done many years ago. Now I could see things differently and allow myself to take another risk. A risk that had a much higher reward than I could imagine. It was time to stop hiding behind fear. It was time to stop being afraid. My daddy always told me that nothing in life worth having ever came easy. For a rare moment I found myself agreeing with my daddy. Angela was worth fighting for. In normal fashion I was back at my place taking my shower in preparation for another day at the office. My gym routine was done and I had eaten a balanced breakfast. It was time to go to work. Time to see patients and help them with their respective issues. The several days that I haven't spoken with Angela began to seem like an eternity. I needed to see her in the worst way; needed to be in her presence. When I got to my office I proceeded to check my email and logged onto a few websites. I decided to do something uncharacteristic and spontaneous by my own standards. I called Maxiene into my office with my schedule. After I looked over my appointments for the day I promptly told her to cancel them. When she saw that I wasn't joking she looked at me as if I needed therapy. "What will I tell your patients Mr. Adams?"

"Just tell them I had a very urgent matter that couldn't wait.......reschedule them for next week. Just think of something?

I left Maxiene with the responsibility of rearranging my day. Today she would really earn her paycheck. My next stop led me to a nearby florist. I was going to surprise Angela and bring her flowers to her job. She would never expect that. Normally I would have them delivered. I have never taken flowers to a woman myself. Angela absolutely loved Tulips. I bought her fifty Tulips in assorted colors. Had the florist to make sure that they were not in full bloom. They were as fresh as possible. The Korean florist smiled.

"She must be pretty special lady....these beautiful flower."

I didn't have the heart to tell her that more than one flower became plural so they were now flowers. Instead I smiled and nodded.

"She is very beautiful."

I hurried out of the floral shop in search of the bank where she worked at. Had to fight back the urges that would normally make me succumb to the fear associated with being vulnerable. I wasn't sure if these flowers would even be well received by Angela; wasn't even sure if she would be glad to see me. I swallowed those fears and proceeded into the bank's lobby. Every women inside the bank marveled at the arrangement and stared as if they would be the lucky recipient. Maybe their significant other picked today to surprise them.

"May I help you sir?"

It was one of the floor tellers. I cleared my throat.

"Sure.....I am here to see Ms. Craven. Is she in?"

The lady looked at the flowers and then me.

"Certainly, I will get her for you."

I had never been by her job so her co-workers didn't know me. For a moment that uncertain feeling crept back in. I thought about leaving before she even came out. Before I could even turn around the scent of Chanel number 5 was imbedded in my olfactory. I inhaled her essence. Angela looked at me with a surprised look. She was probably as surprised as I was for showing up unannounced. She was finishing up with a customer. Angela smiled. I couldn't remember a time she ever looked prettier. She was Halle, Beyonce, Gabrielle, and Kerry Washington all in that moment. She embodied all of the qualities that made those women beautiful. I could tell she was slightly embarrassed. There was that awkward moment of silence between us.

"These are for you."

"Thank you. They're my favorite."

She smiled and invited me into her office. There weren't a set of eyes in that bank that didn't follow us as we walked into her office. I decided that I would lay my cards on the table.

"I wanna talk about that night you left my house."

"I don't think this is the time or the place."

"Just hear me out. I realize what you were asking me Angela. I have been dealing with some things that made it difficult to be what you needed me to be."

"Would those things be called Samantha?"

This wasn't about to be easy I thought to myself.

"Actually it had more to do with me than anything else. The truth is Angela; there hasn't been a second that has gone by without you being on my mind. I want us to start over. I want things to be like they were before."

Angela sat on those words. Then she responded.

"I hear what you are saying Jason. I do. The problem is I don't want things to be like they were. I am not at the point in my life where I can invest myself in a relationship stuck in neutral."

She couldn't make eye contact with me. Angela looked at the Tulips and smelled her bouquet.

"Listen to me Angela. You don't understand what I am telling you. Today......standing in your office I know that I love you."

I couldn't believe how smooth those words flew off my lips. For once I was telling the truth.

"Not only that, but I am in love with you. I am not ready to give up on us."

My words had apparently stunned her. I was never more transparent with anyone the way that I was right now. She began to sob lightly.

"I told you that this wasn't the appropriate place to deal with this."

Suddenly there was a knock at her door. It startled us both. One of her male co-workers peeked inside.

"Hey Angela….. Didn't mean to interrupt. Don't forget about the meeting with the corporate big wigs. You're presenting."

I rarely if ever forgot faces. It was the reject that I'd seen her with the other night. This was her replacement of me. In crept that old familiar feeling that resided in me. That "I told you so feeling." The feeling that I got in Atlanta at Spelman let me know that spontaneity had never served me well. Opening myself up had once again made me look like a damn fool.

"Jason……can we talk later?"

"Hey, I understand you're busy. I think we've said all that needs to be said. Take care Angela."

I held my head up high and left her office. I needed to vent. Needed to blow off some steam. I would go to the only place where I could get some privacy. I headed back home to be alone with my thoughts. Decided to give Kevin a call. The problems he was facing would make my issues seem microscopic. Kevin was good at giving good feedback, but there was no answer for him on his cell phone. I tried him at the hospital and there was no answer on the number registered to Sharon's room. There was no use in trying to

get any information from the nurses regarding patients unless you were immediate family. Those HIPPA people made
sure of that. I tried to drown out thoughts of Angela with
music, but it was useless because every song reminded me
of her. I fought that battle until I was home. A good stiff
drink was what I needed. It would make me numb. That
way I wouldn't have to worry about drinking and driving. I
was at home. I mixed a couple of vodka, peach schnapps,
and cranberry juice drinks together. Savored its flavor. They
went down one after the other. After my second drink I began to ease up. Decided to log onto my computer and pass
some time. That was when it hit me. I needed to get away. It
was a minute since my last real vacation. Had spent so much
time fixing other people I was damn near broken myself.
Thought about the weekend plans that me and Angela had
that I blew off. Thought about how she loved beaches. She
always felt they meant new beginnings. Maybe they did, maybe they didn't. I needed to get away. Needed to put as much
distance between myself and my problems. I wanted to go
somewhere with clear blue water, nice weather, and most important nobody I knew. I called my travel agent and booked
one round trip ticket to Trinidad and Tobago. That sounded
far enough. I remembered this girl from undergrad having
Trinidadian decent. Maybe I would meet me an island girl or
two. I would get spa treatment after my morning workout.
Maybe I would even snorkel and go site seeing to appreciate
the finer points of Trinidad. I booked that ticket and secured
my reservation at a five star resort. This trip would provide
the closure that I needed with Angela and all things related to
my past. I would leave in a couple weeks. That way I could
get my patients transitioned with an on-call therapist while I
was gone. I couldn't wait to leave.

Kevin

32

It was funny how much clearer my head became following an orgasm. Guess it helped having the return of blood flow back to my brain. As I exited from my bathroom to get dressed, I noticed that Sharon was sobbing with her head in her hands. I just figured that she was feeling the ebbs and flows of her emotional uncertainty since the accident.

"It's okay baby, you will be back to your old self in no time."

She was not responsive to those words. It was as if my words had not been uttered. That's when Sharon handed me the source of her emotional discomfort. The main article on the front page of the State paper had bold print that read "Local businessman gunned down in carjacking." Beneath the article was a familiar face. It was the face of a man that I had the unfortunate pleasure of getting to know several days earlier. It was the face of the man who had an affair with my wife. James was dead. It was in big bold print.

An indescribable chill ran up my spine with the speed of a performance enhanced sprinter trying to win gold at the Olympics. The man that I was propositioned to kill just days ago was dead. He was killed on the same night that I was led to his den of lust to ambush him myself. Thankfully Lisa's call broke me out of that trance. She kept me from making a terrible mistake. I was still unsettled. Couldn't shake that feeling. James was dead. My wife was upset. She was grieving. Not the normal grief associated with losing a co-worker. This was the grief associated with losing someone you cared for. Amnesia may have robbed her of any short term memory, but it couldn't lay its fingers on her true feelings. "Looks like I have to go another route to get my closure." Same Boat's words bum rushed their way in my mind. This was no coincidence. She was no joke. Guess James found out the hard way what happens when a woman get's fed up. Things were making sense at once. She wanted me to kill James because of my emotional ties to him and Sharon's affair. I was a part of her calculated plan from the beginning. A plan that she obviously was going to get done one way or the other. The timing of the murder told me that she was the type of woman who believed in having a backup plan in place in case the first option didn't work out. Staring at Sharon's injuries made me think for the first time that her accident wasn't an accident at all. Maybe Same Boat wanted Sharon and James dead. Maybe Sharon surviving has proved to be an inconvenience to her.

"Kevin, there is a detective here. He said he wants to talk with you."

My mother in-law had a panicked look on her face as she delivered those words. I knew that I would immediately be a suspect in this unsolved murder. When you publically beat someone down days before they are gunned down, you may have to answer a few questions from a detective.

"Tell him I'll be right out."

Sharon wiped her tears. She looked at me like someone looks at a person talking to them in a foreign language.

"Why do the police wanna talk to you Kevin?"

"I am about to find out."

I knew that I would be a suspect if something ever happened to James. I told Sharon's mom to let him know that I needed to get dressed. I put on some jeans and a tank top. I despised the way some people made it colloquial to refer to tanks as wife beaters. That thought danced in my head as I left my bedroom and headed towards the family room. Sharon's mom took my place and kept her company. I greeted the inquisitive detective. "You Kevin Wade?"

He was sizing me up, obviously intimidated by my physical stature and figuring I was guilty.

"In the flesh. How can I help you?"

"You mind if I ask you a couple of questions?

I wanted to get smart with him. Wanted to tell him that he had already asked me a couple of questions. I couldn't help being mildly suspicious when it came to police lately.

Somehow I didn't think now was the time to piss a cop off. Besides I knew that I was totally innocent and there was nothing to hide. I invited him to our formal dining room and closed the French doors so that we could have privacy.

"My name is Michael Turner. I am a homicide detective with the Columbia Police department. I heard that you got into an altercation several days ago with a gentleman named James Riley. Wanna tell me what happened."

Detective Turner was trying his best to intimidate me. He was less than impressive.

"I have already been arrested for that charge several days ago and I'm betting that you've seen that police report already. It's over as far as I am concerned."

He smirked and continued his police probe, searching for the one mistake on my part so that he could link me to James's murder.

"Where is this going detective?"

"Well Mr. Wade. It turns out that James Riley was murdered last night. Wanna tell me where you were between 10 pm and 2 am? A simple question that requires a simple answer Mr. Wade."

"Actually I was at my wife's bedside at the hospital where she's been the last several days. She was in a pretty serious car accident. In fact she was released earlier today."

He slid two pictures of James slumped over the steering wheel of his black BMW 745. Just like the paper read he was shot at point blank range in the chest. It was up close and personal. Those pictures of death shook me up; made me feel like hurling right on my dining room table. I was in need of composure as I searched for the words to give this detective.

I remembered Libby. She could verify my words if need be.

"You mind if I speak to your wife."

"Actually I do mind. She has been through enough the last few days. She has Dr's orders to get rest and avoid stress. You could check with a hospital employee named Libby that works in the trauma unit."

I watched the detective as he jotted down his notes, and then there were two more photos. They had me leaving the hospital during the time in question as he cleverly marked the date and time. Damn hospital parking garage cameras were no joke.

"I don't think Libby can explain this Mr. Wade. You previously stated that you were at your wife's bedside and yet you weren't. Now I asked you very simple questions and you haven't provided me with simple answers. I've done some digging and it seems that you definitely had a motive to kill the deceased, a history of violence, and the opportunity to pull the whole thing off." He exhaled. I was becoming nervous by the second. It actually looked like I murdered James. In this country prosecutors gave less than a damn about who did it, they only wanted a conviction. Maybe Same Boat was trying to set me up to take the fall that she wasn't willing to take herself. I was starting to feel used; like I was targeted from the start.

"Listen Detective Turner like I said before, I was at the hospital with my wife. I did leave very briefly to make sure that my kids were taken care of. Things have been less than ideal for my family the past several days. I can assure you that I'm no murderer."

The paper said that there were no suspects, so I knew that I was no more than a person of interest. That was the new term for "we think you did it, however at the moment we don't have sufficient evidence to lock you up."

"Thank you for your cooperation Mr. Wade. I will be in touch with you."

"I am sure you will. Good luck solving your case."

Detective Turner left my house. I breathed a huge sigh of relief. Glad that I was not arrested. Couldn't stand being in handcuffs in the back of a police cruiser. The bullet wounds to James's chest remained a vivid illustration in my mind. It was no coincident that he was shot twice in the chest, in the heart at that. His murder screamed more of a personal slaying than a random act. I never really believed in karma, but it seems that Same Boat did. Her heart had been shattered by James and she made sure that his was to. His transgressions wounded her heart in the figurative sense. Her revenge was delivered in the form of two slugs that literally burst his heart. My watch served as a reminder that it was nearly time to pick up India and K.J. from school. Their schedule provided the distraction that I needed to avoid having to detail my talk with a homicide detective to Sharon. It would be kinda hard not to confront her about having an affair with a dead man that I was suspected of killing. I couldn't see how that would keep her stress level down one bit. I told my mother in-law that I was leaving to pick up the kids. All of a sudden my home had become increasingly more uncomfortable. Needed to take a drive and clear my head. Needed to put things in perspective. I jumped in my Nissan 300 Z and shifted gears through my subdivision in search of my crumb snatchers.

I whipped out my cell to make a call to Jason. He wouldn't believe what was going on. My phone was receiving an incoming call before I could dial out. I smiled when I saw that it was from the 704 area code. The sound of her voice served as a calming influence for me. I answered the phone like a teenage boy does when the girl he likes finally calls him back.

"Hello, this is Kevin."

"Hey Kevin, this is Lisa Ellis."

She spoke with a youthful exuberance about herself this time. It was almost the kind of excitement that a kid has on Christmas Eve.

"Guess what" she said.

I was not in much of a guessing mood after what I have been going through lately. She didn't even wait for me to say anything before her excitement got the best of her.

"The board unanimously approved your proposal" she exclaimed!

I was speechless.

"They wanna fund your sports management firm."

I searched for words. Partly in shock by what she had just said to me.

"Are you kidding me?"

"No, they loved it. They wanna meet you."

I could not believe what Lisa was saying to me. Partly I was excited by the words, but there was part of me that was moved at how she was genuinely happy for me. She believed in me. Didn't even really know me, yet she believed in me. Lisa's news had provided me with the kind of opportunity to forever change my life and give my kids the kind of life I've always dreamed of. We continued talking over the particulars concerning the next steps to putting all of this together. Lisa urged me to get to Charlotte like yesterday so that I could meet with her board members. I told her that I would be there tomorrow if they wanted me to. I'd be there with bells on. Heck, I'd even bring 'em coffee and serve it myself. I was so damn excited that it was a struggle to contain my emotions. It was hard to keep my car in my lane and talk. Now I knew how Will Smith's character in the Pursuit of Happyness felt when he got the job. Didn't know whether to scream or whether to stop my car and break out into one of those praise dances my momma would do at revival. A huge feeling of

disbelief was abounding, but Lisa's words served as my confirmation. This woman who had only met me two times had
more faith in me than a woman that I gave two kids and my
last name did. Momma would always say that God has a sense
of humor. This would have to be one of his finer moments
when I thought about my life. The call with Lisa lasted until
I arrived to pick up India and K.J. As usual my kids were
elated to see me. They provided me the type of joy that would
always prevail no matter how bad things looked.

"Daddy can we go to McDonalds", asked India.

"Of course we can baby."

They both celebrated that small victory in the manner
that some people celebrate the end of a war. After picking
up two Happy Meals, and some KFC for my in-laws I headed
back home to face the madness known as Sharon. Once I got
home and settled the kids I began my mental preparation for
my big day with Lisa's board. I had to be impressive. Had
to be on top of my game. You never get a second chance to
make a first impression. My in-laws were in the family room
dining on KFC watching TV. Those nervous feelings crept
back in when the news report was covering James's murder
again. They were interviewing people from his company
and people from near the crime scene who discovered him.
Initially it was ruled an attempted car jacking, but now the
police seemed totally clueless to what really happened. The
killer left behind an 80,000 dollar car, credit cards, and cash.
The only thing that was stolen was the man's wedding band.
A lady began answering questions before a camera crew in
front of her huge Lake Murray home. It looked like a scene in

front of the White House lawn. The woman was Same Boat.
This time her name was not disguised. Amanda Riley read a
statement no doubt prepared by her attorney to the crowd of
reporters. This woman played the role of a grieving widow
with the grace of a top notch actress. She even became tearful
which prompted her attorney to finish the statement. He told
the reporters that there was a $200,000.00 dollar reward for
information leading to the arrest of the person responsible.
I chuckled inside. She had offered me $1,000,000.00 dollars
to end his life days earlier and this was the prize to find the
person responsible. I started to call the police and collect that
200 grand my damn self. I tuned that broadcast out and took
Sharon some chicken to see if her appetite was improved any.
She was watching the same news report in our bedroom. I
took the remote and turned the TV off.

"That's enough news for one day, you need to try and eat
something."

Sharon stared at me as if she had seen a ghost.

"It makes perfect sense", she exclaimed!

"What's that?"

"The police…they think you killed James. Don't they?"

"Who told you that?"

"I remember….just before my accident. You two fought.
You tried to kill James that day."

Sharon was getting her memory back in the midst of her grief.

"Is that all you remember? Do you remember why we fought?"

Silence stole her words and held them hostage. I ignored Dr. Glading's plea for stress reduction. It was time to grab this bull by the horns once and for all.

"Do you remember me confronting you about sleeping with James? What do you have to say about that?"

Her expression told me that she was getting all of her memory back in that instant. The tears began streaming down her face.

"You got some nerve to question me about any of this shit, when you have yet to explain yourself Sharon. You are the one who fucked up, not me. You are the one that had an affair with your boss. You are the one who got pregnant by another man."

My words were sharp like scalpels digging into tender flesh. Each truth I spoke went deeper and deeper and opened her up.

"I know everything Sharon. That's why I came to your office to confront you about it. When James walked in he caught my wrath and fury. I gave him what I wanted to give to you. Although a part of me wished he was dead, I didn't have nothing to do with him dying."

She halted her tears long enough to speak clear. Even though there was nothing that she could say to ease my pain I still wanted some type of justification to her actions. Sharon issued a lame ass apology and said all the cliché things that people who get caught cheating spew from their lying mouths.

"We haven't been happy for a long time Kevin. You never tell me I'm beautiful anymore. You don't look at me like you desire me anymore. I felt very lonely and vulnerable.......it made me paranoid that you were having an affair with someone else. That shit was driving me crazy. You know that I would never do anything to hurt you Kevin."

Was that the best that she could do, I asked myself? My wife had given herself to another man and this was the bullshit she offered me. Her words were just as hurtful to me as my words had been to her. Maybe I had stopped loving my wife the way that she needed to be loved like she said. Maybe all of her reasons to seek love elsewhere were true. Sometimes in life the person who actually has the affair outside of the relationship does so because their partner has withdrawn their emotional output. Usually the physical part of the affair is simply a microcosm of the bigger realization that their love was not returned the same way in which it was given. Call me crazy, even call me philosophical but I totally understood Sharon's actions. We had a marriage based on a love that was not equal. A love that over the years was reduced to a tolerance for one another. While this would always be a valuable lesson to both of us, I knew we both deserved better. Sharon was beautiful and I knew that she would find a man to love her in a way that I did not. I was sure I'd find that in a woman myself. I knew that I couldn't forgive her enough to look past her infidelity. That simply was not going to happen. We were both on the threshold of our thirties, which by some standards meant that we were just entering into adulthood. We were college sweethearts that probably took our fling one step too far. In a crazy kind of way as we talked and cleared our respective air, I found myself with no regrets. Despite everything that happened, even my trip to jail I realized had a purpose in helping me to come to grips with a reality that I was very much in denial of. I thought of the hook to Kanye West's song "Stronger." I realized the strength that I had gained from the way our relationship dissolved before our eyes. I thought of the precious gifts that we have combined to create in India and K.J. While I knew that they would forever bond Sharon and me together, I knew that the period of our lives as husband and wife was over. We needed to bring closure to this period of pain and betrayal. We stayed up most of the night just talking. It was like old times, without all of the distractions of life that sometimes cloud communication. In that moment we evolved to another level. A place where we could be friendly despite what happened. A place that would allow us to co-parent our two children and make decisions in their best interest without the court system. There was no bitterness or vindictiveness between us. Only peace and understanding. We had our peace with the past including our marriage and looked forward to a new beginning. We found closure.

Nearly two weeks had passed since Angela and I last talked. She still weighed heavily on my mind. I was convinced that it was for the best to let that situation burn and move on. My plane for Trinidad was boarding later on this evening and I still had a few people I wanted to see before my two week hiatus. I had to catch up with Kevin so that I could extend congratulations on his new venture. He was always there for me and I wanted to appear as supportive as possible. I had a laundry list of things to do before my flight. Maxiene and I made sure that all of my patients were booked for two weeks out. Whatever problems they had in between that would have to wait till I got back. I even paid for Maxiene to go on a much needed vacation. She said that she wanted to see the bright lights of Las Vegas, so I bought her and her husband two first class tickets and paid for a week's stay at the MGM Grand. She deserved it. My phone was blowing up all morning as usual. My Blackberry would not be making it out of my carry on luggage once I arrived in Trinidad. No worries, no stress is what I repeated to myself. Samantha was calling me.

"Hey Jason, just wanted to call you to say have a nice trip and enjoy yourself."

"Thanks Sam, I'll do that. What are you doing with your-self this weekend?" "Well…..I kinda…sorda…have a date. This guy from work asked me out."

"Well, well you make sure he has you home at a decent hour now. Don't make me call yo momma and tell her you being fast."

We both laughed at my attempt at humor. This was proof that we were both growing past our differences. We were friends who used to be lovers. I knew that Samantha would do well. I was happy for her moving on.

"Ohh, I almost forgot Jason. I ran into Angela two days ago while I was in the bank. You didn't tell me that yall broke up. She didn't even know about Trinidad."

I didn't tell Sam about me and Angela because I didn't feel like any heavy dialogue like we were about to have.

"It's kinda complicated Sam. It is what it is basically. You know?"

She rested on those words, sensing that I didn't wanna really go further.

"It is what it is. Gotcha man. Have fun anyway, and don't bring me back no lousy t-shirt. I want a real gift. I know they got Gucci over there." We laughed again.

"Okay, I will make sure I get you something nice. Something like Gucci."

She kept laughing as we ended our call. We talked all the way to momma's house. Had to see my folks before I left town for two weeks. I was more nervous about my multiple flights than I let on. It was still triple digit heat with no rain in sight. I would not miss this humidity one bit. My daddy was sitting on the front porch when I pulled up reading the paper.

"Hey daddy, what's up?" He shook his head.

"It's a damn shame dey ain't caught the hoodlums responsible for that man's murder yet."

He was talking about James Riley. The husband of my former client Amanda Riley. The man who broke her heart had been murdered in cold blood and there was no trace of a suspect. My now former client the grieving widow decided to terminate therapy after her husband was killed. She said that she knew how to get in touch with me if she wanted to talk.

"Hey son."

"Where 's momma?"

"She in the back of the house tending to laundry."

Me and daddy made small talk on the porch. He told me that he and momma had a long talk several weeks ago after dinner when everyone left. Daddy said that momma helped him realize some things. I wondered where this was going.

"Son...sometimes it takes a real man to admit he's wrong. To admit the errors of his ways. I know that I have always been hard on you. You remind me so much of myself. So headstrong. So stubborn. I didn't do a good enough job embracing that in you. The truth is.....I am proud of you. I wanted things for my two boys that I never had myself. I may have pushed too hard. May have pushed you away from me. I am proud of the man you done become. I love you son."

My daddy's words caught me off guard and stunned me. Felt like I was seven years old again. In that moment I wasn't a grown man just shy of his thirtieth birthday. I struggled to fight the tears back. Daddy taught me that a man wasn't supposed to cry. I held on to his words. Told him I loved him too. I couldn't remember ever hearing my daddy tell me he loved me. He suddenly appeared human in my eyes, no longer robotic. We shook hands and I went inside to see my momma. Daddy went back to reading his paper. His disgust of an unsolved murder was now the focus of his attention once again. Momma was in her bedroom looking through old photo albums when I walked in. Holding onto memories of yesterday.

"Hey baby. You all packed for your trip?"

"Hey momma. I'm all set and ready to go."

We hugged each other not naïve of the fact that there was mutual apprehension of possible danger where long travel was involved.

"I wish you was going with somebody else. Why you going by yo self?"

"I just need some time away to clear my head. I'll be okay. Don't worry so much."

She wore that look of worry in her eyes that a concerned mother would. Momma was looking at old photos of me Darryl and Tonya growing up. Each of us had our own photo album. She treasured those memories like Saudis did oil.

"Son...even though you the oldest....you gone always be my baby. I just want you to be happy. Do whatever it takes to make sho you happy."

She made me look into her eyes. Did that to search for the truth in my response. I nodded in accordance with what she asked of me.

"I got some running to do before I leave. I love you momma. I will call once I get there to let you know I made it safe."

We hugged and I was back in my SUV. Back in the triple digit heat that made summers crazy in Columbia, S.C. This summer had been one of the hottest ever on record and in recent memory as far as I was concerned. I returned the missed call that I'd gotten from Elise. She wanted to tell me that she made her decision regarding law school. Elise decided to accept the offer to go to Georgetown instead of U.S.C. She said that she couldn't take the heat. I could read between the lines of the words she fed me. We both knew it would be difficult for her to be in the same city as me without wanting to act on feelings that she had expressed to me several weeks ago. Life was funny like that. Love was funny like that. You had no control over how you felt about someone, and even less control about the way in which they felt about you. That's what made true love even more special. Having two people feel the exact way about each other at the same time was priceless. I had most of the things crossed off of my to do list. Made sure Dre hooked me up with a fresh cut. Had all of my mail forwarded to my P.O. Box until I got back. Daryl was coming to house sit off and on while I was gone. Kevin said that he would take me to the airport so that I wouldn't have to pay for two weeks of airport parking. That would give us an opportunity to catch up on the places that life has taken us over the last several weeks. I walked around my house and double checked to make sure I was properly packed. My house phone rang out to let me know it required my attention. I knew that it was someone close to me. I never gave that number out. It was Tonya.

"Hey big bro?"

"What's up baby sis?"

"Nothing.....was just calling to tell you to have a safe trip."

"Awe that's so sweet. Before you ask I will make sure to get you something nice." She laughed.

"I wasn't even gonna say that, but since you did...thanks. I wanted to tell you the good news."

"What good news? You finally graduating?"

"Ha Ha funny man. No. Winston asked me to marry him." I was speechless.

"Yeah, did he already ask daddy?" "Wow......I'm happy for you Tonya. I really am. Winston seems to be a good guy. Tell him he still has to talk to me when I get back." She laughed again.

"I love you Jay."

"I love you to Tee."

I was happy for Tonya. My baby sister was growing up before my eyes. Kevin was ringing my doorbell as I hung up with Tonya. He had interrupted my urge to call Angela before I left. I opened the door to let him in. It felt like ages since I had seen my best friend. He looked like life was treating him better. We dapped each other, did our manly embrace that signified mutually straight adoration. Kevin grabbed my bags and we headed outside to his car.

"Damn...when did you scoop this up player?"

"Just got it about a week ago."

Kevin was pushing a brand new Range Rover. Talk about an upgrade from a Ford Expedition. He told me all about how he and Sharon decided to part ways after her affair with her boss. They were gonna split custody of the kids and do what was in their best interest. It seemed like a happy ending all around I thought, until Kevin said what he said next.

"I decided that I need to get out of Columbia. I'm moving back to Atlanta for a minute to plot my next move. I bought a crib in Conyers so my momma can move in and help take care of the kids until I get things settled with my business."

My best friend was leaving. We had a close friendship that spanned over a decade. We never lived in separate cities or states during that time. Although Atlanta was less than three hours away, I knew that things would never be the same. It was bittersweet. I knew it was what Kevin needed the most. I was happy for my friend, but I was gonna miss my brother from another mother. Kevin told me that he and Lisa have grown close and that they were quietly pursuing one another. I was not the least bit surprised. Guess I would have to make frequent trips to Atlanta to see my pseudo niece and nephew. We talked all the way to the airport. Kevin helped me get my luggage to the correct terminal, but TSA regulations only allowed him to go so far.

"I guess this is goodbye...at least for now."

"No, it's not goodbye....it's see ya later.

"Good luck with the business man. Tell my niece and nephew that Uncle Jay is only a phone call away. Better yet we can just Skype. Tell them that I will bring them souvenirs from Trinidad."

We dapped again, kept it moving, kept it masculine. I watched him drive away in his new ride. BFF I said to myself. Best Friends Forever. Once I checked my bags and went through security screening I took my carry-on bag to

the bar to get a drink. This time I called Angela. I needed
to hear her voice. Needed to talk to her before the distance grew between even greater. When her phone went
to voicemail I decided against leaving a message. Some
things needed to be said directly not via voicemail. I ordered a Red Stripe and a vodka and cranberry to help ease
my flight anxiety and numb my mind from the realities of
the world I was leaving behind. I felt a tap on the shoulder. Was hoping in some crazy way it was Angela. No
such luck. It was my childhood friend Reggie that owned
the detail shop. He was decked out in an all white linen
suit. Clean shaven, no braids. He looked like a million
bucks.

"Where you headed man?"

I am going to Trinidad for a few weeks. Need a vacation.
You know?"

"Yeah, I dig."

"Where are you going? Don't you have some cars to detail
or something?"

He smiled like he had something up his sleeve.

"I am headed to Paris man."

It seemed a little odd for Reggie to be able to take a trip
like that, let alone even know how to find France on a globe.
I didn't even have the energy to question him. Couldn't care
less really.

"Have fun man."

He went to the end of the bar and did his thing. I lost my-self inside of the influence of vodka and Jamaica's best. They began boarding the flight that would take me from Columbia to Trinidad by way of Atlanta. At the same time they were calling for the flight from Columbia to Paris by way of New York. I watched Reggie head in one direction while I headed in the other one. He had a female companion with him and I was alone. They kissed one another and held hands as they headed towards their terminal. Such familiarity as if I knew her. At second glance I realized that Reggie was walking hand and hand with Amanda Riley. My former patient the grieving widow was all smiles. She obviously was a quick healer. "42 CFR Mr. Adams." I laughed to myself as I remem-bered her words. Again I couldn't care less. That was their business. Love was definitely a crazy thing. I boarded my flight under the influence of alcohol and scarred by love gone wrong. After settling into my seat I put on my iPod and be-came hypnotized by the sounds of my favorite artists. Prince, Sade, 2pac, Outkast, Corrine Bailey Rae and a host of others were all making the trip with me. We were all on vacation. When I got to Trinidad I would be able to put all that wasn't right in my life into perspective and move forward. I would enjoy the culture of the island and all it had to offer. The flight attendant gave me a pillow after I downed one more beer. 40,000 feet later we were at our cruising altitude. I was high above all the problems of my world. I had awakened to a tap on my shoulder. This flight attendant was getting on my nerves I thought. She smelled like heaven I thought before I opened my eyes and removed my headphones to tell her I didn't want anything else. I knew the scent of Chanel number 5 anywhere. When I looked up it was Angela. She motioned to sit beside me.

"You promised me a trip to the beach. I'm not letting you get off that easy." She smiled.

I thought I was dreaming, glad I wasn't. She told me how she ran into Samantha the other day and she told her about me going to Trinidad. Samantha also told her all about how we were two friends that used to be lovers. Angela even told me about her co-worker that I saw her out with. She explained that he was fabulously gay and he even thought that I was cute. I told her that part wasn't funny. I told her to stop talking and to kiss me. That was the longest kiss I'd ever had. The best kiss I'd ever had. I thought about our debate over whether beaches represented beginnings or the endings. That all of a sudden didn't matter anymore. All that mattered was that we had a second chance at love. A second chance to get things right. I had finally got my closure to what seemed like a lifetime of frustration at 40,000 feet in the sky.

CHAPTER 35

Kevin

My decision to relocate to Atlanta was a difficult one. Jason has proven to be very dependable. He has been like family. I knew that I would miss that type of friendship being back in Atlanta. While I was excited about the new beginnings in my life, it was difficult to say goodbye to the past. I watched as Jason's plane took off. Watched my brother's plane ascend to heights that made it difficult to still see him. I knew that we would work hard to still remain a close part of each other's lives. He was the only uncle my kids had. My momma was excited about being able to be close to India and K.J. by living with us. My dreams of retiring her from her duties as a bus driver have now come true. With the advance on my business I was able to tell her to quit her job and to come live with me and the kids. To Sharon's credit she didn't try to fight me regarding where the kids would stay. I told her that I absolutely refused to live without them. She understood that she was the one that jeopardized things. I promised her that she could visit anytime and that we would be fair with weekends and holidays. Sharon had flown back home to Philadelphia with her parents to continue with her rehabilitation physically, emotionally, and spiritually. Her memory was back and the doctors all expected her to make a full recovery with no permanent damage to her leg. Even her scratches were healing. She could shower on her own and do her makeup and hair. I knew that it would take time, but she would eventually find the love that she couldn't get from me. I could see that his death had her in pain. I sent India and K.J. with Sharon for the rest of the summer while I got things straight with my company. I would be completely moved to Atlanta in one week. By the time Jason got back I would not be in his home town. My old boss Steve was in the process of selling my house. Life had a way of coming full circle a time or two. Sharon and I decided to bank whatever profit we got from the equity accumulated to benefit our kid's college fund. A billboard on I-26 served as a reminder of the life that was no more. It was a picture of James and the $200,000 reward for information leading to the person's arrest. I never heard from Detective Turner again concerning the death of James Riley and I was glad. When I pulled up to my home I stared at the for sale sign on my lawn. I remembered the day Sharon and I closed on this house. Thought about our plans to be a family and raise our children. Guess that those dreams would never materialize. Although part of me was disappointed, I wasn't bitter. We had two reasons to make sure we did right by one another and that was what was most important.

I checked the mail in anticipation of news from my attorney about our uncontested divorce being finalized. I was eager to close that chapter of my life. My heart danced when I read that letter which confirmed that our divorce was final in the state of Pennsylvania where we were married. I ignored the other final bills and put them in my left hand. I had another letter. This letter had no returned address. Instantly I recognized the hand writing.

Mr. Wade,

I hope that this letter finds you in perfect peace. Don't worry; I will never try to contact you again. In fact I wish that we had never met, at least not under these circumstances. I sincerely apologize for any pain that I may have caused you. I feel that you deserved better and I hope you get what you deserve. The world is a better place with guys like you in it. I am glad you proved to be better than I even gave you credit for. In a strange way I guess I want to thank you for what you didn't do. By the time you read this, I will be on my way to greener pastures. If we should meet again, I hope it will be on better terms. Take care and best wishes in all that you do.

P.S. I have enclosed a small token of my sincerest appreciation for you. This should be a tremendous boost for your new endeavor. It's the least I could do.

Sincerely,

Same Boat no more!

I reached inside to retrieve her token of appreciation with much skepticism and apprehension. There was a note with a locker number 71 and a three digit combination 12-2-18. The instructions were to use the code to access locker 71 at Golds Gym to retrieve my mysterious prize. I was to bring my gym bag into the gym like any other day and swap it with the one inside of the locker. Although I was pressed for time, my curiosity was getting the best of me and I proceeded to the gym with bag in hand. I walked to locker 71 and input the combination as it was written on the note. Sure enough it unlocked and there was the exact same black duffel bag that I used. Looking around cautiously I unzipped the other bag to see what was inside. The contents nearly made my heart leap from inside of my chest. There was more cash money than I have ever seen in my life. I quickly zipped it up and swapped the bags and exited in the same manner that I came inside. One final note from Same Boat told me that there was $500,000.00 total. It was half of what she offered me to kill James, even though I didn't kill James. Same Boat was making sure that there was nothing to connect our respective dots; there was no paper trail. She was very calculated and deliberate. There was nothing she hadn't thought of. Dealing with her would forever have me on my toes and make me paranoid about who was watching me. I hurried back home with the weight of her letter and my duffel bag. This would be a nice cushion to help support my business. I finished packing some boxes in preparation of my move. Lisa and I were meeting for dinner later on. I told her that I wanted to take her somewhere special. This would be the first of many dates with this wonderful woman. For nostalgia's sake I drove us down I-26 east towards Charleston, S.C. We took the 145-A exit to Orangeburg. I wanted to give Lisa a glimpse into my world. Wanted her to see that side of me, the place where it all started. It was the place where Jason and I met as freshmen. The place where I played football for four years. The place I met my now ex-wife Sharon the mother of my two beautiful children. I wanted to show Lisa a part of my past so that she could appreciate me in the present. After we rode through campus in my new SUV I stopped in front of the football stadium that housed so many good memories for me. I took a breathe and breathed in all those old memories. Held onto them for a while. In that moment I was good. Good with all that happened in my past. It was perfect closure. I was ready for a new beginning. That's when I looked at Lisa Ellis. Stared in her beautiful eyes and kissed her for the first time. It felt like the first time I had ever kissed someone. Later on that night we would tour the finer points of Charleston, eat seafood, walk on the beach and make love. Lisa believed in me the way that I needed her to. I could give myself to her totally and completely without fear of being betrayed again. That night we bonded with one another in a way that Sharon and I had never been able to. We committed to the moment and what was not what might or could be. I realized that in life all we really have are the moments in which we presently exist, and right now we existed in a perfect place. For the first time in my life I wasn't concerned about having a plan, I was just fine with right now. Tomorrow would just have to wait.

Epilogue

Amanda abruptly ended her phone call with Kevin Wade. It became apparent that he wasn't going to help her to get what she wanted. He wasn't going to kill her husband as she previously thought and planned for him to do so. Kevin's kind nature and forgiving spirit was something that even she seemed to underestimate. Although it pissed her off, there was a part of her that needed to know that redeeming qualities were still in some people. It was too bad that she couldn't say the same for her cheating husband, who had only taken her kindness as weakness. He would know that this scorned woman was not to be screwed over. She had planned her husband's murder for months after discovering his affair with Sharon. She carefully crafted every detail from the place and time to the actual murderer. Despite detailed planning she was learning through Kevin Wade that some things didn't always go according to plan. Most men would have killed James without thinking twice for what he had done, except Kevin. Amanda sat on her deck smoking and reflecting on her regrets that Sharon had even survived her car accident. She tisked in disgust that Reggie somehow screwed that assignment up. He was supposed to cut her brake line which wouldn't allow her to slow her enormous SUV down when he purposely cut her off on the interstate. Her near death injuries didn't quite satisfy her the way her actual death would. She wondered just how reliable Reggie would be if she really needed him. She'd give him a second chance to redeem

himself she thought. Reggie was weak minded and thus easy
for her to manipulate. Amanda called Reggie after learning
the disappointment of Kevin's decision not to be manipulated
by her. He was down and surprisingly eager to prove his loy-
alty and street credibility. This was the moment of truth for
Amanda Riley. It was time for her to kill her husband. She
was a woman determined to get what she wanted at all costs,
so naturally she had a back up plan, and it was time to put it
in motion. Amanda lit another cigarette as she changed into
her all black wet suit. She wrapped her hair and put on a
swimmer's cap.

"Drop everything and let's move now." She asserted calm-
ly in between controlled puffs of her cigarette, and hung up
before Reggie could reply or have time to change his mind.

Amanda made sure that she had dotted her I's and crossed
her T's. She knew that she would be a prime suspect in her
husband's demise, so she naturally created an alibi. Her car
never left their home and she created the illusion that she
hadn't either. The only way that she was going to be able to
leave her home without being seen was to become one with
the night. She carefully walked to the edge of her water front
property and climbed down the steps of her dock into the
cold and dark waters of Lake Murray. Amanda swam the
two miles it took to get to the other side of the lake where
she was to meet Reggie. When she made it to the other side
Reggie wasn't there. Her anxiety heightened as she pondered
thoughts of him backing out or being sloppy. Moments
later the thumping of his music announced his arrival. He
dimmed the lights and wheeled his vehicle in her direction.
She climbed in the back of his boxed Chevy.

"What took you so long Reggie?"

"I didn't think you could swim that far as fast as you did."

"You shouldn't underestimate me,"   she teased as she took his already lit cigarette and took a few drags, not even slightly winded.

Amanda was zipped out of her wetsuit and dressed in jeans and a tank in no time. She pulled her hair out of the cap and let it flow down her back. She climbed into the front with Reggie and gave him a kiss that was both affectionate and bordered on erotic. She rehearsed the plan from A to Z to ensure that there were no glitches. It was obvious that Reggie was agitated and slightly nervous. Although he had served time and committed an assortment of petty crimes she knew that pre-meditated murder was new ground for him.

"What's wrong with you?" She asked.

"I'm just tired of you sweatin me like I don't know what I'm doing. I told you I got this." He stated in an agitated manner as he drew longer drags from his cigarette. Reggie turned up the volume to his favorite gangster rapper's profanity laced tirade about another person's street exploits to both keep him grounded and to block out Amanda's rhetoric. Loud bass that rattled his classic but dated car and smoke from the filtered cigarettes they smoked filled the car and rested between them. It was their buffer for the moment.

Tension rested between them. In fact this was there first moment of awkwardness. It's not everyday a guy gets asked to murder his girlfriend's husband. Nobody needed to state the obvious. Amanda used the Google device on her phone to track James's exact coordinates. He was not at the condo. He was at a place he frequented downtown called Rust Whiskey Bar. Reggie and Amanda parked where they could keep an eye on him once she spotted his black BMW. Reggie parked across the street in a furniture store's parking lot.

After nearly a pack of cigarettes later it was obvious that either Reggie had grown more anxious, or he was possibly having second thoughts. "Let me go inside to see what's going on." Amanda nodded even though she didn't totally agree with Reggie's sudden good idea. She sat and waited with increased determination to get her closure.

Reggie entered Rust and began scoping the place in search of James. There were less than ten people inside so he wouldn't be hard to find at this time of night going on morning. Anybody out drinking this late either had a really bad day or they were trying to get laid. Maybe it was both for James; regardless his day was about to get worst. Reggie remembered what he looked like from the photos he had seen while inside of his home. He had layed with James' wife in his bed, while in his home; thus they knew each other better than either of them wanted to admit. Reggie climbed the stairs to the restroom to empty his nervous bladder. He washed his face with cold water trying to convince himself of what he was actually about to do. It was a long way from distributing narcotics, and running a few credit card and merchandising scams. He opened the door to exit the restroom and he was face to face with his adversary; it was surreal. James was waiting to come inside to use the bathroom.

"My bad man, I didn't know anyone was in here. I gotta go so bad it feels like I am about to die."

"Help yourself. It's all yours."

Sometimes words really had power. Reggie sat downstairs at the tiny bar with his back to the wall so that he saw everything that went on in Rust. The crowd had mostly dissipated and many of the workers were cleaning up and closing down their registers. Aside from his drink order he was hardly paid any attention. Reggie ordered a double shot of Patron and a Heineken. He took the shot with a grimaced look and chased it with his beer. James came in and sat two chairs down from Reggie. He was nursing a glass filled with brown spirits. He wore the look of a man very deep in thought as if he owned the world's problems. The sleeves from his dress shirt were rolled up past his elbows and his shirt was untucked. He had a bandage on the bridge of his nose and some scarring on his right eye that appeared to be healing. It was clear that James Riley had seen better days. He wore physical wounds from the husband of his love interest. His lover was lying in a hospital with injuries of her own. James blamed himself for what had happened to Sharon. He could never forgive himself if she didn't manage to recover. His thoughts weighed heavier than the nation's debt. He was drowning his sorrows inside of the most expensive cognac Rust could provide him. Reggie watched him ignore at least a dozen calls on his cell phone with a disgusted look. James put his American Express black card on the bar as he ordered one more drink.

"Clear my tab…..and clear his tab as well."

James had taken care of Reggie's tab as well. Reggie was surprised by the gesture since he and James had not been formally introduced although they shared a lot in common. Reggie nodded towards James in acceptance of his gesture. For a minute he almost felt saddened about what he had to do, but he felt the need to prove himself worthy to Amanda. She had shown him a world that he never knew existed during their short romance. After his third shot of Patron his mind felt the type of numbness that he needed it to feel in order to do the type of heartless act that he needed to do. Reggie thought of the scene from his favorite movie New Jack City when Nino Brown said that it was always business, and never personal. Killing James would be business, he wouldn't make it personal. Drinking his liquor, sleeping with his wife and essentially taking his place weren't personal in the mind of Reggie and now murdering James wouldn't be either. That thought gave him comfort . It gave him peace of mind. Whatever a person could rationalize in their mind made sense to them no matter how twisted and irrational it truly was. Reggie watched as James exited Rust. He didn't want to seem obvious, so he waited a few moments before he left knowing that Amanda would have her eye on him.

Moments later Reggie drew the disgust of Amanda when he returned to the car. "Which way did he go?" Amanda offered him no words in response, only pointed in the direction where James was. She had grown further irritated because James sent her calls to voicemail when he saw that it was her calling him. Nothing irritated Amanda more than being ignored. If he had a chance to avoid her death penalty, it was safe to say that he blew it.

Reggie tailed James at a safe distance through several traffic lights down Gervais. He was turning right onto Huger. It appeared that James was heading in the direction of his home then he swerved in reaction to his cell phone vibrating. In his response he overcorrected and his passenger side wheel struck a raised curb. James was pissed about damaging his car; pissed even more to see that it was his wife calling him again. He turned off the main road and pulled into the Trustus Theatre parking lot to assess the damage to his vehicle. The parking lot was dark and deserted without a soul in sight. Amanda Riley seized the moment that her husband's poor judgment and blatant disregard of her feelings had now afforded her. With James focused on his beloved vehicle he was totally unaware that Reggie's car was less than 20 feet away from his. By the time James returned to his car and closed his door in preparation to leave a now eager Reggie was on him before he knew it with a look of death in his eyes and a widow maker in his right hand. There were no words uttered from either man, but their eyes said everything. Two shots to James's chest later was all that was needed to seal the deal. In that moment not only was James's soul leaving his body, but in a way so was Reggie's and neither of them would ever be the same. Just as James rested his head atop his steering wheel his loving wife swooped in to not only see the look of death upon his face, but also to make sure that she removed the ring from his finger. It was the same ring that her father had given to her and now she was taking it back. "Consider this our divorce." She said with conviction and walked away satisfied with the final results. Amanda Riley had found the closure that she sought all along.

Excerpts from "In The Moment"

By Aaron L. Ashford

(Releasing 2012)

Chapter One

My life had become a sick joke. I had contemplated at least a dozen ways to end my suffering, but I just couldn't bring myself to acting on any of them. It wouldn't be fair to my family; especially my son. For once in my life I just didn't have all the answers; only had questions. I didn't own a gun, hated swallowing pills, was afraid of heights, and I definitely wasn't gonna hang myself. How could I have allowed myself to end up on the verge of suicide, in a state of depression no less? In these moments I couldn't magnify my blessings to be bigger than my problems. Normally I would just take a long run and forget about everything and everyone. That was how I escaped my problems. Not even I could outrun this pain; this hurt. I was searching for a reason to go on. That's when my phone rang. I looked at the caller ID in disappointment. It wasn't her. It was Marcus. My best friend and now he was my agent. I really didn't wanna be bothered with either version.

"Hello."

"Kennedy.....you sound like crap. That doesn't sound like happiness to hear from your agent. I have some good news man!"

"Good news," I replied sarcastically.

"Clean the wax out of your ears and listen up. I fished your book to a couple of producers to gauge their interest and we appear to have a bite!"

I paused for several moments. This had been the opportunity that I have been waiting on all my life. I should be bursting at the seams with excitement and doing a serious Holy Ghost dance all while speaking in tongues. I was excited deep down, just not like I thought I would be. Not like I should be. Not even news this good could wake me from this state of depression that has consumed me for the last few weeks. I couldn't stop thinking of Jacqueline Tate. Breaking up with her has been the hardest thing that I have ever had to do. Falling in love had to be the invention of a fool, not a sane or rational person. My life made no sense whatsoever.

"Say something man. I am gonna take your silence as you being speechless."

"I am here.......excited man that's all, just excited. You are the man Marcus."

"This I know", he said with all of the arrogance and bravado that I have come to expect from him. "On another note......you ain't still trippin over that Jackie broad are you?"

"Her name is Jacqueline and I would appreciate if you didn't refer to her or any other woman as a broad. To answer your question I just have a lot on my mind, none of which you would understand."

"Yeah yeah whatever. I do know one thing."

"What's that?"

"I know that a new woman is the quickest way for you to get over Jacqueline or anybody else. Besides.........she is a married woman for goodness sake."

That big dose of reality hit me like a ton of bricks falling from the Empire State building. It reminded me of why I did what I did. I had to pull away, because in spite of what we felt the fact was that she was a married woman with a husband and two children. As much as I hated to admit it, Marcus was absolutely correct. At least about the fact that I needed to move on and get pass Jacqueline. I needed to focus on my career and getting my affairs in order; literally and figuratively. I had been separated from my wife Marley for the last year and a half after being married for 14 years. For some reason we have not made our divorce official despite the reality that happily ever after had ended for us. We both wanted what was best for our son Miles.

"So.....who took the bait on the screen play?"

"None other than Tyler Perry himself. Mr. Madea."

"Tyler Perry as in the Tyler Perry? Your kidding right?"

"Kennedy King, would I pull your leg about business? You know I don't play about my paper, so I wouldn't joke about yours, especially since in this case they are co-mingled. Anyway, he said that he wants to meet you ASAP!"

"Wow, was all I could get out of my mouth. I couldn't believe that this was happening. Since I could remember I have always loved writing and to think that someone else was finally seeing my potential was so surreal. My mood began to improve with those thoughts in mind. I could finally put Jacqueline out of my mind and focus on my happiness for a moment. I knew that Marcus was serious because it was the first time in nearly 15 years he called me by my entire name. He had been calling me K2 since I can remember. I had one of those weird double last names. My mother said she wanted to name me Martin after Dr. Martin Luther King, Jr. but decided against Martin since my last name was already King. She said that she didn't want to make me have to walk around hearing all the MLK jokes from the other kids. She named me Kennedy instead. My mom thought that JFK, and MLK were two of the most selfless and influential people of her time and she thought the name would be perfect. When you are named after two men that were both assassinated in their prime it makes you a little suspicious and you hope it's not in the name.

"Just set up the meeting, you know I am on board. Good job," I said with much more enthusiasm.

"Okay, I will hit you with all the particulars. One more thing."

"What's that?"

"Who da man?"

We both laughed at his humorous side.

"You da man Marcus! You da man."

We hung up the phone still laughing. That was what I needed, it actually helped me to feel better. Marcus was a workaholic and even though it wasn't quite 9:00 AM, he was making things happen. I opened the blinds to allow some sunlight into my dark and cluttered condo. The sunlight revealed both a gorgeous day on the outside and a person's life in disarray inside. From my view I could oversee Centennial Park, The Atlanta Aquarium and the Coca Cola Factory. There was so much life going on; children playing and people going about their normal day in the pursuit of their respective happiness. Meanwhile doom and gloom consumed my world. Nothing resembled life in here. I hadn't cleaned my place in about two weeks, there was clutter everywhere. There was a stack of Atlanta Journal Constitution papers that I hadn't even read, my voicemail was full, the sink was full of dishes, and I had trash that needed to be taken out. My postal mail, email, and hygiene had all been neglected at this point. As I began to think of Jacqueline I decided to do the one thing I enjoyed the most other than writing or being with her and that's running.

I figured that I was already in need of a shower, and that it could wait until I really worked up a sweat. I threw on my tights, a tank top, reached for my I-pod, and grabbed my best running shoes. Since my life was already an uphill battle, I figured that I needed a challenge. I would conquer Stone Mountain. Going into the bright sun that Atlanta had offered on this day was almost blinding. I felt like a vampire at daybreak. I ran back in for my shades and I was set to go. It had been at least a couple of days since I have left my home, so it felt good to get out. I had risen from the dead. My GPS device told me that Stone Mountain was a little over 15 miles from downtown Atlanta, which would take about 27 minutes. What would I do without this Garmin? Even though it was nearly fall, this down south heat and humidity was for the birds. Didn't think that I could get used to it. I had only been in Atlanta for a year and a half since leaving my hometown of Lorton, VA.

Marcus urged me to come to Atlanta as a way of getting a fresh start and refocusing. He was like many other young aspiring professionals that migrated to Atlanta in search of something bigger and better. We had both gone to Hampton University for undergrad. Marcus and I were not only good friends; we were fraternity brothers as well. We pledged together, thus we have experienced nearly a lifetime worth of memories. Some of which I would just as soon forget.

I shielded thoughts of Jacqueline as I pulled up to Stone Mountain.

This paid parking pass came in handy since I frequently ran either around the mountain or up the mountain. I didn't have to pay a daily rate. In a moment of weakness I decided to send her a text to let her know I was thinking about her and wondered if she was thinking of me. Naw...I thought to myself as I tossed my G1 on the floor of my car along with the keys and began stretching in preparation for my run. I've had my Honda Accord since I graduated college. It hasn't let me down yet as I approached nearly 300,000 miles. Didn't figure anyone would be looking to steal it now.

I drowned out all thoughts of Jacqueline and our two year affair by turning up my iPod full blast. Track after track was a reminder of her since she loaded nearly all of the songs. Our playlists mirrored one another. The truth was that although I was closer to 40 than I was to 30 reminded me of the importance of keeping my body in shape. People thought that I was lying when they found out my age. I stretched my hamstrings, calves, and groin muscles; didn't wanna risk pulling one. I admired a few women either walking or jogging that were worthy of another look, but all that did was remind me of what I was trying to forget. Every woman that I meet I find myself comparing her to Jacqueline, and the truth is they don't even compare. I was pathetic. I was in love with another man's wife. What a disgrace I thought to myself; embarrassing. I knew that I was better than this.

Chapter 2

I took off on my quest to scale the 1,686 feet of elevation that made up Stone Mountain. In spite of a nice mix of my favorite tunes across nearly every genre of music, my mind settled on Jacqueline. I could not get her image out of my mind. I was married to a woman for 14 years of my life, gave her my last name and a child and I have never felt for her what I feel for Jacqueline. That was crazy. The sad thing was that it wasn't a knock on Marley. She was no slouch at all. Marley and I met back in college at a Mid-eastern Athletic conference track meet. She went to Norfolk State University by way of Jamaica. We were both runners; in fact we both ran the same events. We were sprinters. We ran the 100 and 200 meters and we anchored the 4 by 100 meter relay teams. Speed was our greatest asset and probably our biggest detriment. We definitely hurried things in the relationship department as well.

We had everything in common at the time. That was a time when running was all I really cared about, and it was how my education was paid for. Marley and I would train during summers and spend alternating weekends either in Hampton or Norfolk Virginia. Most of my undergrad experience aside from pledging pretty much centered around her. It didn't take long for our romance to blossom. Marcus was always trying to get me to be with other women. He said that it wasn't natural for a man to be with one woman. Those are words that he still lives by today. Guess I was a bit more traditional. If that were the case, how could I have shared a man's wife for 2 years? I felt like a huge "S" was branded on my forehead which stood for Stupid or maybe sucker. Either one could apply to me right now. I pondered those thoughts as I climbed in altitude along my run.

I was getting some stares which could have had many interpretations. Not many guys wore tights uncovered, which made me suspect that maybe some of the guys were enjoying the view a bit too much. This was Atlanta after all. Not that I had anything personally against gay guys, just as long as they missed me completely with it. On the other hand I was appreciative of the not so subtle stares I garnered from the beautiful women that I passed along the way. I began to pick up my pace as the mountain steepened.

I was beginning to get perspired, which let me know that I had neglected both my passion for running and my personal hygiene a little too long. Nonetheless I kept on climbing; kept on going. I envisioned that I was climbing higher than all the problems this life had offered me. The more I thought of Jacqueline the more I ran; the harder I pressed. I ignored the burning in my legs and within my lungs. Struggled to maintain my perfect running form.

It was funny, but I could even smell Jacqueline. If 100 women wore her trademark fragrance I could pick her out blindfolded. Nobody wore Juicy Couture quite the way that she did. Just the thought of her drove me crazy. It made blood flow to places that it didn't need to right now; especially wearing these tights. Before I knew it I was mentally back in the place in time that we first met. Marcus and I were hanging out in Charlotte, North Carolina for the CIAA weekend. Once again he was trying to mix a little business

with pleasure. We were celebrating another of his clients
who he had recently signed. At the time Marley and I were
still together under the same roof, but far from the illusion
of being each other's soul mate. Marcus was getting on me
to finish writing my book which at the time was very in-
complete. Writer's block definitely had the best of me. It
was beating me down like Kimbo Slice. I was facing some
difficult realities in my life and writing was the furthest
thing from my mind.

Reluctantly I hung out with Marcus and we frequented
most of the events throughout the weekend affiliated with
the tournament, all VIP access of course. Even though
I wasn't the flashy type like Marcus was I had to admit
that it beat standing in those long lines just to get into
all the venues. The CIAA was a big deal in this region of
the country judging by the huge crowds of people, probably most of which didn't even go to CIAA schools but
just liked having a good time. I was a MEAC type of guy
myself, but I had to admit that there was a lot to be desired as far as our tournament went. We were hanging out
at a spot called Club 935 that had a line wrapped around
the corner just waiting to get in. Over the years I had lost
my attraction for what clubs used to provide in terms of
excitement. It was mostly the same tired looking guys saying played out lines, while women just wanted free drinks
and gave out fake names. I mulled over that thought as we
found our way inside.

Pretty nice I thought to myself as I looked around. We
passed a bar with a smaller dance floor off set by a huge pro-
jection screen showing the video to the song that the DJ was

spinning, or should I say programming on his fruit themed laptop. Nobody spins records anymore; guess technology has even advanced DJs. I will always be a fan of the needle to vinyl sound from back in the day. I stopped at the bar and ordered a drink. I wasn't a heavy drinker so I ordered a beer. Marcus got a dirty martini. That was one drink that looked like it was appropriately named. It looked very unsanitary.

"I see your still a Heineken fan," he said referring to my beer selection.

"Yeah, I like to stay consistent."

"I hear ya. You need to be looking for some new talent. From where I stand there is a lot to choose from. I may even hold an audition for a spot or two on my roster," he said while nearly breaking his neck looking around.

"Man there is nothing for me in here...not trying to re-place one problem with the next one," I said as I thought about the realistic possibility of officially splitting up with Marley and divorcing.

Marcus just looked at me as he rested on my words. He didn't even comment. He was focused on scouting new tal-ent. Marcus was a guy who worked hard, but played even harder. He enjoyed the life that he was living. I was a guy who prided himself on stability and being consistent and it was hard to have that interrupted. We walked to the coat check area and surrendered our jackets as we embraced the warmth that this many people under one roof had suddenly provided. I was wearing a nice buttoned down shirt with some dark Guess jeans; not flashy at all. Marcus on the other hand stayed decked out. He was wearing a nice designer suit, expensive shoes, and monogrammed shirt with his initials on the sleeves, and no tie. He definitely dressed the part of an entertainment agent. We made it to the VIP area that was really only slightly elevated and separated by a velvet rope with some plush lounge chairs to sit down. It didn't seem that exclusive to me.

I became mesmerized by the women dancing onstage separate from everybody else to pass time. Marcus entertained more than a few women and wooed them with free drinks for the majority of the night. I didn't see the sense of it all. Men buying drinks and telling lies, while women accept the drinks and tell their own lies. It seemed like nobody told the truth anymore. A big waste of time I thought. Women put themselves in awkward predicaments time after time without even knowing it. A man would buy drinks all night if he felt like it would get him closer to the inside of a woman's panties. Why couldn't people just meet and say "let's screw a few times and see where this goes?" It seems like it would save everyone time and money. I sipped more than a few beers and eye danced with the stage dancers, song after song, move for move. Although it frightened me to fathom being in the 21st Century dating game, I knew deep down that it would be my reality. I cringed at the prospect of dating in an era where Facebook, camera phones, and Skype existed. Marley and I were on borrowed time, and time was coming to collect itself any day now with penalty and interest.

After more beers than I could recall I decided to go to the restroom and get our jackets. Once I had relieved myself and collected our jackets I scanned the crowd for Marcus. He was a party animal and it was obvious that he was having a good time. The crowd was beginning to dissipate and people were moving towards the exit. That was when it happened. I turned in search of Marcus, but what I found was the discovery of a lifetime. Never had a mistake been more perfect. I accidentally stepped on the toes of a young lady. Although I apologized profusely at the time, I would later find out that it was the perfect alignment of the planet and the stars. With the audacity of Columbus I proceeded to explore this new venture.

"I am so sorry," I exclaimed out of sheer embarrassment.

She paused as she looked down to examine her shoes and toes that peeped through her pumps. "I'm okay."

For a moment I feared a nasty response that would have been uncalled for, but she was very different. Her eyes were the brightest most beautiful eyes that I had ever had the pleasure of gazing into. There was so much life. They were both innocent and sensual all at once. We stared into each others eyes for minutes that seemed like hours before we even exchanged names. In that moment the crowd didn't matter. In fact everyone else was moving slow like those scenes from the Matrix trilogy. I only saw her. There was immediate attraction, but not the typical physical attraction that I have experienced since I could remember where beautiful women were involved. This was on a deeper level. It was almost spiritual.

"I'm Kennedy. What's your name?"

"Nice to meet you Kennedy. My name is Jacqueline."

"I didn't mean to step on your foot. In fact I didn't even see you. Guess I was not paying attention."

"You sure that's not how you pick up women?" She smiled. "just step on their feet and play like you didn't see 'em…. Is that it?"

"I can assure you that that's not how I do it." We both laughed.

Jacqueline told me that she was out with her friends for a girl's night out. I told her that I was out with Marcus, pretty much doing the same thing I guess. We both looked at each other with the "married people don't do this stare" and probably dismissed it just as easy. Every relationship was different, that's for sure. Jacqueline told me about her job, her twin boys, and her 7 year marriage. She told me that she used to be a social worker until she realized that her student loan payments exceeded her salary. She figured that since she loved helping people that she might want to start with her self first. She told me that she was into marketing but didn't really elaborate. I told her about Miles, Marley, and my never ending job as a pharmaceutical sales rep. That was just a government sanctioned version of a drug dealer. I guess if the FDA could regulate a drug and Uncle Sam could tax it, it was legal. Told her about my on again off again novel that was far from complete. I was no more than an aspiring author. Anytime you aspired to do something it just meant that you hadn't done it yet. There was just something about her that made me comfortable sharing that.

We became engaged in conversation totally oblivious of elapsing time. It may have been the beer that I consumed or whatever she was drinking, but I don't even remember whose idea it was to exchange numbers but we did. In retrospect I guess we both blamed it on the alcohol and kept moving. I noticed Marcus from my peripheral waiting on me. Jacqueline and I parted ways reluctantly. I was not looking forward to the interrogation that Marcus had waiting, but I was looking forward to hearing from Jacqueline Tate very soon.

Chapter 3

As the crowd dissipated Marcus and I went in the direction of once eager party goers, who were now just intoxicated people in search of the nearest Waffle House or hotel room toward the exit. All the while I wanted to look back to steal a glimpse of Jacqueline. Wondered what she looked like from afar; wondered if she was looking at me. That was silly I thought to myself as I fought that urge with everything inside of me. I just couldn't help but feel a moment of awkwardness and intrigue. I know that didn't make sense, but I was trying to wrap my mind around what just happened inside a night club of all places. This woman I didn't know from Eve or her sister had piqued my curiosity in the worst way.

"I'm starved man let's get some grub," Marcus demanded as he yawned a tired man's yawn.

"That's cool," I asserted and kept it moving.

The temperature outside seemed like it dropped at least twenty degrees and the rain from earlier had returned in the form of sleet. A cold front moved through the area bringing in temperatures that made me see my breath when I spoke. I clutched my jacket and pulled it tighter to keep my warmth from being consumed by the hawk that was out tonight. I was used to cold growing up in Northern Virginia, but I did not expect it to be this cold in Charlotte. Right now I was one cold dude ready to get to inside of something that provided me with warmth. I blew into my hands and rubbed them together as Marcus and I waited on the valet to bring his car around. We boarded his Lexus GS 460. There were more horses under this hood, than on an average sized farm. The heated seats were just what I needed as my body melted and seemed to come back to life in no time. Times like this made me wish I had bought a new car because my dated Accord would have both of us freezing damn near to death. I chuck-led inside and decided to keep that thought concealed where it belonged. Marcus used his voice activated GPS system that guided us to the nearest IHOP.

Her fragrance lingered on my hands. It was not one that I wasn't familiar with, but was suddenly growing on me with every passing moment. I inhaled and exhaled her with every breath. Marcus and I made small talk over veggie om-elets and cheese grits at 3 AM. IHOP was packed like a club. I tried to imagine the money that Charlotte was making as a result of all the people who attended the CIAA. Marcus was busy yapping about how many women he had met and what his plans were for them. He never stopped. He was so busy talking about himself that he never bought Jacqueline up, which was great for me. The times that he was inter-rupted by calls or texts on his I phone gave me opportunities to think of her.

I was at the top of Stone Mountain overlooking the best view in which to see Atlanta. With my hands on my hips I began stretching again to control my breathing and to en-sure that I didn't pull anything. Not even running could to-tally clear my mind of Jacqueline, but my mood overall was greatly improved. My brain was suddenly overtaken by en-dorphins and for the first time in weeks I felt like I had a purpose. I trotted back down in the same manner in which I had climbed. Only this time it was easier to reverse what I had done in the first place. At least this applied to running, not as much in relationships. Before I knew it I was back in my dated but reliable Accord heading back to my condo.

With my sunroof open I enjoyed the breeze that 85 miles per hour granted me as I crossed multiple stretches of high-ways to get back downtown. Once inside I decided to give my place a much needed cleaning. I plucked my iPod in its stationary dock so that my tunes could blare and fill every square foot with noise. It felt as though I had been in si-lence for too long. I listened to random tunes from Alicia, Ledisi, Laura Izibor, Maxwell, Jill Scott, John Legend, Muziq Soul child, Michael Jackson, Marvin Gaye, Miles Davis, Lenny Kravitz, and Mary J. I even had some New Edition pumping. Although the music helped me to restore my place to a sense of cleanliness, it also kept me in a place where I was once again filled with thoughts of Jacqueline. I took my phone out and decided to call my son. The most difficult part of being

separated was not being able to see Miles everyday. Now that
I was in a different state all together made that even more
painful. He was a great kid and to Marley's credit she helped
with the transition. I had tons of frequent flier miles going
back and forth to Virginia to see him. Miles was 14 years
old now and I knew that he needed me more than ever at
this point in his development. He was extremely resilient in
handling the separation so far. At his age most kids are so
consumed with a rush of hormones and bad information that
they screw things up literally and figuratively. I was much
younger than Miles when my parents split and it was not a
smooth transition whatsoever.

My folks argued like any other couple, but I had to admit that I didn't see that coming. I just remember one day
my dad did not come home. That day turned to weeks,
which turned to months and eventually he was remarried
with a family of his own. Talk about one to grow on. I
hated his ass for years. To this day I have never gotten over
how a man could just walk away from his family like it was
nothing. To add insult to injury he left my mom for a white
woman. Not a glamorous woman like Pam Anderson or
pretty like Jennifer Anniston; he picked a Meredith Baxter
reject. I wasn't racist in the least bit, but he obviously had
issues with color. That's the straw that breaks the camel's
back when it comes to black women. My mom could pass
for white in some circles and compared to my dad she was.
My mom is beautiful like a doll baby. She is the type of
woman that wakes up flawless. She looks like an older version of the singer Tamia. My dad is as dark as the keys on a
piano. He made Richard Roundtree look light skinned. At
the end of the day he felt as though he needed the real thing

and despite my mom's complexion she was what she was. A light skinned black woman. It was sad that people still saw color and that prejudices even existed within races.

Daddy grew up in a small town in Mississippi called Natchez. He told me that he got called nigger in every way possible for a person to be called nigger. So much that he thought nigger was his first name. The weight of those jokes and taunts destroyed any self esteem that he may have had. He hated the word and anyone who used it. He even hated himself deep down. It offended me like hell when he told me that he married my mother because he thought that she was light enough that his kids wouldn't have to go through what he went through. Wouldn't have to be called spooks, darkies, jiggaboos, and porch monkeys like he was. Even by other blacks. He fed me that lame excuse as if it would help me somehow feel better that he just walked out on his family. I hated him then, now I just feel sorry for his ass. His theory proved wrong because I ended up being only a shade or two lighter than him, but dark nonetheless. The difference is that I love the skin I'm in. It is what it is. Thanks to him I have a white stepmom named Jane and three half siblings Richard, Charles, and Catherine.

Despite his flawed ways I never rejected them no matter their makeup. Kids didn't ask to come here in the first place. I already knew what that was like. I already knew that having him for a father was enough of a burden to bear. There were many nights that I had cried myself to sleep wishing I was never born. The pain of his absence was too much initially. Maybe not having him in my life was a blessing in disguise because I seemed to be the only one of his children that's never been on drugs, arrested, or with children out of wedlock. That thought gave me some solace when it came to that situation. I dialed the number to the residence that used to be where I layed my head. The phone rang a few times before someone answered. It was Marley.

"Miles is not here Ken." She said that with some attitude.

"Well hello to you too Marley. How do you know I am not calling to talk to you?"

She hissed at my question. I could tell that she had one of her major "tudes" in full effect.

"Look," she paused. "If you were truly concerned about me....then you would be here and not in Atlanta or wherever the hell you are so save it. Miles is out with his friends so call him on his cell phone arie." Her Jamaican accent increased its presence which let me know that she was in rare form. I decided that I didn't want to take part in the latest episode of back and forth. Especially not over stuff that was not going to change. I took the out that she had provided and decided to cut this conversation short. I ended that call and called Miles on his cell. I laughed to myself thinking about how technology has spoiled everyone. At 14 my mom knew where I was gonna be from dusk till dawn. There were no cell phones. You went to school and came home. You played until the street lights came on and you went home to do it all again the next day. Now you have to text your own kids and hope that they respond on the phone that you pay for. Something just didn't make sense about that, but here I was texting my son who didn't pick up my previous call.

Acknowledgements:

First things first, I am forever thankful to GOD for continuing to show me daily that all things are possible through his divine intervention and wisdom. I am so thankful that you bare the burden of perfection so that I don't have to. I want to thank my mother Ola Mae Ashford; my first love for her unconditional love, patience and soul food on demand. To my beautiful wife Tamala for A.J. and Arrington and being a great mother, but also for being better to me than I probably deserve. I am forever grateful of the bond I share with my sister Sherani and brother Aubrey, Jr. All the fights through the years have served to make us into the people we are today. I hope Patrick and Asmarette know what they are dealing with. I can truly say that I love you both and that I wouldn't trade you for anyone. Man we had some knock down drag out battles. To my nieces Aja, Kaliegh, Peyton, and Lorin and my nephews Aubrey, I'll just say Tre to keep the confusion down and Terrance I love you guys. To my paternal grandmother Carrie Lee Ashford and my maternal grandmother Bertha Lee Broome. Thank you both for your examples of matriarchal leadership, courage, wisdom, and longevity. To my extended family of uncles, aunts, and cousins I thank you; too many to name here. Just know that there are several Ashfords, Broomes, Williams, and Hayes that have had some form of contribution to my life and I didn't want to leave them out. Thanks for being a part of the village it took to raise me. I probably have the best in-laws in the world. Jeff and Joan Murrill, the entire Murrill and Phillips family I extend heartfelt gratitude and appreciation for your support. Kenneth Simmons and Christopher

Young; my partners in business. Eight years in business, I guess that we are doing something right. Hang in there. Special thanks to my select readers, you know who you are. Thank you to the total strangers I've met during book signings in malls or at expos who thought it not robbery to support a starving artist by buying his book. I am truly humbled and grateful for the support that you have shown from the beginning and I hope that you continue to support me in what I hope will be a long and prosperous career in writing. New York Times here we come! Thanks to the bookstores that support new authors and understand that everybody has to have a starting point no matter where they eventually end up. As much as I want to list each name here, I know that I will unintentionally leave someone out and get myself in trouble. Just know that I do appreciate you and I have not forgotten you, so here is your chance to shine. Kindly insert your name in the space provided. Thank you so much (your name here) for your contribution to this project. Special shout to Omega Psi Phi Fraternity, Inc. which is only the best frat in the world. Thanks to my 3rd grade teacher Mrs. Sullivan who even back then recognized and encouraged both my creativity and my literary aptitude. We should never take for granted our ability to spark the mind of a child and encourage them to bring forth their talents. To my line brothers from Epsilon Omega's Spring 99 line, DeJaun, Tyrone, Irick, Gerald, Howard, Jason, Willis, Bernard, Charles, Gordon(RIP), and Don; I couldn't have hand picked a better line to be a part of. Roooo! To my alma mater South Carolina State University, thank you for giving me an opportunity to attend college when it didn't seem that I was college material. Thank you for recognizing that I was more than the reflections of my high school transcript. You made

the right choice. To my many friends and associates throughout the years I appreciate you. To the people who understand that it is easier to catch a rocket before it launches I
especially thank you. Now about the book that you are
holding in your hand; it's been a long time coming. This
book has gone through many transformations since that
night back in 2001 when insomnia had the best of me and I
just started pecking away with no idea whatsoever in mind.
I just knew that I wanted to write. Since I've been a kid
creative writing was what I have enjoyed doing so it is really
not far fetched that we are at this point. What started out as
Momma's Boy became Closure, which is now Getting
Closure. This is the product of hard work, determination,
growth, and acceptance of constructive criticism. Together
these ingredients combined for a suspenseful thrill ride
laced with a little sex; just a little. LOL. I wanted to take a
topic like infidelity and put a different spin on it. Most people only see the obvious, which is that someone cheated.
Very few people will look a bit closer and see that if people
are broken and never heal themselves, the only thing they
know is how to hurt other people. So what happens is that
this cycle is repeated over and over. Yes that's the therapist
in me. The truth is that women much like men cheat themselves. Men really do have feelings, they do get hurt and they
in turn hurt. Getting Closure is necessary to move on, not
only in relationships but life in general. Okay that's all the
free therapy I'm giving here. If you want more it's gonna
cost you; Obamacare accepted. The book is fiction, I repeat
fiction. I can't say that enough. I am neither Kevin nor
Jason. Yes I am married with two children, but I wasn't
when I wrote this. Yes I am a licensed therapist who co-
owns his own practice. Again I wasn't when I wrote this. In

fact I didn't even have a Masters Degree. See where I'm going here? Life simply has a way of taking us places we never
thought we would go. When I started writing I wanted to
frame a story around characters that were not the stereotypical characters that African American males normally get
casted for. I wanted these guys to have education, be on the
right side of the law; for the most part and show the type of
male that too often is not portrayed in mainstream media.
Let's face it, everybody is not selling drugs, and not raising
their children, and disrespecting women. Jason prided himself in being self sufficient, being his own boss, and having
the type of lifestyle that his parent's couldn't provide him.
He was very grounded and valued his friendship with Kevin.
Like all of us he had his share of flaws. He was very self ab-
sorbed and even materialistic and guarded. Then there is
Kevin who is a family man, he is really preoccupied with not
repeating the cycle of father absence and infidelity when it
comes to his children and his wife. Even though they have a
decade long friendship that has endured ups and downs the
common fiber is their unresolved issues with infidelity. For
Jason it happened in the first relationship that he considered
to be serious because he never got closure and wasn't able to
process that hurt, he put up a wall and in turn only gave hurt
in future relationships. For Kevin it was seeing the hurt that
his father's cheating inflicted upon his mother and ultimate-
ly him so indirectly infidelity made him want to go the extra
mile to somehow redeem his father by being a good dad and
a faithful spouse even in a marriage that he wasn't happy in.
When his wife cheats it nearly drives him to murder. For
Kevin and Jason getting closure closure was necessary for
each of them, and their closure impacted so many other people from Sharon, Samantha, Lisa, Elise, and of course

Amanda. It shows how the actions of one can have a pro-
found impact on many. Although the story is fiction, these
issues are very real and they play themselves out everyday.
In fact as a therapist in my day job....I am betting that you'd
be hard pressed to encounter someone who has not been
directly impacted by infidelity in a relationship. Like it or
not we are all impacted by a relationship at some point in
our lives. For anyone with unresolved issues regarding relationships, it's imperative that you find closure needed from
past relationships in order to make present and future relationships thrive. As for what's next there are no plans currently for a sequel, but there is no telling when any of these
guys will show up again. Life has a way of bringing people
together. Thank you for allowing me to take you on this
literary voyage to my hometown of Columbia, SC hopefully
it provided a glimpse of some of the finer points of this small
city with big city crime. Quality fiction writing should in-
corporate each of the five senses. I believe that you must
bring those black words on white paper to life and help the
reader anticipate turning the next page. If I have done that,
then my hours of typing and re-typing have not been in vain.
Hopefully you saw the characters, you smelled something
different, felt lots of Carolina heat, tasted the finer points of
Columbia, and heard all that you needed to hear while reading this. I realize that this literary work may not be suitable
for all tastes and for that I offer no apologies. That's why
many genres exist. We all have different tastes and I could
not possibly have written a work that everyone would enjoy
and that wasn't my aim. I wrote this book for those who
enjoy creative writing, aren't offended by sex, drama, and
real story telling. Those people are my audience and it is my
audience that I will strive to keep and improve my craft for.

Again I thank your sincerely and ask that you stay tuned, because this thing only gets better. Thank you Katrice Hatten for putting up with me and pointing out errors while leaving room for creative differences. Smile. It was especially gratifying to create this title as the first book to be published by i Write publishing. I wouldn't have had it any other way. Signing off officially at 6:57 p.m. on September 28, 2011; location is my office of all places and not Starbucks. Go figure.

Much love,

Aaron L. Ashford

www.ingramcontent.com/pod-product-compliance
Lightning Source LLC
Chambersburg PA
CBHW020907200626
46814CB00001BA/218